SILV[...]

STILETTO SM

OVER 100
GREAT NOVELS
OF
EROTIC DOMINATION

If you like one you will probably like the rest

NEW TITLES EVERY MONTH

If you want to be on our confidential mailing list for our Readers' Club Magazine (with extracts from past and forthcoming titles) write to:

SILVER MOON READER SERVICES
The Shadowline Building
6 Wembley Street
Gainsborough
DN21 2AJ
United Kingdom
or
info@babash.com

or leave details on our 24hr UK answer-phone
08700 10 90 60
International access code then +44 08700 10 90 60

NEW AUTHORS WELCOME
Please send submissions to
Silver Moon Books Ltd.
PO Box 5663
Nottingham
NG3 6PJ
or
editor@babash.com

First published 2003 Silver Moon Books
ISBN 1-897809-84-0
© 2003 Mark Stewart
The right of Mark Stewart to be identified as the author of this book has been asserted in accordance with Section 77 and 78 of the Copyrights and Patents Act 1988

NO JUSTICE FOR JULIETTE

BY

MARK STEWART

ALSO BY MARK STEWART
Desert Discipline
Submission of a Clan Girl
Theatre of Slaves
Trained in the Harem
Pain & Passion

CHAPTER 1.

They came for her at nine o'clock the next morning. She heard booted footsteps outside the dank cell. Heavy bolts were drawn back. She held her breath. Two large, stern faced, warders entered the cell and she cringed away into a corner, hiding her face in her hands.

"You will come with us," the senior of the warders commanded sharply.

"Is it time now?" the girl asked plaintively, unable to stop her voice betraying the dread that raged within her. Ever since she had been thrown in the cell the previous afternoon, her fear had been mounting. Fear that her story would not be believed. She was not guilty of the charge they were to bring against her, but she had no proof, or witnesses to testify for her. She hoped that the crowd she had been with would come to her rescue but, knowing them, there was little or no hope that they would. She was on her own and she felt so alone and helpless.

Ever so reluctantly, she rose to her feet and followed the two men from the cell, clutching the thin blanket around her young body. It was the only covering she had been allowed since she had been made to strip for the doctor's examination when she had arrived at the House of Correction. She was led along a corridor, up a flight of stairs, and into the white tiled room where the doctor had seen her the day before. She remembered fleetingly the smile of satisfaction on his face when, after the most intimate examination, he had pronounced her fit for trial and subsequent punishment should she be found guilty.

"Hand me that," the senior warder said, pointing to the blanket, which she automatically clutched tighter to her.

They had to take the blanket from her forcibly. It was warm in the room but, as she stood there with their devouring eyes roving over her nakedness, she could not suppress a shudder. The House of Correction served as both a courtroom and prison and she had heard dreadful tales of the things that were supposed to have happened within its

5

walls. The door opened and the same doctor entered.

"So, young lady, your time has come," he said with undisguised pleasure. His face was sharp and lean, like a rat she thought with a shudder, but with lust in his eyes as he looked her over. "You are to be made ready. Come with me."

She followed him into an adjoining ablutions room.

"You must be cleansed inside and out," the doctor said with relish, running his hands over her body. He liked what he saw and felt, even though she shrank away from him. "First the inside. Stand here, facing me, with your hands high above your head. Nice! Now turn round. Place your feet wide apart. Bend and hold your ankles." He pushed down on her shoulders and caressingly ran his hands over her legs, pulling them back and straightening them. "Do not move."

The girl was at a loss to understand what this was all about. Then she flinched as she felt a long tube inserted into her anus, making her squirm. Then a deluge of warm water flooded into her body and, as the tube was withdrawn, some sort of plug pushed into her opening, imprisoning the liquid inside her. It was only then that she realised what this preparation was for. He was certain she would be found guilty and was preparing her for punishment! Panic flowed over her at the thought.

"Stand up. Begin running on the spot," the doctor ordered, licking his lips. "Hands on your head! Raise your knees higher. Faster! Faster!"

Completely at a loss to believe what was happening, the girl obeyed his commands. That she had been brought to the House of Correction would have been natural. It was here that offenders were brought to await trial as well as the prison where convicted offenders were punished and detained for the period of their sentence. The thing that concerned her was that it appeared she was being prepared for punishment before she had even been put on trial! She was conscious that, while she was obeying the order to run on the spot, the doctor and warders were staring at her breasts as they bounced with the motion. Then as the effort began to tell on her, she felt the liquid forcing the plug from its position. She bit her lip as she strained to keep it from falling out

"Not yet!" shouted the doctor. "Wait!" sensing what was amiss, as he reached for her. But he was too late. The plug shot out of her and the flood that followed squirted all over his hand.

"Bitch!" he shouted at her. "Dirty, filthy little bitch!"

Before Juliette realised what was happening, he had dragged her across the room, sat down on a chair and pulled her over his knee. With one hand gripped tight round one breast, he began to spank her hard across her buttocks with the other. She struggled to escape, yelling at him to stop, but he was too strong and she was no match for him. Her rounded bottom writhed under the onslaught, reddening fast. It was the first time in her life she had ever been spoken to like that or hit there! The sensation that rode upon the pain and humiliation was strange to her.

The doctor, fortunately for her, soon ran out of breath and his fury subsided. She was made to shave off her pubic hair and, after a short but thorough bath, ordered to dry herself and brush out her hair and apply cosmetics to her face. The latter made her feel more naked in one place and over painted in the other. These preparations completed, she was made to stand while the senior warder carefully inspected her. He saw a young naked girl, just twenty years old, standing five feet seven inches in her bare feet. She had a slim figure with well-developed but firm breasts, nicely rounded and firm tempting buttocks and long shapely legs. Her attractive oval face, with large blue eyes, was crowned by dark brown hair that fell in natural waves below straight shoulders.

She was certainly far better to look at than most that came under his control. He was on the verge of breaking the rules and raping her when the door opening stopped him. Two more warders entered. Unlike he and his colleague, they were dressed in smart uniforms, bedecked with gold braid.

"Is she ready?" one enquired.

7

"She is," answered the doctor. "I have cleansed her body, now it is up to the Court to deal with her soul, and may God have mercy on her." The last was his usual joke but, in this girl's case, his expression did not echo his words.

The new warder who had spoken approached the trembling girl and secured leather straps, each fitted with a metal ring, round her wrists and ankles. Her arms were pulled behind her and the rings snapped together, pinioning her wrists between her shoulder blades. Then taking an arm each, the new warders marched her from the room, along a passage, up a flight of stairs until they arrived outside a large wooden door on which their leader rapped loudly. The door opened slightly and, after an exchange between the warder and someone inside, the door swung open and she was marched through. They had entered a large hall. At the far end, on a raised platform, the magistrate sat behind a long table, with an assistant on either side. Along one side of the hall sat some fifty men and women who, judging by their attire, were from the wealthier section of the community. In the centre of the hall was a heavy wooden stool, bolted to the floor, with a padded leather top. The girl's face palled beneath the make up as she saw this. The small procession halted before the magistrate and her escort having unshackled her wrists, took two paces back.

The magistrate put on his spectacles and glared at the girl over the top of them. His eyes were steely and the girl thought they showed a person without mercy or understanding and her heart sank. She began to tremble.

"Juliette Savart," the magistrate said, looking hard at her.

She stood meekly silent, not knowing what to do or say.

"Juliette Savart!" the man barked at her, making her jump.

"Oh! Oh!" she gasped. "Yes!"

"You will address me as 'Your Worship'," he shouted at her. "I will not tolerate dumb insolence in my Court. It will only make your sentence all the harder, do you understand?"

"Y…yes, Your Worship," Juliette stammered. "I didn't mean…"

"Don't answer me back," he interrupted her, his face reddening with anger. "Do not dare to. Why are you naked?"

"My clothes were taken from me when I was arrested," she began to explain.

"Ah, yes! When you were arrested," he said, returning his mind to the business in hand. "You painted a red nose on the statue of our gracious Leader. Drunk on alcohol at the time I presume."

"No, your Worship," Juliette said. "My friends did it before I arrived. I was late and I didn't know anything about it then. When the lawmen came, they all ran off. I certainly was not drunk," she added, beginning to lose her temper.

"The lawmen saw no others," the magistrate shouted, looking sharply at her. "So stop telling lies. What excuse have you for this heinous crime?"

"But it wasn't me!" Juliette protested, shouting back at him.

"But it wasn't me!" he mimicked her voice scornfully. He turned to his assistants. "It wasn't me. It wasn't me." Still imitating her voice. "They all say that, thinking we are fools enough to believe them. Guilty, I think?"

The others nodded solemnly. They were younger men and enjoying the sight of the delicious naked girl standing before them, frightened and alone.

The magistrate banged his gavel on the table.

"Juliette Savart," he began in a very pompous voice, looking menacingly at the girl. "We find you guilty of sacrilege against our gracious Leader. You are now sentenced to…" He turned to his assistants. "…shall we say twenty?" There was a short pause while they debated quietly together, then the magistrate looked again at the girl, "…to twenty-five strokes of the cane across your buttocks."

The girl' face turned a deathly pallor as she gasped at the enormity of what they intended to do to her. Her legs trembled and the knuckles on her small hands were white as

9

she clenched her fists.

"The sentence to be carried out forthwith," the magistrate added, his piggy eyes lit up as he gazed down at the girl and saw that she had nearly collapsed.

The girl suddenly found her voice. "No!" she screamed at the man leering at her. "No! No! No! That's not fair. I didn't do it! I am innocent! Is this what you call justice?"

Her two warders grasped an arm each, preventing her from turning and running. She was still shouting for justice, protesting at her innocence, almost hysterical, when one of her escort slapped her hard across her face. She fell silent, stunned by the blow. The magistrate raised his gavel and banged three times on the table. A door at the side of the room opened and a heavily built man entered. He was naked from the waist upwards, displaying muscular arms and chest, except for his face that was hidden behind a mask. It was thought best by the Court that offenders did not know the identity of the person who flogged them! The girl saw him approach out of the corner of her eye and started to scream again as she saw the long thin cane he carried. He stopped before the magistrate.

The audience was pleased. It was rare that one so attractive as this one came before the Court. Not only was she to be flogged but there was something else, something which they knew and she didn't, that had caused the hall to be full to capacity this morning.

"The sentence is twenty-five," the magistrate said, looking with glee at the slender rod. "Proceed, and do your duty thoroughly," he added.

Juliette's escort turned her to face into the hall. She saw the stool that she was to be bent over. She looked round at the expectant faces of her audience, at the stern looks on her escorts' faces. Finally she accepted the inevitable. They intended to flog her, come what may. So the sooner it was over and done with and she could retreat to her lodgings and nurse her wounded pride and bottom the better. I still have my dignity left, She tried to console herself. She had to cling on to something or she would be screaming all the time. With a show of bravado that belied the dread that

10

consumed her, she shrugged off the warders' hands and walked slowly towards where her ordeal was to take place.

She came to a halt against the stool. Her legs were pulled apart and the rings snapped to others at the base of the stool. With one last terrified glance she looked at the cane in the executioner's hand as she felt a light push between her shoulders. She bent over and the rings on her wrists were attached to the stool. She realised that her buttocks were now perfectly positioned and a feeling of rebellion surged through her. This was so unjust! Her parents had always taught her that justice was important, and she had always dealt fairly with friends and enemies alike. She resolved that, if the gloating ogres in the audience expected her to yell for mercy, she would not give them that satisfaction. She shut her eyes and gripped the stool tight with her small hands, her buttocks quivering, as she waited for the onslaught to begin.

She heard the executioner walk across the hall and take his position to her left. She felt her legs shaking and her buttocks clenched in anticipation She couldn't control them.

Swish. Thwack.

Nothing could have prepared her for the searing pain that erupted in her backside. It was as if a white-hot poker had been laid across the full width of her soft cheeks.

Swish. Crack.

Another line of fire joined the first. She felt hot tears escape from between her tightly closed eyelids. Yet, she tried to console herself, apart from a quick gasp as the cane struck, she had remained defiantly silent.

Thwack.

Only three strokes taken. Her bottom already felt as if she was sitting in boiling oil and she had twenty-five strokes to endure! How could she survive such a beating?

Crack.

Her lithe body jerked in its bonds as the rattan curled around her burning cheeks. A loud sob sounded from between her tightly closed lips.

Thwack.

She had deliberately clenched her bottom cheeks as the

cane descended in a frantic attempt to reduce the pain, but it had only made the stroke hurt more. A cry, more of frustration than pain, escaped her lips.

Crack.

Thwack.

The executioner had noticed the audience's annoyance at the girl's stubborn silence. The two strokes, without any reduction in force, were delivered in quick succession. His effort was rewarded as the girl gave up the struggle and, as she surrendered to the pain, a wail of agony rebounded round the hall. Some of the audience clapped!

Swish. Crack.

Eight!

To her surprise, part of the girl's brain was keeping count of her progress.

Thwack.

Crack.

Juliette's agonised body began to writhe frantically on the stool, trying to avoid the punishing rod. Each stroke was drawing a loud yell of agony and protest from her and the nearer watchers could see a fine sheen of sweat covering her fair skin.

Thwack.

Crack.

This, the twelfth stroke, finally broke the girl's control as she turned her head to the ceiling and a shrill scream echoed round the hall.

Crack.

Thwack.

The girl screamed as her thrashing passed the half way mark. The strokes were now landing on the raised weals left by the rod and her abused body was struggling to avoid further agony being heaped upon it. Her erratic movements were spoiling the executioner's aim and he stopped for a minute to secure a leather strap round her waist and the stool.

Four more times the long punishing rod whistled through the air to land with a resounding report adding another searing line of fire across her immobile cheeks.

Scream after scream was forced from her lungs. She could not now writhe or squirm to ease the agony. Some of the audience, those in the back row, had risen to their feet to get a better view. After the eighteenth stroke had laced across her cheeks, the girl's eyes momentarily cleared of tears. She turned her head and looked at the executioner over her shoulder. The concentration on his face, and the sweat on his brow, testified to the effort he was putting into his task. She looked over the other shoulder, at the audience, hoping to see some sign of sympathy or pity. There was none!

Thwack.

Thwack.

Relentlessly, the rod lashed her swollen cheeks as her screams echoed in the hall. Her body was wringing with sweat, rivulets of which ran down her hanging breasts to fall from her nipples to the floor. Only five more to come, her brain informed her. She had never dreamed such agony could exist. Yet here she was, a young tender twenty year old, her bottom absorbing the flogging as if it were a regular occurrence.

Crack.

Another line of exquisite agony flared in her bottom sending another scream rebounding through the air. Despite the agony that raged in her bottom and was radiating through her body, she realised there was something wrong. Her breasts ached with the hardness of her erect nipples and her sex lips were soaking wet! She was sexually aroused just as she had been when her boyfriend tenderly stroked her body before taking his pleasure of her. But this was different and a surge of shame and humiliation swept through her.

Swish. Thwack.

The girl jerked rigid as the pain wracked her body then, with a final scream of agony and surrender, she collapsed over the stool. The shuddering of her body and the low mewing and moaning that came from her open mouth showed that she was still conscious and aware of what was being done to her.

Three more times the punishing rattan lashed her across

13

her bottom. Her body jerked violently against the restraints and her mewing and moaning increased in volume. Sweat poured from her body, dripping to the floor from her erect nipples to join the dark stains on the floor where her tears had fallen. Her brain, now aware only of the terrible agony that flooded through her body, had given up the count. She was, therefore, unaware that her sentence had been completed and, for a minute or two, her body continued to jerk as if the cane was still lashing her bottom. Through the mist of pain that engulfed her, she felt the strap removed from her waist and her ankles and wrists released. Her hands flew behind her, seeking out her throbbing cheeks to rub them to try and ease the pain.

She continued to lie over the stool as she fought to regain control of herself. Slowly the mist cleared, leaving her fully conscious of the raging fire in her bottom. Again, she became aware of her hardened nipples and the wetness oozing from her sex lips. This couldn't be, she tried to tell herself. Her backside had just been painfully flogged, yet her body had become aroused. Her brain refused to believe it could have happened, but the evidence was there. Her erect nipples and the juices that had run down the inside of her thighs were undeniable. Shame and humiliation flooded through her. All she wanted was to get out of the hall, away from the eyes of these disgusting people who had witnessed her shame.

She placed her hands on the top of the stool and gradually eased her body upright. The movement sending fresh waves of pain through her bottom. She turned to face the magistrate and the audience that had so plainly enjoyed watching her beating. She looked at the man who had just beaten her and the cane hanging loose in his hand. His thick torso was covered in sweat and his chest heaved with his heavy breathing as he made his way from the hall, to the applause of the audience. The two warders grasped her arms and marched her back to stand facing the magistrate. She tried to blank out the spasms of pain each movement caused to flare up, but she just couldn't obliterate from her mind the knowledge that her thighs carried the evidence of her body's strange behaviour during the flogging.

"Juliette Savart!" the magistrate's voice broke into her thoughts.

"Y…yes, Your Worship." Juliette looked up at him and, before he could speak, continued. "I have taken the punishment to which you so unjustly sentenced me. Now may I go home?"

For a moment, she thought she saw a hint of laughter in his cruel eyes. A ripple of amusement came from the audience. Juliette shook her head, disgusted at this reaction to her words. They had seen her thrashed, what more could they want?

"No!" the magistrate announced. "It seems you have not lost your haughty attitude and, were it not that there is more to your sentence, I would summon the executioner back and have you flogged again."

Juliette looked at him, utter astonishment and disbelief in her expression. She had taken the beating, what more could there be?

"No, Juliette Savart," the magistrate continued, looking hard at her. "You may not go home, not now or ever. Your offence was a very grave one." He paused to clear his throat. "Sacrilege is a matter that cannot be dealt with merely by a flogging. You are now to be sold into servitude, by auction, as the Laws of the State prescribe for the offence of sacrilege."

"Sold! Into servitude!" Juliette stammered, not believing what she had heard. "You said a flogging and I took it, even though I was innocent of any crime," she shouted indignantly at him. "You have no right to sell me. This is not the justice I was brought up to expect."

"The Law is clear and will be upheld," the magistrate spluttered, angry at her audacity in questioning his judgement. A thunderous scowl had replaced the lecherous look on his face as he had watched her naked body squirming under the rod. He turned to the warders. "Take the slut away and have her cleaned up ready for the sale. Then bring her back here. If you have any trouble with her, you will report the matter to me and she will get another flogging. Perhaps a taste of the lash on her back will teach her respect."

The warders marched Juliette from the hall and took her to a nearby wash room. Here she was ordered to bathe. In a complete mental daze at what she had just learned, she did as they ordered. The hot water at first stung her swollen buttocks dreadfully but, after a minute or two, it began to have a soothing effect. The warders supervised her closely and she was not allowed long in the bath. She was ordered out and, having dried herself, ordered to brush out her hair and repair the cosmetics. The two men made the most of the opportunity. It was rare that they had such a young and attractive girl in their custody, most unlike the usual hags that came their way. Although they did not make her hurry, they stretched the time as much as they dared as their eyes devoured the luxury of her naked body. Their ribald comments on her attributes, and the good fortune of her future master, sent shivers of fear and disgust down her spine.

When they were satisfied that she was again presentable, they marched her back into the hall where she had been flogged and halted her in front of the magistrate. The dignitary thumped the table with his gavel, bringing silence to the hall.

"Juliette Savart," he announced in a loud voice. "You are now to be sold into servitude by auction. You will become the property of the highest bidder, who will become your master or mistress, to do with you as they choose. If you should be so foolish as to try and escape, the mandatory punishment for a recaptured slave is death. Do you understand?"

The girl, stunned by his words, looked straight into his eyes not trying to hide the loathing that shone there. At first, as she had bathed, she had not really believed what he had said before dismissing her.

"Understand?" the magistrate barked at her, annoyed at the delay in her response and the expression on her face.

"I heard you," Juliette replied sullenly.

"I will have respect from you," he stormed at her. Then,

forcing his temper to cool down, he turned and whispered to one of his assistants. The man rose and left the hall. He returned a moment or so later, accompanied by the executioner who held a vicious whip in his hands. "Now," the magistrate resumed. "Do I have to have you whipped before you learn?"

"No, your Worship," Juliette replied, trying to make her voice sound meek and respectful. The sight of the whip had banished any rebelliousness from her.

"Proceed with the auction."

The two warders marched Juliette to the centre of the hall. The stool, over which she had been thrashed, had been removed. In its place was a raised dais. They led her to this and made her stand in the centre facing the audience. The manacles on her wrists were again snapped together and attached to a chain that hung from the roof rafter. The chain was pulled tight stretching her arms above her head and raising her up onto her toes. The magistrate's assistant mounted the dais and faced the audience.

"Ladies and Gentlemen," he began. "Juliette Savart is twenty years old. The doctor has fully examined her and assessed that she is in perfect health. She is not a virgin but, he assures us, she had not conceived."

As the man paused for breath, the chain by which she was suspended began to slowly, making her rotate with it.

"Look well, Ladies and Gentlemen," he continued. "You can see her obvious charms and you have seen how well she comports herself when under discipline. With the right persuasion, she will, I am sure, provide many hours of pleasure to whoever acquires her. You did not fail, I am sure, to notice the unusual reaction of her body to the cane. Surely this promises well and adds to her attractions."

Juliette blushed with shame at this last observation, which drew forth many sniggers from the audience.

"Now, Ladies and Gentlemen. What am I bid for this delightful animal? Who will start the bidding?"

As the audience began to shout their bids to the assistant, Juliette felt a deep revulsion sweep through her. It was her, her body, which they were bidding for! She felt

17

like a prize cow, or mare, which they sought to own. But she was not a cow, nor a mare! She was a human being, just like them! But she was not! In their eyes she had ceased to be a human being by the sentence of the Court. From now on she was merely an animal, and not a prize one at that. She hated all of them for the degradation to which she was being subjected. Sell her as a slave they might, but she would never, never, be anyone's slave. At least, not in her own mind no matter how hard they tried to break her.

The bidding, which had been fast and furious at first, had slowed down. Now there were only three bidders, two men and one woman, left in contention for her. She could see that both men were of middle age and, she had to admit to herself that one was quite handsome. The woman, on the other hand, was quite young and was looking at Juliette's naked body with unconcealed lust.

The assistant continued to praise, unnecessarily Juliette thought, the charms and attractions of owning such a delicious piece of 'slave meat', as he referred to her, trying his hardest to raise the price. Now only two contenders continued to outbid each other until finally, to Juliette's relief, the woman dropped out and the assistant announced that she had been sold to the remaining man. Her wrists were released from the chain and she was hurried to a side room. Here, her purchaser completed the transaction and ordered her to kneel at his feet. He replaced the manacles on her wrists with his own and then closed a metal collar, from which hung a long chain, round her neck. Holding the chain, the man led her from the building. As they emerged, Juliette saw the young woman who had lost in the bidding.

"Not so lucky, this time, Lady Moona," her owner called out to the woman. "As a consolation, in time, I may loan the slave to you for a few days so you may enjoy her."

"That is most generous of you, Lord Reythal," the woman replied graciously. "She is a fine piece and I look forward to trying her for myself."

Juliette's new master chuckled to himself as he mounted his horse. He set off at a slow trot, forcing the still naked slave to keep pace alongside his mount. They passed along the dust covered road and she heard several voices calling out complimenting her owner on his acquisition. Keeping pace with the horse, trying not to stumble, Juliette felt ashamed of her nakedness. Her firm full breasts bounced invitingly with the motion and her bottom, which still burned and throbbed from the caning, was on full view to all who chose to look. Hatred for those who had brought her to this sorry state seethed inside her. Just as she thought that her lungs would burst and she would end up being dragged behind the horse, they approached a pair of heavy gates set in a high wall. The gates swung open and, slowing his mount, her master led his naked slave through the opening.

Inside the gate, the scene changed dramatically. Either side of a long driveway, which led to a large mansion, green lawns grew, intersected by well-tended flowerbeds, full of exotic blossoms. Juliette walked beside the horse until, having passed round to the rear of the building they entered a large yard, bounded by what were obviously stables and store sheds. A tall thickset man, clearly the head groom, took the horse's reins as her master dismounted.

"'Morning, Quinell," her master addressed the man. "This is the new slave. She is called Juliette. Take her and give her the usual introduction, then bring her to my study."

"Yes, My Lord," the man replied, then turned to the girl. "Follow me."

Juliette followed the man across the yard and into one of the stables. As they crossed the yard, she noticed a high thick wooden post, erected in the centre and, nearby, another, about a meter high with a round log fixed along the top. Inside the stable, Quinell pushed the girl towards one of the supporting pillars. He pulled her arms up above her head and hooked her manacles over a hook, the chain from the collar hanging down between her breasts. He parted her hair and draped it forward to hang over her upthrust breasts.

"The introduction for a new slave is ten lashes," Quinell said in her ear. "This is to teach you that, here, you are a slave and what your fate will be if you fail to please those you serve."

Juliette shook with fear. Her buttocks were still

19

throbbing from the earlier caning and now, for no reason, she was to be beaten again. That her hair had been pulled forward over her breasts warned her that, this time, it was her back that was to suffer. She watched in alarm as the head groom strode across the stable and picked up a bundle of leather reins. As he shook them loose, the girl trembled with terror. As he approached her, she gritted her teeth and screwed her eyes tight shut.

The force of the blow across her back jerked her up onto her toes as her body was thrown against the pillar, separating her breasts. A sheet of fire exploded in her back and shoulders as the leathers burned a path across her flesh. She heard a loud scream, her scream, echo round the stable. Again she was thrown against the post and again she screamed as the pain raged in her back. Eight more times the head groom lashed the leathers across her back, sending sheets of fire through her body. Such a flogging, which she was to learn later was a mere token, on top of the caning she had received that morning was too much for her young body to bear and, although still conscious, she hung limp from her wrists as the final lashes were laid on. Her wrists were released and she slid slowly down the pillar, sobbing and moaning.

Her wrists were again manacled together in front of her body and she was led by the chain back across the yard and into the rear of the building. As they passed through the kitchens, Juliette saw other girls attending to their duties under the supervision of the head cook. They paid little attention to the new arrival, only casting secretive glances in her direction as she passed. She did not fail to notice the thin cane that hung on the wall by the door, nor that one or two of the girls were naked, their bottoms decorated with dark red stripes where they had been beaten. She shuddered with apprehension as she observed these details. She knew that slavery was legal and, among the richer people, widespread in the Country, but she had never dreamed that such would be her fate.

She followed the head groom, along passages and up a flight of stairs until he halted outside a door on which he knocked. A voice from within bade them enter. She was led into a large room that, judging from the number of books lining the walls and the other furniture, was clearly a study and library. Seated behind a desk was Lord Reythal, the man who had purchased her at the auction. The groom kicked lightly at the back of her knees and ordered her to kneel.

"She has been taught her place?" Lord Reythal asked.

"She has, My Lord. Ten lashes with the leathers as usual."

"Let me see."

Obeying the groom's orders, Juliette rose and turned, presenting her rear to her Master. Quinell drew her hair forward, exposing her back. Lord Reythal looked at the mass of weals left by the leathers and then his eyes lowered to inspect her bruised buttocks.

"Very satisfactory, Quinell," he said. "How did she take it?" he asked, thoughtfully.

"She screamed on each stroke, My Lord. They usually do until they become used to being disciplined."

"Turn and kneel, slave."

Juliette heard her Master's order and quickly obeyed, the movement rekindling the fire in her back and bottom. She kept her eyes lowered, staring at the floor, not daring to meet his gaze in case he saw the hatred in her own, which she knew she could not hide.

"I am Lord Reythal." His voice sounded firm and hard. A man who was used to being obeyed without question, she realised. "You are now my slave, my property. You will serve me, and my family and staff, without hesitation or question." The tone of his voice left Juliette in no doubt that he meant every word. Although she had been caned and whipped that very day, she still found it hard to believe that she was now nothing more than a slave. An animal! "You were warned by the magistrate of the punishment for attempting to escape. There is no escape from my holding! You are confined to the buildings and grounds and, if you ever disobey this order, you will be severely dealt with. Do you understand?"

"Yes." Juliette had hardly murmured the word when she received a sound slap across the side of her head from Quinell that sent her sliding across the floor.

"You will address me as 'Master'," Lord Reythal's voice thundered.

"Yes, Master," Juliette replied, regaining her kneeling position.

"I detect a strain of defiance in her bearing, Quinell," Lord Reythal mused. "Take her away and put her in cook's charge. She can scrub the kitchen floors until she learns how to behave. She will remain naked and sleep in the kennels until further notice."

The head groom ordered Juliette to rise and follow him. At the door, Lord Reythal's voice halted them.

"Quinell. Put her in the belt and, at night, manacle her wrists behind her back."

Quinell led her back to the stables. He ordered her to stand with her legs wide apart. Juliette shuddered with horror as he took a strange contraption from a hook. A thick leather belt was put round her waist and fastened behind her back. From the front hung a 'U' shaped metal bar which he drew up between her legs, pulled it tight, and locked the end to the fastening on the belt. The whole was then locked in place. As Quinell turned his back on her, Juliette quickly ran her hands over the metal. It fitted so snugly that she could not get even her small finger beneath it. She found that it was designed so that she could relieve herself without the thing being removed. To her dismay, it prevented her from getting her fingers anywhere near her sex. A low moan of despair came from her as her heart sank in dismay. Ever since she had surrendered her virginity, it had been one of her secret pleasures, when she was in bed and alone, to stroke herself there and feel the delicious sensations coursing through her body.

"That's right, my beauty," Quinell said sneering. "That will stop you playing with yourself."

Quinell looked her up and down. From the moment he had seen her arrive, he had anticipated the pleasure of using her. That pleasure was now denied him. It seemed that, contrary to his usual practice, the Master had earmarked this one for his personal service before she had spent time available to the staff. He could hardly blame Lord Reythal! This one was an unusually attractive piece of slave meat. Putting his regrets aside, he picked up the chain and led her back to the kitchens, where, removing the chain from the collar, he handed her over to cook.

Gretta, as Juliette soon discovered was the cook's name, looked the new arrival over carefully. The weals left by the leathers on the girl's back did not surprise her. That was usual for new arrivals! What did surprise her, however, was the state of the girl's heavily bruised and swollen buttocks.

"What did you do to be flogged that badly, girl?" the cook demanded.

"Nothing," Juliette replied. "I was accused of something I did not do and the magistrate found me guilty of sacrilege."

"That is what they all say," cook said scornfully. "Sacrilege, you said! Then you deserved all you got, and more." She did not try to hide the contempt she felt at the girl's crime. She reached out and took the cane down from the hook by the door. "Bend over and hold your ankles."

Juliette saw the hate in the woman's eyes and was sorely tempted to refuse. Then she remembered the no-nonsense attitude of her owner. The last thing she needed was another severe thrashing on her sore bottom. Better take what the 'cow' might do rather than that! Reluctantly she obeyed, gripping her ankles tight.

"Straighten those legs and keep still. Three strokes to teach you that you are now a slave. In future, you will address me as 'madam'."

Juliette braced herself as cook took up her position. All those in the kitchen had stopped what they were doing to watch. Juliette heard the cane swish through the air. It landed with surprising force across her bottom. But for the state of her bottom, the stroke would have been bearable but, landing as it did on cheeks made swollen and sore by the morning's caning, she could not suppress a shrill yell. She just managed to keep hold of her ankles as the cook

23

lashed her buttocks twice more. The lesson over, Juliette was set to work scrubbing the kitchen floor. To ensure that she did it properly, cook delegated one of the kitchen staff to stand over her, cane in hand, to discourage any slackness in her efforts.

As she worked, Juliette seethed inwardly. In less than thirty hours since her so called friends had run off and left her to the mercy of the law men, she had been falsely accused, caned terribly and severely lashed with those leathers and now caned again. Their cowardice had deposited her in this terrible predicament and now, like it or not, she was condemned to be a slave for the rest of her life. It wasn't fair and she silently cursed them. Her trial had been a mockery of justice. Her conviction, sentence and the terrible future from which there was no escape were a nightmare. In this land, the law was the whim of those who seized and held on to power.

There was no justice. Certainly no justice for Juliette.

CHAPTER 2

Juliette laboured in the kitchens for four weeks. She worked from sun up to dusk, all the time under the watchful eyes of cook or one of her underlings. Any sign of slacking earned her a sharp cut with the cane. The signs of her judicial beating faded gradually, but her buttocks were never free from the fresh tramlines, which gave evidence of the strict regime she was put under. Inwardly, she burned with the injustice of her plight, but she soon learned to hide her feelings and work hard, if only to save her tender bottom from further punishment. It seemed to her that everyone in the household had been told of her 'crime', of which only she knew she was innocent, and despised her for it and took every opportunity to increase her suffering.

At night, along with the other menial female slaves owned by Lord Reythal, she was locked in the kennels. These were cages, constructed of metal bars spaced close together and mounted on blocks above the stone floor. The slaves were kept naked at night and allowed no covering, other than some straw that littered the floor and which had a tendency to fall between the bars. It was the night time that caused Juliette the worst suffering. Apart from the discomfort caused by the barred floor, with her hands secured behind her back, she had no way to satisfy the needs that her body was prone to. The kennels were not constructed for comfort. Each was a mere three feet high and wide and six feet long. The stone floor ensured that, even on the hottest night, the slaves were never warm. She soon came to terms with the frequent attacks on her behind, but the tight fitting belt ensured that she had no way to give her body the satisfaction it craved.

Her frustration was not helped by the strange change that had come over her body. As she had, to her shame, discovered at the House of Correction, the kiss of a cane on her bottom caused her body to become aroused. She was ashamed that the application of pain to her bottom could arouse her sexually. She did not understand this and so tried

25

her best to conceal it to the best of her ability. Her shame and frustration fuelled the hatred she felt, both for those who seemed to delight in ordering, and administering the pain, and for her body for responding the way it did.

It was during her fifth week in the kitchens that a dramatic change occurred to her routine. Instead of being taken to the kitchen after she had scrubbed out her cage, Quinell fastened a chain to the collar round her neck and took her to a different part of the house. She eventually ended up in a large washroom. Here a severe looking man, well dressed, awaited them. Quinell removed the belt from her waist and the collar and chain from her neck and handed her over to this man and departed.

"I am Lord Reythal's major-domo," the man announced. "My name is Abaddon. I trust that your time in the kitchens has taught you your place and how a slave should behave."

"Yes," Juliette replied. There was something about this man that made her instinctively dislike him. It was the first time she had met him but she had heard him spoken of by the other slaves. She was aware that his name was also an alternative name for the Devil and, judging by what she had heard, he lived up to his name.

"You will address me as 'Master' when we are alone. At other times you will call me 'Sir'," he thundered. "Do not forget again or I will have you thrashed."

Juliette shivered at the sheer malevolence in his voice and the overt way he looked lustfully at her naked body.

"You are to be transferred to the Lord's personal service. See that you do not displease him or you will be flogged and returned permanently to the kitchens." He clapped his hands and two young female slaves entered the room and knelt in front of him. "This slave, she is named Juliette, is to join the Master's personal service," he informed them. "See that she is thoroughly washed and prepared to be presented to him."

One of the girls led her to a long low bench and made her lie along it. Her body and limbs were coated with a thick lather then, picking up a sharp looking knife, one girl proceeded to shave her until only her head boasted any hair.

Then she was ordered to bathe and wash her body and hair thoroughly. Having dried her hair and body, she was stood in front of a full-length mirror. She watched, resignedly, as the girls brushed out her hair and applied cosmetics to her face and body. She nearly forgot herself and objected when a girl knelt in front of her and proceeded to outline her sex lips with kohl, and the other rubbed rouge into her nipples and aureoles. When the girls had finished, Juliette hardly recognised the reflection that looked back at her in the mirror. All this was done under the close scrutiny of Abaddon. When he was satisfied, a short transparent skirt that only reached to mid thigh, was placed round her hips and cups, of the same material, suspended from her neck by thin gold chains, covered her breasts. The transparency of the material seemed to emphasise the black outline of the kohl and rouge.

Apart from the occasional order from Abaddon, the whole process had been carried out in silence. But for the exaggerating effect of the cosmetics, Juliette was now attired the same as the other two girls. This, she assumed, was the 'uniform' worn by the female slaves in the Master's personal service. She wondered who the other two could be. She dared not ask for, since she had arrived at the mansion, none of the other slaves had spoken to her except to relay an order. The one time she had dared to speak to one of them, she had received three hard cuts of Gretta's cane.

Finally satisfied with her appearance, Abaddon ordered her to follow him. With the other two a step behind her, Juliette obeyed until the man halted in front of an ornately carved door on which he knocked. A summons came from within and he opened the door and the small procession entered the room beyond. She was halted in front of a throne like chair on which Lord Reythal was seated.

"Do not kneel. Stand still," Abaddon ordered.

Juliette was conscious of the critical survey that her Master made of her and her legs began to shake as she looked into his dark eyes. In obedience to his command, she turned slowly round until she faced him again. Abaddon gave a signal to the two girls, who stepped forward and

27

deftly removed the filmy coverings from her hips and breasts. She stood naked, perfectly still, keeping her eyes lowered so she might not see the disapproving look on her Master's face.

"Look at me," her Master ordered.

Slowly, with mounting dread, Juliette raised her gaze until her eyes met his. Her knees suddenly felt weak at the sheer lust and savagery she saw in his eyes and the cruel twist on his mouth.

"You have done well, Abaddon. She will do very nicely. If she proves satisfactory, she may join my personal service," Lord Reythal finally said.

"Thank you, My Lord," the major-domo replied. "I trust you will not be disappointed with her. As you so rightly assessed, she has displayed all the signs that indicate her body can provide perfect satisfaction." He turned to the two slave girls. "Prepare her."

The two girls rose from the kneeling position they had adopted since stripping her, and led Juliette to a large divan in an adjoining room. Before she realised what was happening, they had forced her down on the divan, placed a thick cushion under her buttocks and, spreading her limbs wide, secured her wrists and ankles to ropes at the four corners. They pulled the ropes tight, stretching her body taut. Juliette began to tremble as a cloth was placed over her head. She could see nothing but immediately felt soft fingers stroking her thighs and breasts. Her body, having been deprived of any form of satisfaction for so long, responded almost immediately. The girls played her body, as a skilled musician plays his instrument. Juliette, ashamed at the way her body betrayed her, despite her efforts to prevent it, moaned and writhed as her arousal increased. They worked on her until her nipples felt as if they would burst and her sex lips gaped wide and wet. The girls were skilful, making sure that her arousal did not rise too high, making her moan as her body demanded release from the exquisite agony that coursed through her.

Just as suddenly as they had started, their attentions ceased and the cloth was whisked away from her face and another cushion placed under her head. Looking along her body, between her aching breasts, Juliette gasped in disbelief. Standing at the foot of the divan was Lord Reythal, naked, his penis erect and swollen so much that the prone girl shuddered in awe. She trembled as he mounted the divan and lowered himself onto his slave. Despite the attentions of the girls, Juliette's gaping sex was not prepared for the first thrust of his massive organ. It felt as if she was being torn apart as he entered and forced himself deep into her love tunnel. Slowly at first, then with increasing momentum, he took his pleasure of her. His hands grasped her breasts, causing her to gasp in pain so fierce was his grip.

"Do not, on any account, permit yourself to come. It is the Master's order," Juliette heard one of the girls whisper in her ear.

Shocked by the sudden realisation that there was still an audience to her taking, Juliette tried desperately to control the orgasm that was threatening to overcome her. She felt her face redden with embarrassment and shame as her muscles tightened round the invader and began to milk it. This is rape! Her brain screamed in her head. Never in her life had she been taken by force. Her body twisted under the weight of her Master. She tried to scream her hatred of him but only a low moan of pleasure escaped her mouth as her body denied her and welcomed the possession it had craved for so long. Then the thrusting stopped as her Master's body arched rigid above her for a moment, only to recommence more violent than before. She felt her Master's satisfaction jet into her in rapid spurts until she thought he would never stop. Slowly he withdrew, her muscles trying to hold him inside her until she came too. He eased himself forward until he knelt over her breasts.

"Cleanse your Master," the girl whispered in her ear.

Juliette sensed what was required of her, although she had never done such a thing before. She had always refused to fellate her boyfriends in the past even though her own sex had been no stranger to their tongues. But now she had no choice if she was not to incur his displeasure. She leaned her head forward, mouth open and, as the still rigid shaft descended, took it in. For the first time she tasted the saltiness of a man's secretion, mixed with her own muskiness. To her astonishment she did not find it unpleasant. She used her tongue, just as she had seen her cat clean her kittens, and licked his manhood clean. As the shaft finally started to become flaccid, she felt a few drops of his juices slide along her tongue. As he eased himself off her body, she felt a hard object inserted between her sex lips. This was moved back and forth, teasing her arousal to uncontrollable heights until the room spun and her body climaxed in a series of shattering orgasms and a blackness fell over her eyes. Just as the last strands of consciousness left her, she remembered the order. Her orgasm had been forced totally out of her control, but she had disobeyed and her mind's eye saw the terrible whip that she knew would punish her for her transgression.

She began to emerge from the delicious mist that had engulfed her in the orgasm's wake. Her body felt wonderful, its craving having been satisfied after so long an abstinence. She was still in the same room, still on the divan, but she had been turned face down, her limbs again secured to the corners, and the cushions that her been under her behind and head were now under her stomach, raising her buttocks high in the air. Still muzzy from the orgasm, she turned her head and looked round, just in time to see one of the girls hand a long thin switch to Abaddon. The cruel smile on his face made her stomach churn.

"Fortunately for you, the Master was pleased with your body," Abaddon sneered at her. "That is why, to my regret, he has not ordered a whipping for your disobedience. Instead all you are to have is ten cuts with this," he said regretfully, waving the switch before her eyes.

So saying, he raised his arm and brought the switch down, cutting across her proffered buttocks with a resounding report. Still weak from her taking, she was unable to stop a shrill cry of pain following the sound of the first impact.

Thwack.

Crack.

Thwack.

The slave's body writhed as the four livid lines burned in her soft cheeks. Her shrill cries sounded loud in the otherwise silent room.

Thwack.

Crack.

Although the girl was writhing, Abaddon admired the accuracy of his marksmanship. The slave's buttocks, which had been pale and smooth, devoid of any sign of flagellation when she had entered the room, now displayed six bright red lines running parallel across her cheeks, the weals stretching round both sides. Even though he hard laid the strokes on hard, because her buttocks had not been stretched taut, the leather covered rod had not cut the skin. Also, to his displeasure, the softer underside had escaped the rod's attention. The only way to attack that region would to bring the rod across sideways. But she was too low down to achieve the optimum force that way! A wicked smile spread his lips. He would try something he had wanted to do for a long time. He beckoned one of the girls to him and whispered in her ear. A look of astonishment appeared on the girl's face but she was too frightened of him to question his order. She knelt at the side of the divan and, without disturbing the cushions, insinuated her body forward, until her own buttocks were directly under the prone girl's stomach and arched her back.

Abaddon looked at the result. It was a modification he had thought about often. With the girl under her arching her back, Juliette's buttocks had been raised so that the vulnerable underside was perfectly positioned. Taking his time and putting his weight behind each, Abaddon brought the riding switch down across the soft underhang of the slave's buttocks for the final four strokes of her beating. To his great pleasure Juliette screamed shrilly each time the switch lashed her behind. She writhed and squirmed delightfully, and the picturesque pattern on her cheeks was a joy for him to behold.

Abaddon ordered the girl to extricate herself from the

divan just as Lord Reythal, now fully dressed, returned to the room. He surveyed Juliette's buttocks, running his fingers lightly over the weals, making her flinch at the touch.

"Excellent, Abaddon," he said. "Education can be, and should be, painful. I trust you have learned a lesson from it, slave?"

"Yes, Master," Juliette replied through the sobs that she was unable to control. Those last four strokes had been 'hell'. She hated this man who had ordered the thrashing, and he who had applied it, with all her heart. Her only regret was that she was too terrified of them to spit her hatred at them. That the beating had only been a mild one, made no difference.

"See that she is attended to, Abaddon. She is to wait on table this evening," Lord Reythal said.

"Yes, My Lord," he replied. "But there is something which you should know," he whispered in the Lord's ear.

"Are you sure, man?"

"Yes, My Lord. Feel for yourself."

Lord Reythal stooped down and slipped his hand under the prone girl. His fingers sought her nipples, which he found were hard and engorged. His other hand slid down between her thighs and found her sex lips open and oozing juice. He straightened up, a look of astonishment on his face.

"By Jove," he said, turning to his major-domo. "You are right, Abaddon. I saw the same thing when she was publicly flogged, but thought it had, somehow, been induced. That magistrate is a crafty fellow and is quite capable of doing anything to make his wares more attractive. This is food for thought." So saying he turned and strolled pensively from the room.

Juliette felt her limbs released and, immediately, her hands flew to her backside, gingerly rubbing to ease the pain. She felt the raised weals and the stickiness on the soft underside where the switch had cut the skin. Abaddon watched with a smile of satisfaction on his face. He was aware of the pressure of his penis against his breeches and he regretted he had been prevented from using this tasty morsel when she had been in the kitchens. She was, by far, the best he had ever seen and he silently vowed that somehow, one day, his manhood would sample the flavour of her body. But that was in the future, at present he had to satisfy his needs. He gave orders to the two slave girls and hurriedly left the room on his way to the kitchens to seek out a young female on whom to assuage his desires.

The two young slave girls assisted Juliette to rise and took her to the quarters assigned to Lord Reythal's personal slaves. As they tenderly applied cold towels to Juliette's bottom, they introduced themselves as Sarita and Maya. Juliette turned to look at them properly for the first time. She saw that they were both young, a year younger than herself she found out later, shapely, and the same height with long golden hair flowing in waves down their backs. Their skins were pale, like alabaster, and, looking at them together, they were almost identical. A well matched pair! As soon as they had assured her that, in their quarters, they were free from the restriction of silence, Juliette plied them with many questions. She learned that they were not related, as she had first imagined. They had both been victims of the injustice of the Courts, sentenced to a flogging and slavery, and bought by their Master.

The three became instant friends. The two blondes explained their duties and the rules to Juliette, and the best ways of keeping out of trouble and avoid being beaten. They warned her that the Master, whilst being fair, was very strict but to beware of Abaddon who, as she had already found out, enjoyed beating the female slaves. Also, they warned her to stay clear of the Master's younger son. He, they said in a whisper, was a spoilt brat who enjoyed getting them, especially Sarita for some unknown reason, into trouble and watching them beaten. Also, they added with a shudder, he was sometimes allowed to administer their thrashings. The truth, at least part, of this was to be brought home to Juliette sooner than she expected.

Soon it was time to prepare to serve during the evening meal. Juliette, informed that the whole of the Master's family would be present, was somewhat apprehensive when she was given the costume she would be required to wear for the evening. This was so minimal that it hardly existed and her apprehension increased when she surveyed herself in a long mirror. A thin gold chain hung from her hips with a narrow panel of gossamer material suspended from the front. The material was so fine that the girls' sex lips and bush were clearly visible. Two thin chains, drawn tight, circled the base of her breasts making them swell and her nipples stand proud and erect, the ends being pulled up behind her neck and linked together. Apart from this, they were naked. The two blondes were clearly used to being trussed like this but Juliette felt more embarrassed than if she had been totally naked.

Her feelings were further disturbed when Abaddon arrived and inspected them closely, adjusting the chains here and there until he was satisfied. The new girl, much to the man's annoyance, cringed as his stubby fingers touched her body. Only the threat of a beating made her submit passively. Once satisfied, he conducted the three to the dining hall where he gave them their instructions for the evening. The two blondes were detailed to serve the food while the new girl would dispense the wine. They were then told to stand at the side of the hall. After a short wait, Lord Reythal, accompanied by his wife and two sons, entered and took their places at the table. Juliette took the opportunity, as they arranged themselves, to study her Master's family. The wife was not by any standards attractive, being over dressed in finery with a petulant look on her face that never seemed to change. It was the two sons that held her attention. The younger looked thoroughly spoiled and bad tempered and she recalled the warning her two friends had given her about him. Little did she know that, before the evening was over, she would find out the truth of what they had said. The older son was quite handsome. He had his father's looks, even to the slight cruel curl to his mouth. Under other circumstances, she thought, she might have fancied him. The object of her gaze turned his head and looked in her direction.

"So that is the new girl?" he said, turning to his father. "She looks quite appetising. I would like to try her out sometime, if you agree."

"She is not bad," Lord Reythal responded. "A little untrained as yet, but promising. I will consider your request in time."

"I want her also," the younger son chimed in. "She has a nice backside!"

"All in good time, my boy," the boy's father replied, looking fondly at his son. "If you are good, I might let you discipline her sometime, if the need arises."

"Oh yes please!" the boy answered quickly, giving Juliette a leering look.

Juliette, who had heard the exchange between both sons and their father, felt both ashamed and revolted as she listened to them. They were discussing her as if she were some animal. The very idea of that brat touching and beating her made her feel sick. Fortunately, Abaddon gave the signal for the food and wine to be served and her mind was taken of the revolting idea as she concentrated on her task. She did not fail to notice the older boy slide his hand up Maya's thigh as she served him and this prepared her for similar treatment as she leaned close to him and filled his glass. To her surprise, she found his touch gentle and pleasant.

As the meal progressed, the younger boy's behaviour became more objectionable. Lord Reythal seemed to be trying hard to ignore it, but the doting mother seemed intent on encouraging the little brat. The youth's behaviour got progressively worse and it was clear that, one way or another, he was intent on causing mischief. The disaster occurred as Sarita was serving him his sweet. She suddenly jumped back, letting out a cry and some of the younger son's sweet spilled over the tablecloth. Sarita's face immediately turned white with fear. Abaddon, whose back had been turned at the moment, looked over his shoulder. He hurried across to the table, cloth in hand to clear up the mess, giving the hapless girl a ferocious glare.

"I am sorry, My Lord," he flustered. "The slave will be

35

severely punished for her clumsiness. I will see to it immediately, myself." His eyes fastened on the unfortunate girl, gloating with anticipation.

"That can wait until later, when we have finished eating," Lord Reythal said slowly.

Juliette was aghast that Sarita was to be punished, She had clearly seen the boy jab something sharp into Sarita's thigh. She was about to move forward and protest, when Maya held her back, shaking her head. The meal came to an end without further incident. The three slaves cleared the table and stood to one side waiting to be dismissed.

"Maya and Juliette!" Abaddon announced. "You may return to your quarters. Sarita, you will go immediately to the yard and await your punishment."

The slaves were about to obey, when the younger son's voice halted them in their tracks.

"Father. It is nearly dark outside and I won't be able to see anything properly from the window here. Tell Abaddon to have the birch and 'horse' brought in and the punishment done in here."

Lord Reythal thought for a moment and then turned to Abaddon. "My son is right. It is too dark outside and the slave should not be made to wait until the morning. Better to do it now, while the offence is still fresh in her mind. Do as my son says. The other slaves will stay and watch. It may encourage them to be careful in their duties."

Abaddon hurried from the hall to do the Lord's bidding. The diners rearranged their seats so they would have a clear view of the proceedings. The young son, his face glowing with excitement, ensured that he managed to get the best position. Abaddon reappeared a few minutes later followed by two lackeys carrying the 'horse'. This turned out to be a heavy carpenter's trestle with a smooth round log fixed across one end. Sarita, at her side, began to shake as she saw the instrument that Abaddon held in his hand. He held it aloft for the family's inspection. The lackeys set the horse down and left the room.

"Since it was your tablecloth that was damaged, my dear," Lord Reythal said, turning to his wife. "You may

36

decide the slave's punishment."

"She must be taught to be more careful, and control herself," the wife said quietly. "Let her bend free for six strokes. If she moves, put her on the horse and give her another dozen." The wife's voice was soft and gentle, totally in contrast with the cruelty of the beating she was ordering for the young slave.

"Sound thinking, my dear," Lord Reythal said, then turned to Abaddon. "Proceed."

"You heard the Mistress's order, slave. Prepare yourself," Abaddon commanded, his eyes shining with sadistic cruelty.

Casting a fleeting look at her sister slaves, Sarita walked to the centre of the hall, between the trestle and the family, turned, spread her legs wide and bent over, grasping her ankles tightly. Her legs and buttocks trembled visibly.

"Straighten your legs. Stick your behind out more and keep still," Abaddon barked the command. He waited until the slave had obeyed then held the birch against her proffered buttocks, making them clench with fear. "Are you ready?"

"Master," Sarita's voice trembled. "Your slave is sorry and begs to be soundly beaten for her clumsiness."

"Lay it on hard, Abaddon," the younger son called out gleefully

Juliette had watched the preparations with mounting horror. She was not sure which was worse, hearing Sarita begging to be thrashed or the young boy egging Abaddon on. She was to learn later that it was required of any of the Lord's personal slaves, who was to be punished, to apologise for her offence and beg to be soundly beaten. Appalled by the dreadful scene in front of her, Juliette watched as Abaddon raised the birch rods high and brought them swishing down with a resounding 'thwack' across the slave's buttocks. A loud gasp escaped the slave's clenched teeth as a bright red swathe appeared on her cheeks. The force of the blow made her rock so much that Juliette thought she was about to fall over. The grinning major-domo lashed down three more strokes, the sharp reports echoing in the hall. Still Sarita had not moved nor cried out, only a loud gasp as each laid a swathe of pain across her cheeks.

The slave had now managed to survive four of the six stipulated strokes. Juliette was silently praying that she would not move, shuddering as she saw her friends knuckles turn white as each stroke landed. The younger son, who wanted the slave to get the dozen extra, was not amused by the slave's tenacity.

"Harder Abaddon," he called out. "You're not trying. Give it to her much harder."

Abaddon, too, was not happy with the slave's stubbornness. The jibe from the boy hurt and annoyed him immensely. A mere six strokes would not satisfy his appetite. He looked hard at the quivering buttocks, provocatively thrust out at him, and raised his arm. Again the report echoed round the hall, followed by a deep groan from the slave. Her body rocked back and forth but her hands remained glued stubbornly to her ankles.

Sarita rocked under the stroke. Her buttocks were writhing frantically as the agony burning in her cheeks escalated to the limit of her endurance. The last stroke had hurt so much that she let out a loud groan of despair followed by 'God help me!' as she fought to keep hold of her ankles. Spurred on by the fear of being tied to the trestle for another dozen, she knew that she had only one more of those terrible strokes to survive. She also knew that her stubbornness would fuel Abaddon's arm. She sensed the birch raised and clenched her teeth, closed her eyes tight and gripped her ankles even tighter.

Juliette held her breath as she saw the look of determination on Abaddon's face as the birch rose. She mentally willed her friend to stay in position for just the one more. She saw the birch lash down across her friend's bottom, heard the terrible report of the impact and the strangled scream as Sarita's buttocks absorbed the sheer agony the stroke caused. She was about to let out her breath with a sigh of relief, when she saw Sarita's hands fly back and rub her flaming bottom.

"She moved! She moved!" the younger son was on his feet shouting with glee. "Give her the rest. Give her the rest."

Abaddon flicked the birch across Sarita's knuckles as she rubbed her burning cheeks. Quickly she grasped her ankles again.

"Stand and face your Master, slave," Abaddon commanded.

Slowly, dreading what she knew must follow, Sarita straightened up and turned to face her Master, her face running with the tears that flowed from her eyes. She had disobeyed and moved and knew the next order would herald a full thrashing with the birch across her already flaming bottom.

"You disobeyed your Mistress's order, slave, and moved before given permission. You will now be punished for your disobedience with twelve strokes. Further, you blasphemed during the beating. That will earn you another six strokes." Lord Reythal nodded to his major-domo.

Sarita visibly shook as the younger son chuckled with glee at the further entertainment to come. The look of anticipation on his face made her feel sick. As Abaddon gave her the order to prepare, she raised her shaking hands behind her neck and released the clasp on the chains. They fell away, allowing the girl's breasts to adopt their normal seductive position. The gossamer strip followed as the chain round her hips followed the first. Although the chains and strip barely concealed any of her body, and would certainly have given no protection from the birch, it was mandatory that a slave strip naked for a formal punishment. Casting a fleeting glance for mercy at her Master, she walked to the end of the 'horse' where the log was attached. She braced her shoulders and bent over, feeling the smooth cool wood against her stomach, and reached forward and gripped the end of the plank with her small hands.

Abaddon secured her wrists to the plank, then moved behind her. He reached down and spread her legs wide and shackled her ankles to the stout trestle supports. Due to the log on top of the plank, Sarita's buttocks were thrust up and out, the skin stretched taut and exposing her anus and sex to the family seated behind her. Abaddon stepped back and inspected her to ensure she was properly positioned for the flogging. She presented a perfect target and he smiled and nodded with anticipation.

"Don't forget the waist strap, Abaddon," the younger son called out. He was bouncing up and down on his chair, his eyes wide open and a savage grin on his face. "It stretches them better," the boy added.

A sadistic smile flitted across the man's face. The boy had learned well. He could almost be his own son. He looked at Lord Reythal, who hesitated to reply as he looked hard at his son.

"If that is what my darling wants, let him have it." Lady Reythal's gentle voice rose in support of the son to whom she denied nothing.

A scowl of anger passed across Lord Reythal's face. He disliked the way his wife spoiled the boy and, though the boy was his own son, he abhorred the sadistic streak he seemed to have caught from Abaddon. Rather than get involved in a family squabble, he looked at Abaddon and nodded.

Sarita, whose eyes had cleared of tears, had watched the exchange in dreadful trepidation. As she saw her Master nodding his agreement, her self control snapped. "Oh no! No! Please not that! Please! Please not that!"

"Silence, slave," Abaddon shouted at her. Grinning evilly, he reached for the long strap attached to the underneath of the plank. He buckled the ends together and pulled it tight, forcing the slave's breasts hard down on the plank and thrusting her buttocks even higher in the air.

Juliette shook her head in disbelief and disgust as she saw her friend's buttocks, already red and sore from the earlier strokes, stretched even tighter. The look of abject terror on Sarita's face and the soft whimpering sound that came from her closed mouth was too much for her to bear. She might have to listen to the noise of the flogging but she did not have to watch. She turned her head to one side.

"Do not look away," Maya whispered urgently at her

side. "Abaddon will be watching and if he sees it will mean extra strokes for Sarita and you will take her place next."

Juliette forced her eyes to focus on the dreadful scene, Abaddon, the dreadful birch in hand, had taken up his position. Sarita's legs were visibly shaking, despite the restrictive bonds securing them, as Abaddon laid the birch lightly on her bottom. He kept it there for a few seconds, savouring the terror the touch was instilling in the slave. Juliette nearly screamed herself as she watched the man raise the rods high in the air and bring them down with a resounding report across her friend's bottom. Sarita's body jerked violently against the strap and a shrill scream followed the report as the fire in her cheeks was rekindled.

Although Juliette had been beaten often herself, and seen the weals on the other girls' bottoms, it was the first time she had actually seen a formal thrashing administered. The way her friend writhed and screamed as each stroke was applied made her shudder and cringe, but it was the utter concentration on the family's faces, and the glee on the younger sons, that made her feel sick. She had never dreamed, perhaps because she had never given it any thought, that one human being could get so much pleasure by the infliction of pain on another. She had rebelled at the injustice of her own fate. Now she was forced to admit that she was not the only one for whom justice did not exist. She had silently been counting the strokes. Her friend's bottom had now received, in all, fourteen strokes of that terrible instrument and she still had ten more to come. The sharp report of each stroke had been followed by an agonised scream from the slave, whose body was writhing and squirming, despite the strap, trying to avoid the wicked rods. Sweat poured from her and her buttocks, stretched to the limit, were suffering terribly. Many of the strokes had split the skin and globules of bright red glistened on her cheeks, some already becoming thin rivulets running down on to her quivering thighs.

Abaddon, although deprived of his intention to punish the slave with a whip was, nonetheless, thoroughly enjoying himself. His forehead glistened with perspiration, evidencing the effort he was putting into the task. The large bulge in his breeches showed the arousing effect his labours were having on his libido. But he was not the only one to be affected. To her horror, Juliette suddenly realised that her breathing had quickened and become shallower. Even worse, her breasts were aching and her nipples were swollen, and not because of the chains, and there was a definite tingling in her sex tunnel. Her disgust at the way her body was reacting did not quench the arousal. That the erotic scene being enacted in front of her could arouse her body in that fashion shocked her. Her body was being aroused by the sight of her new-found friend suffering such a terrible flogging! It can't be, she tried to tell herself. She wouldn't believe it! But the undeniable signs were there.

Not daring to take her eyes off the scene, Juliette cursed silently as the young boy urged the major-domo to greater efforts, the flogging continued. Sarita's buttocks were in a terrible state. The birch rods were beginning to snap and the jagged ends were seeking out and finding her anus bud and sex lips. Her agonised screams seemed to run one into another as she absorbed the terrible pain. After the eighteenth stroke had seared its swathe of pain, Sarita had slumped along the trestle, exhausted by her struggles. Juliette was praying that the girl would lose consciousness when she felt her own arm nudged. She glanced sideways at Maya. The girl's face was a picture of alarm and disgust as she stared at Juliette's hips. Juliette followed the gaze and looked down. Her face turned red with shame. Her hand was under the gossamer strip, pressed against her mound and her fingers were lightly stroking her sex. Feeling her face burning, she quickly removed her hand, hoping that no one else had noticed her disgusting act.

She returned her eyes to the girl on the trestle, who was moaning and mewing loudly, her flaccid body jerking each time the birch rods cut into her tortured flesh. Despite her illicit preoccupation, Juliette's brain had continued to keep count. It was with relief that she realised that Sarita only had one more stroke to take before her ordeal was over.

"Only one more to go," the younger boy called out.

"Make it a good one, Abaddon."

The major-domo, now sweating profusely and panting heavily with the effort, stepped back to survey his handiwork. He was glad he was nearing the end of the flogging. The pressure of his penis against his breeches was getting too uncomfortable and he was anxious to hasten to the kennels and wake up a certain slave and fuck her to assuage the burning desires in his loins. A demonic grin appeared on his face and lit up his eyes. To Juliette's intense horror, she watched, too scared to shout a warning, as Abaddon brought the vicious birch rods down for the last time. Without any reduction in speed of force, he swept the rods down behind the bent girl then, sweeping upwards, lashed them across the soft underside of Sarita's cheeks and her thighs. The blow lifted the girl off her feet and a terrible scream was forced from her lungs as her sex received the worst of the stroke. Sarita's body, which had arched backwards against the strap, collapsed again along the trestle, sobbing violently.

"Well done, Abaddon," Lord Reythal said, although his words seemed to lack sincerity. "Perhaps that will teach her to be more careful in future. Have her taken away and seen to." Inwardly, he was a little worried in case the major-domo's enthusiasm had done too much damage to the girl. She had a lovely backside and it would be a pity if it were permanently marked.

At a signal from Abaddon, Juliette and Maya hurried forward and released the shaking girl's bonds. Slowly, trying not to aggravate the poor girl's agony, they eased her upright and, picking up her discarded chains, led her from the hall and back to their own quarters. They laid the sobbing girl down on her bed and, while Juliette bathed her tear stained face, Maya did her best with cold cloths to soothe the burning buttocks.

"That was grossly unfair," Juliette whispered. "That little swine needs a lesson of his own. He deliberately made you spill the food and then had the nerve to egg Abaddon on. He needs a taste of the birch himself, then he would know what it feels like."

43

"Shush!" Sarita replied between the sobs that were now gradually abating. "I have had far worse at his hands. But you must not speak thoughts like that. If anyone hears you they will have you properly whipped."

"I still think it was wicked of him."

"Please do not talk like that," Maya interrupted. "The last girl, whose place you took, was heard saying something similar. They had Quinell give her thirty lashes with a heavy whip. The poor thing is now scarred for life and has been sold to a brothel in the port."

"Poor girl," Juliette kept her voice low. "That is no way to treat a human being."

"We are slaves, not humans," Maya replied. "They have the law on their side and can do anything they like to us, even kill us, if the notion takes them. So be careful what you say and do. We wouldn't want anything like that to happen to you. To them we are nothing. Even less than their animals."

"I will try and remember," Juliette whispered back. "But I still think it is wrong." She shuddered as she remembered the lashing she had received on arrival. That had been bad enough. The thought of a heavy whip being used on her soft body was beyond her comprehension.

They made Sarita as comfortable as they could and settled down for the night. Before sleep came, Juliette remembered, to her shame, the feelings that Sarita's beating had aroused in her. She said a silent thanks to Maya for not letting on about what she had caught her doing. She eventually fell into a troubled sleep. In her dream, she was tied to the post in the yard and Abaddon was wielding a heavy whip across her back. As each stroke fell and the pain built up, her breasts hardened and her love tunnel felt on fire with the desire that burned within her. Her body ached to be used. As much as she hated the devil, who was whipping her, she cried out to him, begging him to put her onto her back and fuck her. True to his sadistic nature, he continued to lash her, taunting her all the time that her needs would not be satisfied until she declared herself to him as his true, complete and loving slave. The dream

44

suddenly ceased and she woke up, her body drenched in sweat and her clitoris and breasts aching with unfulfilled desire. She looked quickly round, frightened that she may have called out in her sleep, but her friends were fast asleep.

She lay there for sometime, trying to understand the message her body was sending out. She hated the pain she suffered when beaten and was horrified that, at the same time, her body became aroused more than anyone, or anything, had ever done before. But it was not only her pain that had this effect! This evening had shown her that watching another suffering had the same result. She seemed to be a different person to what she was before her arrest. In the relatively short time since then, she had discovered many strange latent things about herself that puzzled her. Was there something weird about her? With the riddle still spinning, unresolved, in her mind she again drifted off into sleep.

CHAPTER 3.

One morning, three months after her introduction into Lord Reythal's household, Juliette was summoned before her Master. His eyes passed slowly over his slave as she knelt before him, her eyes demurely lowered. The thin working shift that she was wearing did nothing to hide her considerable charms. Charms that he had enjoyed many times since she had graduated to his personal service. He was reluctant to do what he was about to, but a promise was a promise, even to that weird one, Lady Moona. If it was not for the fact that he wanted to know more about what really went on inside her house, he was quite prepared to break the promise. He had waited some time for the right moment, and the right girl, to come along and now that she had, he had to go through with it.

"You are to be sent to the Lady Moona today," Lord Reythal said, bringing his mind back to the business in hand. "You will be on loan to her for two weeks. See that you serve her well. She has my full permission to punish you if she is displeased with you. If she reports that you did not live up to her expectations, I will have Abaddon whip you on your return."

Juliette was unaware of the suspicions her Master held about the Lady Moona and had no idea what she was going to. But his last words sent a shiver of terror down her spine.

"Do you understand me, slave?" he said, his voice tinged with anger.

"Yes, Master," Juliette replied meekly. "I will do my best to please the Lady."

"See that you do! Abaddon will take you to her dwelling this afternoon. When you return, I will require a full account of what happens there during your stay. But you must, on no account, let her know that I have given this order. Now go with Abaddon."

Juliette rose from her knees and followed the major-domo from the study. She was taken back to her quarters and ordered to strip.

"Permission to speak, please Master?" she asked, making her voice as demur as she could.

"You may speak, slave," he replied.

"I have never served a Lady before. How will I be expected to serve her? Surely she has slaves of her own."

"That is why you are being sent there. To find out! She saw you naked at the auction and took a fancy to you. She prefers the bodies of young girls to that of a man," Abaddon replied with a knowing smile on his lips at the last remark.

Juliette had heard stories of women like that. Women who preferred female 'friends' instead of men! A shudder of disgust ran down her back at the thought that, this very afternoon, she was to be put into the clutches of such a woman

"She is very hard to please, so I understand," Abaddon continued, the smile on his face turning to one of cruelty. "I look forward to your return for, surely, you will be found unsatisfactory and then I will have the pleasure of using a proper whip on you."

"I intend to please her," Juliette said, without thinking.

"Then you will be deprived of that pleasure. I saw how you enjoyed thrashing Sarita with that birch. You are a sadistic monster."

Abaddon's face turned purple with rage and Juliette realised she had gone too far this time. Her disgust at the fate that awaited her that afternoon had put her off her guard. She trembled with terror at the contorted expression on the man's face. Abaddon was shaking with rage. No slave had ever dared to speak to him in that fashion. His anger was intensified by the Master's order that the slave had to be delivered unmarked.

"I will remember this day," he stormed at her through his rage. "You will regret your outburst when you return and the Master orders a whipping. I will see to it that you never forget your first meeting with the lash. The anticipation during the delay will only serve to increase my pleasure." This thought helped him regain his composure and he returned his attention to the matter in hand. "Now you must be prepared."

Maya and Sarita appeared in answer to his summons. They took Juliette to the washroom and depilated her until, except for the flowing tresses on her head, there was not one hair left on her. A hot bath followed after which they applied cosmetics and perfume and brushed her hair until it shone. She tried to protest when they rubbed rouge on her nipples and kohl to her sex lips, but a fierce glare from Abaddon halted her in time. The two blondes had not been told the reason for these preparations and, since talking was forbidden, their concern for Juliette's future showed on their faces. When he was satisfied with her appearance, Abaddon manacled her wrists together between her shoulder blades and put a long black cloak, with a large hood, over her. The hood was pulled over her face, obstructing her view. She felt a collar buckled round her neck. Holding a chain attached to the collar, Abaddon led her out of the building and hoisted her up onto a cart and locked the chain to the floor.

The cart moved forward. The journey seemed to take ages. In the back of the cart, Juliette was at first aware of the sound of people as they passed through the town then, apart from the sound of the horse's hooves, a menacing silence reigned. Despite her apprehension at what awaited her, Juliette was thankful when the cart finally came to a halt and she was ordered off. The journey had been uncomfortable and she was grateful for the chance to stretch herself to relieve the stiffness. A tug on the collar pulled her forward. She knew they had entered a building when the stones beneath her feet gave way to a smooth surface.

"Is this the slave?" she heard a young voice ask.

"It is," Abaddon replied peevishly at the lack of respect in the voice. "I will be back in two weeks to collect her."

"That is the arrangement. She will be ready," the young voice replied.

She heard Abaddon's footsteps receding as he walked to the door, which was closed behind him. She breathed a silent sigh of relief at his departure. At least she was out of his reach for two weeks and now she was alone with the owner of the young voice who, she assumed, was a slave

48

girl.

"Now. Let me see what we have here!" the young voice spoke at her side.

The collar was unbuckled from her neck and the cloak and hood removed, exposing her nakedness. When her eyes became accustomed to the light again, she was surprised to find that the voice belonged to a young man, who stood in front of her surveying her critically. The youth, who Juliette guessed, was no more than sixteen years old, was stark naked except for a belt at his waist from which a leather band hung down over his stomach and was drawn up to the belt at his back. The band had a split in the front, through which his penis and scrotum, both of which seemed over large for his age, protruded. She did not fail to notice the whippy cane that hung from the belt at his side.

"Not bad! Not bad at all!" the youth mused, his survey complete. "Follow me."

As she walked behind him, Juliette saw several tramlines across his tight buttocks where he had recently been caned. From this she assumed he must also be a slave. Having negotiated the large entrance hall and a wide corridor, both of which were beautifully decorated, the youth halted at a door on which he rapped lightly. A woman's voice bade them enter. The room into which she was led, was large and, like the hall and corridor, beautifully and extravagantly furnished. Reclining on a luxurious sofa, was a young woman who, Juliette recognised from the auction, was the Lady Moona.

When Juliette had seen her that day, she had been dressed in a heavy gown and cloak. Still suffering from the pain of the thrashing and humiliation of the auction, Juliette had taken little notice of her. Now she could see that her temporary Mistress, who now apart from a gorgeous gossamer gown was quite naked, was very beautiful.

"So!" Lady Moona cooed in a low seductive voice. "Lord Reythal has kept his promise after all. You understand that, for the next two weeks, you are my slave?"

"Yes, Mistress," Juliette stammered, still not recovered from the surprise of the woman's lack of clothing and her

49

revealed beauty.

"Your Master has promised you a reward if I find you pleasing, I hope?"

"No, Mistress," Juliette replied. "But I am to be severely whipped if I fail to please you."

"No doubt that was that ogre Abaddon's idea," the Lady mused to herself. "I have heard of his appetite for young girls." Then aloud to Juliette. "Your crime, as I recall, was sacrilege for which you were flogged with twenty-five strokes of the cane."

"Yes, Mistress," Juliette replied. She was about to protest that she was innocent of the crime but held her tongue.

"Also, I recall, you took the thrashing quite well, considering it was the first time. Have you been beaten since?"

"Yes, Mistress," Juliette replied, unable to meet the woman's eyes. "Many times."

"Good," the Lady Moona cooed. "Then you have been well practised. See that you do not disappoint me. Jason, release her wrists."

The youth removed her restraints and she let her arms fall to her sides. She was tempted to try and cover her nakedness, until she remembered the cane at Jason's side.

"Take her away, Jason, and explain her duties to her. I will require her to attend on me after the evening meal. Then we will try her out."

Juliette followed the youth and was taken to a small room, with barred windows. It was pleasantly furnished and comfortable. Jason told her that this was where she would be confined during her stay except when attending on the Mistress. He then went on to explain what her duties were. To her surprise, she found that she would not be required to do any work at all. It was only when Jason explained, in great detail, what she had to do that she wished she had not been sent there. She was left alone until, later in the afternoon, Jason brought her some food and fruit. The food looked very nice but, after hearing from the youth earlier, she had lost her appetite. However, aware of what awaited her, she forced the food down. Jason then took her to a room where he prepared her for the evening, and left her there until she would be required.

All too soon he returned for her and took her to another room in the building. The sight that met her eyes as she looked round astounded her and increased her feeling of dread and horror. The room was devoid of windows, being brilliantly lit by many torches in brackets around the walls. In the centre was a large divan with posts attached to the corners. To one side of the room stood a thick wooden post and a high padded stool. To all these were fixed numerous cords, chains and rings. She felt a shiver of fear and dread as she saw, scattered around the walls, a selection of straps, canes and whips and other instruments, whose sole purpose could only be the infliction of pain.

The youth, Jason, ordered her to kneel, knees wide spread, some distance away from and facing the end of the divan. Although the temperature in the room was comfortably warm, Juliette shivered as if a cold gust of wind had blown over her. After a short while, Jason returned, leading a naked blindfolded girl. He took the girl to the stool and ordered her to bend over. Her wrists and ankles were secured to the legs. Then, to Juliette's surprise, Jason sat on the end of the divan, facing her. Several minutes passed in silence, then the door opened again and the Lady Moona entered. To Juliette's utter astonishment, the Lady was stark naked. She walked across the room and knelt beside her, spreading her knees wide and exposing her shaven sex.

Juliette could hardly believe her eyes and ears at the sequence of events that followed during the evening.

"Moona," Jason's voice seemed deeper and commanding. "Take your position!"

"Yes, Master," she heard the woman's voice at her side, her voice very seductive and submissive.

The Lady Moona rose and walked to the tall post. She pressed her body against the smooth surface and raised her slim arms above her head until her hands were level with one of the rings near the top of the post. She gripped the ring tight.

Juliette gasped as she watched Jason rise and stroll to the side of the room and take down a light whip. Slowly, flicking the end of the whip on the floor, he approached the woman at the post. He parted her long dark hair and draped it forward over her full upthrust breasts, exposing her lovely smooth back.

"How many strokes do you deserve tonight, slave?" Jason demanded, making his voice hard and stern.

"Whatever my Master thinks I deserve," Lady Moona replied softly, a tremor in her voice. "But six, if it pleases you, Master."

The youth turned towards the bent slave and raised the whip. With a resounding 'crack' the lash curled across the back of the bent slave. Juliette heard the girl suck in the air between her clenched teeth. Juliette's eyes opened wide in disbelief as the youth turned, raised the whip and brought the lash down across his Mistress's bare back. Her body jerked against the post as she, also, sucked air between her teeth. Twice more, Jason laid the lash across the backs of the two girls. Neither cried out but Juliette saw the Lady Moona grip the ring so tight that her knuckles turned white as three angry red lines stretched across her pale smooth back.

What she was seeing completely mystified Juliette. A free woman letting her slave whip her back! Although the youth was wielding the whip with some considerable force, the lash was not biting deep enough to break the skin. That it was, nonetheless, causing acute pain to both recipients was undoubted. Two more sharp reports sounded in her ears as each girl's back received another stroke, Again, other than for a loud gasp, both girls remained silent.

Just as she had when watching Sarita being thrashed with the birch, Juliette felt her body becoming aroused. The sheer, unbelievable eroticism of the scene being enacted before her eyes was arousing her. This shocked her but the feelings were undeniably there and they were undoubtedly delicious.

Jason laid two more strokes across each bare back.

Again silence from the slave but the Lady Moona let out a long drawn out 'Aaaaarrrrgh' as the second burned across her back and curled round her side, the tip of the lash flicking her breast and nipple. The girl's body jerked against the post with the force of the stroke.

Each back received its final stroke. The slave still remained silent but the Lady Moona let out another cry as she released her grip on the ring and her body slid slowly down on to her knees, her arms wrapped round the post. The youth looked down on his Mistress's body, shaking his head. He went to the wall and replaced the whip and took down a long thin rattan cane. He went and stood behind his Mistress.

"Stand up, slave," he ordered. "Bend and hold your ankles. Keep your legs straight."

Slowly the Lady Moona eased her body upright then, with a pleading glance at the youth, bent over as he had ordered.

"You failed to hold position and you cried out on two strokes," Juliette heard him say. "That deserves six with the cane. You may cry out but, if you move, the stroke will not count. Understand?"

"Yes, Master," the lady Moona replied, meekly, trembling and soft sobs sounding in her voice.

To Juliette's surprise the Lady Moona managed to absorb all six without releasing the grip on her ankles. Her body rocked back and forth on each and her buttocks clenched and relaxed spasmodically. A shrill cry of agony followed each report as white lines, rapidly turning dark red were etched across the paleness of her buttocks. Tears flowed down her face and a thin sheen glowed on her skin. She continued to maintain position as Jason replaced the cane and turned towards her.

"Spread yourself on the couch, slave," he ordered.

With a moan, Lady Moona straightened up and walked gingerly to the divan, her hands frantically rubbing her sore bottom cheeks that bore six distinct tramlines where the cane had struck. She laid her body, face up, on the divan. The youth tied cords to her wrists and ankles and pulled her limbs taut, spread-eagling his Mistress, and secured the cords to the posts. Jason then lifted her head and placed a thick cushion under it so she could look down her body and, by turning her head, see the slave bent over the stool.

Jason released the manacles that had secured Juliette's wrists behind her back and, thankfully, removed the pressing temptation to stroke her own tingling sex lips.

"Slave," Jason said, looking at her. "Your Mistress is in pain. She needs comforting. Soothe her well or you will be next one to stand at the post."

Slowly, Juliette approached the body of her Mistress stretched on the divan. She saw the tears in the woman's eyes and the expectant expression on her face. Fighting down the nausea that rose in her throat at the task she knew she must perform, she knelt down at the foot of the divan. She looked at the woman and saw that her breasts were rising and falling fast as the woman began breathing heavily as desire flowed in her body. Her nipples were erect and hard and, swallowing down her disgust at her task, Juliette could see tiny drops of moisture glistening on her sex lips. Juliette braced her shoulders and leaned over the divan, between the spread legs. Slowly, careful not to progress too fast, she began licking and kissing the slim ankles and worked her way up along the inside of the calves and over the knees. She heard the woman's breathing rate increase and, as she reached the join of the thighs, the body began to tremble and she could detect the odour of the woman's arousal.

Crack. "Ooooww."

Both Juliette and the body on the divan jumped at the sound, but it was the slave's buttocks that had received the stroke of the cane. Juliette's ministrations had now reached the woman's shaven mound.

Crack. "Aaaaaarrggggh."

Another scream from the bent slave! Juliette, trying hard not to retch, touched her tongue to the edge of the woman's sex lips.

Thwack.

Juliette jumped as the cane cut across her bottom. Jason

had been watching her closely and had detected the reluctance to perform her task and it was her bottom upon which the cane had left its mark.

Acting more from the shock of the stroke than the line of pain it left behind, Juliette forced her tongue into the woman's recess and was rewarded as her Mistress's body began to writhe with the desire that Juliette was arousing in her. Bound as she was, her movements were restricted but, even so, Juliette had great difficulty in stopping her tongue being displaced. To the sound of the cane striking the bent slave's buttocks, and her shrill cry with each stroke, Juliette pressed on with her endeavours.

After the initial insertion of her tongue, Juliette found that the task was not as unpleasant as she had imagined it would be. She felt a sense of power over her Mistress as she realised she could control the arousal she was fuelling and hasten, or prolong, the process as she wished. But, fearful of the cane in the youth's hands, she increased her attentions, making her tongue slide up and down against the inside of her Mistress's body making her moan with the arousal that was growing within her.

There was no doubt in Juliette's mind that the whipping, caning and the pain the woman was still feeling, and watching the slave's buttocks as they received the cane, were the prime cause of the woman's arousal. Her own ministrations were merely the delicious icing on the cake. With this realisation came better understanding of the strange reactions of her own body when under and watching punishment.

The bent slave had ceased crying out for the cane had stopped lashing her buttocks. Jason was now using it to gently tap Juliette's behind, gradually increasing the frequency, exerting her to greater and faster efforts. Then the cane ceased its rhythm on her bottom. She heard a shrill cry come from her Mistress, whose body jerked violently making Juliette lose her position. Juliette looked over her Mistress's body and gasped at what she saw. Jason had replaced the cane with a bundle of birch rods, a wicked grin lighting up his face. He raised his arm and brought the birch down with some force across his Mistress's breasts. Obeying Jason's orders, she inserted her fingers inside her Mistress's opening, moving them quickly up and down, she saw the birch descend across her Mistress's breasts.

Lady Moona uttered a shrill scream of pain and pleasure as her body arched rigid. Juliette felt the woman's muscles tighten round her fingers as the woman's juices flowed over them, and her body went into a series of deep orgasms. Then, with a final cry of satisfaction the woman's body collapsed onto the divan. Juliette was ordered to resume her former kneeling position as the youth gently released his Mistress's limbs from their bonds. Slowly, the Lady Moona emerged from the sea of pleasure and, as she sat up, her small hands gently rubbed her breasts where the birch had struck.

"That was delicious, Jason," she purred. "You may release and dismiss the slave."

Jason did as she ordered and the girl, still blindfolded, collapsed on the floor, rubbing her sore and swollen buttocks. Jason hauled her to her feet and ushered her from the room.

"Was that the first time you have seduced a woman's body?" Lady Moona asked Juliette sweetly

"Yes, Mistress," Juliette answered.

"I thought so," Lady Moona said, looking at the kneeling girl. "You were not too bad for a first attempt, but you need some instruction. Jason will see to that before tomorrow evening. This time you will be let off lightly but, if your technique does not improve, it will go hard with you. When Jason returns you will bend over and ask him for five with the birch. Then you may apply cream to my breasts."

Jason returned at that moment and Juliette obeyed her Mistress's order. She gripped her ankles tight and steeled herself ready to receive the birch. When it came two quick strokes flayed across her bottom leaving a swathe of pain behind and rocking her on her feet. She had seen the youth in action earlier but, even so, was surprised by the force he could put behind the strokes. The third drew a moan from her. A moan not only of pain, but of despair as the heat in her bottom spurred the arousal that had been lingering in her belly most of the evening. Fortunately for her, Jason lost no time in lashing the last two strokes down on her quivering cheeks, bringing tears to her eyes and loud cries from her mouth. Then, all too soon to fuel the arousal too much, it was over and she straightened up, her hands rubbing her glowing cheeks.

"Come here, slave," Lady Moona ordered. "Give her the jar, Jason."

Juliette approached the divan and took the jar from the youth. She was about to kneel down when Lady Moona's command halted her.

"No! Bend over me and keep your legs straight. Do not move."

Juliette, expecting a further onslaught on her behind as she attended to the task, obeyed and braced herself. She was about to dip her fingers into the cream when she felt a hand on her breast and another ease up between her legs.

"Well! Well! What have we here," Lady Moona purred with delight. "You are quite hot and your tits are so hard. What has caused that, I wonder? Was it your own birching or watching others being beaten?"

"I am not…" Juliette was about to protest but was cut short.

"Do not attempt to deny it. Lying will earn you a whipping. Anyway, your body gives you away. Now, the truth!"

"It was a mixture of both," she answered, conscious that her face had turned red with embarrassment.

"Good! I suspected as much the day you were caned at the House of Correction. There is a chance that you will return to Lord Reythal with a good report. Provided, of course, that you put aside all pretence and allow yourself to be guided by your body. Now the cream!"

Juliette dug her fingers into the jar and began to smooth the cream over the weals left by the birch on her Mistress's breasts. The Lady Moona's orbs were larger than her own, but she was surprised at their firmness. The flesh felt hot where the lines showed where the rods had struck but in no place had the skin been broken. As she gently rubbed the cream in, Lady Moona laid back and gave a sigh of contentment.

"That's nice!" she purred. "You have such soft hands. Would you like some cream on your arse?"

"If Mistress wishes," Juliette replied. She was mystified at this apparent concern for a slave.

"It is. Give the jar to Jason. He can attend to you while you cream my back and bottom." She turned over. "The cream is special. It makes the marks disappear quickly so the area is clear and ready for the next beating. I like to see an arse that is unmarked before it is kissed again."

Juliette worked on in the ensuing silence, flinching a little as she felt the cool cream applied to her sore bottom. Gradually the burning began to fade but her gratitude was short lived as the youth's fingers strayed between her crease and lightly pressed her anus bud. Then, as a low moan escaped her mouth, his fingers slipped between her legs, stroking her sex lips. She was unable to control her body and her breathing became lighter and faster as she became aroused. She was taken by surprise as an arm circled her neck and pulled her head down. She lost her footing and fell onto the woman, their breasts touching and her lips met those of her Mistress. The kiss seemed to go on forever! Juliette refrained from resisting, whether from fear or excitement, she could not decide. Even when her Mistress's tongue forced its way between her teeth, she did not feel the revulsion she might have anticipated.

It was a long time before her Mistress indicated that the session was over. As she rose from the divan, she was surprised to see that the weals on her Mistress's breasts had faded and nearly disappeared. The cream was acting like magic and, as the woman stood up, she saw that her back and bottom were clearing equally quickly. As Jason conducted her back to her room, Juliette asked him if her own bottom had healed to the same degree. He stopped her in front of a mirror so she could see for herself. Looking over her shoulder she could see her own cheeks with hardly a mark on them.

In the solitude of her room, before sleep came, she thought over the events of the evening. She was at a loss to understand what had happened there. That a young slave had actually birched his Mistress's bare breasts, after caning her bottom and taking a whip to her back, was beyond her understanding. The way the woman's body had become aroused, both by her own beating and watching the bent slave girl suffer, mirrored her own body's reactions under similar circumstances. So, perhaps, she was not so peculiar after all!

Most evenings during her stay, Juliette was summoned to the same room. The routine varied slightly each evening, the strap replacing the birch and a different slave girl over the stool, but the end result was that both she, and the Lady Moona, ended the evening having been well and truly thrashed. No matter what had occurred the previous evening, at the start of each session both Juliette's and the Lady Moona's bodies were clear of any evidence of the beating they had endured. Juliette took her Mistress's advice and put aside her inhibitions and let her body dictate to her. It came as a shock to her that, not only did she come to enjoy herself, she actually looked forward to the evening summons.

With the threat of a whipping from Abaddon ever present in her mind, Juliette strove to please her Mistress. The only thing that spoiled it for her was that, whilst her Mistress enjoyed many orgasms during the sessions she was not allowed to follow suit. Her frustration must have been apparent for, after that first evening, Lady Moona gave her permission to finish the matter once she had returned to her own room.

It was on her last day there that the routine changed. Juliette was prepared and sent for in the early afternoon. As usual, Jason took her to the same room and ordered her to kneel at the foot of the divan. This time when Jason reappeared, he led in two naked and blindfolded slave girls and sat them down at the side of the room and took up his usual position, sitting on the end of the divan. One girl carried a lute and the other a lyre. Both girls were stunningly beautiful with flawless skins and Juliette could not help but wonder where her Mistress got them from. That she had been forced to drop out of the auction at the House of Correction seemed to prove that the woman's finances were not inexhaustible.

Her thoughts were interrupted as the door opened again and the Lady Moona entered. To Juliette's surprise the woman was not, as usual, naked. A wide belt, studded with many coloured stones, clung to her hips. From the belt, a fine gossamer skirt swept the floor at her unshod feet. It was slit up to the belt in two places at the front so that, as she walked, her shapely legs were revealed. Her full firm breasts were encased in golden cups, held in place by a fine gold chain round the back of her neck and the lower half of her face was covered by a veil, of the same material as the skirt, through which her features were barely hidden. Silver bands, resembling snakes, wound round her upper arms and, round her neck was fastened a silver collar.

Slowly, taking dainty steps, Lady Moona walked across the room approaching the divan where Jason sat, looking at his Mistress with a severe expression on his face. Lady Moona halted in front of him and sank gracefully to her knees, her eyes demurely lowered, and placed her hands, palms up, on her knees. Somehow, to Juliette's surprise, she looked more beautiful, seductive and submissive than ever. For a few minutes the tableau remained static as Jason critically surveyed the kneeling figure. Then he quietly ordered Juliette to move and kneel at the side of the divan, facing into the room.

"Whose collar do you wear, slave?" Jason's stern voice broke the pregnant silence that had fallen in the room.

"Yours, Master," Lady Moona replied, her voice soft and seductive with just a trace of apprehension.

"What is inscribed on the collar?"

"It reads, 'I am the property of Jason', Master."

"Stand, slave, and prepare to entertain your Master," Jason commanded.

The Lady Moona rose gracefully to her feet and walked

to the centre of the room. She raised her arms above her head, her hands touching, back to back. She bent her left leg slightly. Juliette, enthralled at the sheer eroticism, saw the tip of the woman's tongue slide over the lips of her slightly open mouth.

"Play," Jason ordered.

The musicians raised their instruments and, to Juliette's ear, a strange sounding music flooded into the room. For a moment, Lady Moona remained motionless, and then she began to sway to the rhythm. For the next five minutes or so, Juliette watched, fascinated, as her Mistress danced seductively in front of Jason. As the tempo varied, it seemed that she was a new slave girl, reluctant to display her body. Then, as the tempo altered, she became a brazen wench, eager only to seduce the man before whom she danced. At intervals during the dance, one of the musicians slapped her hand on the floor and Juliette saw the woman's body jerk as if struck by a whip. The spectacle was so delightful to watch that Juliette was a little saddened when, to a final flourish, the music stopped and the panting dancer sank to the floor, before the seated youth. Juliette didn't know whether to applaud or not, so refrained.

"Your dancing is slowly improving, slave," Jason commented as he looked down on his slave.

"A slave is grateful that her Master finds her performance pleasing," Lady Moona said, softly.

"I did not say I was pleased," Jason's voice cut through the air. "You presume too much, slave."

"I am sorry, Master. Please do not have me whipped," the Lady Moona begged, frightened, throwing herself to the floor and kissing his feet.

"I will have to think about it. I only said you were improving," he said scornfully.

"That's not fair, Jason. You know that I danced superbly for you," Lady Moona protested.

Juliette was tempted to agree with her Mistress. The dance had been beautifully erotic and a delight to watch.

"Not only do you dare to question my judgement," Jason shouted angrily. "You also addressed me by name.

Two offences and each deserves a sound whipping." Jason's voice had taken on a threatening tone that made the woman tremble with fear.

"Forgive your slave, Master," Lady Moona pleaded. "Please do not whip my soft body."

Despite the content of the sessions of each evening since she had arrived, Juliette was unprepared for what was happening. The atmosphere was different, more menacing, and she was somehow sure that this afternoon, things were going to be very different. But in what way? She had found it strange that, in this room, her Mistress placed herself totally in the hands of, and at the mercy of, this young slave. But, whereas before there seemed to be some unspoken agreement that he would not go too far, this afternoon she got the impression that the youth was under no restraint. Both the aura of fear that seemed to hover over the woman and the more authoritative demeanour of the boy seemed to point to this.

"I will give you one chance to redeem yourself," the youth's harsh voice broke her train of thought. "You will dance again. This time, you will dance to save your back from the 'male' whip." He turned to Juliette. "Fetch me that whip," he ordered, pointing to a whip that hung by itself on the wall, and which Juliette was sure had not been there on other evenings.

Juliette rose and walked to the wall and, with shaking hands, took the whip and handed it to him and returned to her kneeling position. Just holding it had terrified her! It had a thick handle from which hung a long plaited lash, some six feet long. The lash was as thick as a man's thumb and tapered away at the end no thicker than a cat's claw. The youth let the lash uncurl and slide over his Mistress's prone body. She shivered violently at the touch.

"Prepare to save your back, slave," Jason ordered.

With fear clearly showing in the eyes that peered over the veil, Lady Moona rose and positioned herself in the centre of the room as before. Juliette looked at the whip that now lay curled on the floor at the Jason's feet. Surely he was not intending to use that on his Mistress's bare back!

Then, she thought, after the last two weeks, anything that might happen would not surprise her.

"Play," Jason ordered.

The two slaves picked up their instruments. Again the strange music flooded the room but, this time, with a more sinister beat. Juliette watched, more fascinated than ever, as Lady Moona began to move to the rhythm. Her movements were more flowing, more seductive, than before and Juliette was spellbound at the sheer eroticism that was being unfolded before her eyes. Lady Moona's eyes hardly seemed to stray from the terrible whip. At intervals, she stood absolutely stationary in front of him, her stomach undulating to the beat of the music. At others, she fell to the floor, her eyes looking straight into the youth's pleadingly, and writhed there as if being lashed. It was plain to see that her body was becoming aroused. Whether this was because of the erotic movements of the dance or the anticipation of the whip, Juliette could not decide.

One by one, as the dance progressed, Lady Moona discarded the flimsy garments that covered her supple body until she danced naked for a few minutes. As the dance came to an end, she sank to the floor, her arms spread sideways and her lips on the handle of the whip. She was breathing heavily from her exertions and her body trembled, awaiting her Master's verdict on her performance. A dreadful silence filled the room and Juliette found she was shaking also, fearful of the terrible events, which she was certain were to follow.

"Your slave hopes that she has been found pleasing in her Master's eyes," Lady Moona's whispered as she struggled to regain her breath

"We shall see," Jason's voice was toneless, giving nothing of his thoughts away. "Remove the slaves, then I will decide."

Lady Moona rose gracefully and escorted the two slaves, clutching their instruments, from the room. She closed the door behind them and returned to kneel in front of the youth. Knowing how her Mistress reacted during these sessions, Juliette was not surprised as she noticed the signs that the woman was already becoming aroused.

"Your dancing has improved a little, after all," Jason said, quietly but menacingly. "But you are still guilty of the two offences. Perhaps you have earned a little leniency so, this time, I will give you the chance to spare your back from the lash. You will choose your punishment." He paused and looked down on the trembling body kneeling before him. "You will choose between the whipping, twelve lashes, or a caning. Thirty strokes with impalement!" he continued, an evil grin spreading across his face.

Juliette saw the woman's body begin to shake. She did not know what he meant when he said 'with impalement' but clearly this was well known to the kneeling woman. Even without this unknown condition, Juliette thought, the woman had a terrible choice. The grin on Jason's face foretold that, either way, he intended to see that his Mistress suffered considerably.

"If it please you, Master, your slave would choose the cane," Lady Moona replied softly, her voice trembling and her body shaking.

"You understand, slave, that, since your offences were very serious, you will be shown no mercy," Jason spat the words out venomously.

"I fully understand, Master. Your slave neither deserves nor expects any."

Juliette had sensed that, since this was her last evening there, this session was to be a special one. She had come to accept that, for some strange reason, the Lady Moona had, she assumed, orchestrated the previous sessions and the youth had 'played his part' according to her rules. From the tone of the conversation so far, the woman's unfeigned fear that had shown in her voice and in her eyes, for this session Jason would be under no restrictive instructions. She had seen this in the cruel smile on his mouth and the excited look in his eyes, both of which had changed to disappointment as the woman had made her choice.

She watched as the youth rose and fetched a long wooden bench from the side of the room and placed it on top of the divan. The legs of the bench slotted neatly into recesses on the divan so that there was a clear space of some two feet between the base of the bench and the divan. He then took down a strange looking contraption, fitted with straps, from a hook on the wall. He ordered Juliette to stand and fitted the straps round her waist and thighs. Looking down her body, she saw something sticking out from her groin. A gasp of surprise and shock came from her as she realised the 'thing' resembled a thick, erect, man's penis. Jason ordered her to mount the divan and lay, face up on the bench and strapped her to it so that she was unable to move.

"Bring me the cane, then take your position, slave," Jason ordered, turning towards his kneeling Mistress. "The long one!" he added sternly.

Lady Moona rose and fetched the cane from the wall. She knelt in front of the youth and, after kissing it lovingly, offered it to him.

"The cane, Master," Lady Moona said haltingly. "Your slave's bottom begs to atone for her offences. May the kiss of the cane draw forth the juice of her repentance."

"Your wish will be granted, slave." He picked up a piece of white cloth that had been lying on the divan. "The red stains on this will soon bear witness to the sincerity of your repentance."

Jason took the cane from his Mistress's trembling hands. With a final glance of dread at the rod with which she was about to be thrashed, Lady Moona rose and climbed up onto the divan and positioned herself for the ordeal ahead.

Still wondering what was to take place, Juliette saw her Mistress straddle her prone body so that the tip of the leather phallus just brushed her already open sex lips. She slowly leaned forward and reached to the two posts at the head of the divan and clutched them tightly. The woman's breasts hung just above her own and she could see the nipples already hard and erect.

"Remember, slave!" Jason's voice now sounded very menacing in the otherwise silent room. "You will not impale yourself until given permission. Then you will masturbate your body on the phallus. You are forbidden to come. If you fail to comply with these rules, you will still get the whipping with a further six lashes added for disobedience."

"I understand, Master," Lady Moona gasped between her clenched teeth.

By turning her head, Juliette could see the youth take his position at the side of the divan, a beaming smile on his face as he surveyed his Mistress's gorgeous bottom. She could hardly believe her eyes as she saw him raise the cane high in the air and bring it down with a resounding report across the waiting buttocks. To Juliette's utter astonishment, the stroke had been applied with greater force than any other she had seen him give the woman during the last two weeks. Clearly, for this session, no holds were to be barred and the youth intended to take full advantage of the situation. She cringed as she realised the woman was to get thirty such strokes laid across her soft behind. Lady Moona rocked under the force of the stroke, causing the phallus to rub against her sex.

Three more times Juliette felt her Mistress's body jerk as the sharp reports of the rattan striking bare flesh echoed round the room. To her surprise, Lady Moona made no sound other than a quick hissing noise as she sucked in air through her teeth as each struck. The woman's breasts, now mottled with her desire, swayed above her, the nipples just brushing her own.

Swish. Thwack. A loud groan issued from the woman's throat as the fifth stroke blazed across her cheeks and the first tears sprang from her eyes to land on the naked body beneath her. Another five sharp reports echoed round the room, followed by shrill cries, which turned to screams on the last. The woman's body rocked back and forth as the pain built up in her body.

"Do not cheat, slave, or it will be a whipping for you," Jason commanded. He had been watching the slave carefully and had seen her lower herself onto the phallus a little so it brushed harder on her sex.

Five more times the rattan lashed down on the woman's

buttocks, each stroke drawing a loud scream from her lungs and rocking her body back and forth on the tip of the leather. Her body was now dripping with sweat and her tears were flowing freely, droplets falling onto Juliette. Looking up, Juliette could see the woman's face contorted with pain. Her nipples were hard and swollen and her pendant breasts becoming marked as the veins became filled. She had now taken half of the designated thrashing and her body was burning with the pain in her bottom and the arousal that it was inciting in her body.

"You will impale yourself after the next stroke," Jason ordered. "You will masturbate on the penis properly. I do not want to see any signs of you cheating."

Swish. Thwack. A loud scream followed the report and, looking along her body, Juliette saw the woman thrust down on the leather and the phallus disappear into her tunnel. Still gripping the posts tight, Lady Moona immediately began to thrust up and down on the invader, gasping and moaning as the movement drove her arousal soaring. As well as the woman's sweat and tears, she now felt the juices of her arousal dripping down the phallus onto her stomach and seeping between her thighs.

Jason began leaving a longer interval between each stroke now, to allow the buttocks to absorb the full benefit of each before the next added its quota of fuel to the fire raging in his Mistress's bottom. He was putting all his strength behind the cane, the strokes of which were now landing on the hard ridges of previous strokes. He was timing the strokes perfectly, ensuring that each cut across the buttocks at the height of the woman's upward movement and landing at the second that the soft flesh was stretched to the limit. He was rewarded with the sight of thin bright red lines appearing along the top of each weal.

After the fifth stroke since the woman had impaled her body on the leather, Juliette was, herself, gasping for breath as the body above her kept thudding down onto her own driving the air from her lungs. For her own sake, she was glad that the woman only had ten more strokes to come. As the twentieth stroke burned its path across the woman's throbbing bottom, Juliette saw her head turn up towards the ceiling a sudden expression of fear on her face. Juliette sensed that the woman was about to succumb to an orgasm

"No! No more!" Lady Moona's plaintive voice moaned. "No more. I can't take any more."

Jason, seemingly determined to break his Mistress's control and force an orgasm through her body, grinned evilly to himself. Opportunities such as this only presented themselves very rarely. He was still smarting from the injustice of a whipping Lady Moona had given him a month earlier, for something he had not done! This session, when no holds were barred, would give him the perfect opportunity to take his revenge and, for the first time, lay a whip across his Mistress sexy back and let her have a taste of what it was like. But he only had ten more strokes with which to achieve his goal!

Juliette looked sideways at the youth and shuddered. He had taken a couple of steps backwards, then with the cane raised high over his shoulder, his took two quick paces forward and lashed the rod across the rising cheeks. A terrible scream echoed round the room and the Lady Moona's body writhed frantically. Jason repeated the process on each of the remaining strokes. On the twenty sixth, Lady Moona's hands slipped down the post and her mouth descended on to Juliette's, the tongue forcing her teeth apart as the woman screamed her agony into her mouth. As the final stroke was applied, Lady Moona's body arched backwards like a strung bow as she thumped up and down on the phallus, desperately trying to stave off the orgasm that was on the point of exploding inside her. Somehow, to Juliette's astonishment, she succeeded.

Juliette watched the youth replace the cane on its rack and return to stand at the side of his Mistress who was still pumping up and down on the phallus.

"Dismount at once, slave," Jason ordered. Juliette detected disappointment in his voice. Had he really wanted to put his Mistress's back to the whip? He had certainly tried hard enough to break her control!

Slowly, reluctantly, Lady Moona eased her body off the

phallus and climbed down and stood facing him. As Jason walked round her and released Juliette's bonds and removed the bench from the divan, she had a clear view of her Mistress's backside. She just managed to suppress a cry of shock. The cheeks were badly swollen and covered with a mass of hard dark red ridges, most of which boasted thin bright red lines on the top where the cane had cut through the taut skin.

"Moona," Jason ordered. "Bend over, double, and hold your ankles." As the woman obeyed, he turned to Juliette. "Take the cloth and spread it over the slave's backside and press on it firmly. I want to see it well and truly marked with the evidence of her punishment."

Juliette did as she was ordered. Lady Moona flinched and moaned at the light touch of the cloth and let out a sharp cry as Juliette pressed it against her flesh with her hands. She felt the heat radiating from the cheeks and saw the white cloth marked by a pattern of bright red lines. She lifted the cloth away and handed it to the youth. No doubt he would hang it somewhere as a memento of the days enjoyment!

"Moona. Spread yourself on the divan, face up," Jason ordered and when, with a shudder and moan the woman obeyed, he spread her limbs wide apart and tied them to the posts.

"So!" he said, looking down on his Mistress's spread body. "You managed to survive this time. Shall I order this slave to satisfy the needs in your body? You don't really deserve such a nice treat, you know." To her surprise, Juliette expected to hear disappointment and bitterness in his voice, but she detected, instead, a hint of anticipated excitement.

"Yes please, Master," Lady Moona whispered through the sobs that still emitted from her throat. "I have earned it," she continued. "I didn't come during the beating although it was very hard not to."

"I recall that, during the caning, you begged for mercy. Begged for me to stop! You know that to ask for mercy is forbidden."

"No, Master! I didn't ask for mercy. I was telling my body to hold on a bit longer. I wouldn't dare beg for mercy."

"It sounded very like a plea for mercy to me. So, if you want to be satisfied, you must convince me that I am wrong and that you are not lying. How do you suggest you do it?"

"Any way you wish, Master, as long as my needs are satisfied first."

"With the whip?" Jason asked, the smile on his face spreading.

Juliette realised that the youth had very craftily laid the trap and now the Lady Moona was standing on the brink. She was faced with the choice of submitting her soft back to the whip, which, there was no doubt, Jason would wield severely, or spending the night, her wrists chained behind her back and her needs unfulfilled. Juliette saw a shudder of resignation sweep over the woman

"If that is what my Master requires," the Lady Moona replied softly, to Juliette's utter astonishment.

"How many lashes?" Jason demanded, smiling now that the trap had been successfully sprung.

"As many as my Master desires," Lady Moona said resignedly, knowing her fate had now been sealed. It was merely, now, a question of the extent to which she would be made to suffer. "But not with the heavy whip."

"It would have been twelve with the heavy whip if you had disobeyed me," Jason said. "You merely begged for mercy so it will be with the Slave Girl Whip. So, how many lashes is your satisfaction worth?"

"Five, Master?" Lady Moona said tentatively.

"Five?" Jason queried. "Then your needs can't be all that great!" he added, scornfully.

"Ten, then Master. I do not deserve any more," Lady Moona said, pleading.

"You deserve whatever I decide, slave," Jason said with menace in his voice. "Twelve with the Girl Slave Whip to earn your satisfaction. Followed by six with the heavy whip for daring to bargain with your Master."

A heavy silence fell in the room. Juliette, seeing the

cruel glint in the youth's eyes, which her Mistress could not have missed, fully expected the Lady Moona to call a halt to the session. Surely no free woman would submit to a whip being used on her bare back, especially by a slave who was, obviously, fully intending to lay it on as hard as he could. She looked at the woman spread on the divan and saw a fierce shudder pass through the body. Was it only the arousal raging in her or, was she really going to let him whip her?

"Master. I am your slave to do with as you wish," Lady Moona said softly to Juliette's astonishment, a pleading look in her eyes. "But I beg to be satisfied first."

"I will grant that wish, slave. But I still think you begged for mercy under the cane. I ask you again and, this time, I demand the truth. Did you lie to me just now and did you beg for mercy?"

Another short silence hung in the room as Lady Moona considered her reply. If she told the truth this time, she was certain it would result in her whipping being increased dreadfully. If she lied again, however, could it somehow make her predicament any worse? She took a deep breath.

"Yes, Master," her whisper was hardly audible as a series of shudders swept over her body.

"You are therefore guilty of both disobedience and of lying to your Master." The jubilation in Jason's voice made Juliette shudder. She was glad that it was not she that was the object of the youth's vindictiveness. "You will get six additional lashes for each offence," Jason continued. "With the heavy whip."

Lady Moona, realising that her fate was sealed looked up into Jason's eyes. The needs raging inside her were too great for her to invoke her authority and call an end to the session. Further, it was an unwritten rule that, in this room, she was a slave and must accept whatever decision the youth made. But he had never risked sentencing her to any punishment across her back before, let alone a whipping. Perhaps he would back down at the last minute and only hit her very lightly as a token punishment!

"Master," Lady Moona whispered, looking into Jason's

face with utter pleading in her eyes. "I am guilty and have greatly displeased you. I beg to earn your forgiveness. Let the whip teach your slave a severe lesson."

During the last two weeks, Juliette had come to accept many strange things. That, in this room Lady Moona, a free woman, reversed places with her slave and submitted to being punished by him. She had seen the woman's buttocks thrashed with a cane and her breasts with a birch and strap. She had heard the sharp, loud, reports of the strokes landing on her bare flesh and heard the woman scream in pain and agony, and her cries of ecstatic pleasure as her orgasms surged through her body. Now she was to submit to being whipped, and no doubt soundly, across her bare back. Even the most satisfying sexual satisfaction could not be worth that. Juliette would have been even more astounded had she known that it was to be the first time Lady Moona's back had been punished in any way.

Obeying Jason's instructions, Juliette mounted the divan and knelt between the spread legs. Then, as Jason guided the phallus, which was still strapped in place, into the woman's tunnel, Juliette lowered herself until she lay on the woman's body, their breasts crushed against each other. Slowly, Juliette began to lift her hips up and down, driving the phallus back and forth inside Lady Moona's tunnel, making her moan with desire. Then she felt the cane, once again back in Jason's hand, begin to beat a light tattoo on her behind. Gradually she felt the tapping became more frequent, and the force increase, and she matched her momentum to keep pace with it. The body underneath her responded, writhing and bucking with the delicious sensations that were surging through it. Lady Moona's moaning and bucking rapidly grew more insistent until, with a cry of wonderful relief, her body arched raising Juliette high off the divan as a series of shattering orgasms took control of her.

Jason ordered Juliette to dismount and, having removed the leather straps, ordered her to kneel at the side of the divan. The youth left the room and returned in a few moments carrying a bowl of cold water. He untied his

Mistress's limbs and, kneeling at the side of the divan, commenced to gently bathe her face and neck. Slowly, Lady Moona emerged from the misty cloud into which the orgasm had pitched her. She raised her head and looked round, a sublime smile on her lips.

"Thank you slave. That was absolutely delicious," she said, looking at Jason and then turned to look at Juliette. "Thank you also Juliette."

"I am glad you enjoyed this slave's efforts, Moona. Now you must pay for your pleasures and sins," the youth's voice cut into the air. "Get up and stand in the centre of the room."

The Lady Moona had spoken as she usually did at the end of each session. The sublime smile on her face vanished immediately to be replaced with an expression of utter terror. She had spoken too soon, forgetting that the session was not over and she had her worst ordeal yet to face. Shaking visibly she rose from the divan and walked to the centre of the room and stood facing the wall to the side of where Juliette knelt. Jason followed her and, bending down, pulled her legs apart and secured her ankles to rings in the floor. He strode purposefully to the side of the room and unhooked a rope and let it slide through his fingers. A heavy metal ring, on the other end of the rope, slowly descended until it hung at the woman's waist.

Standing at her side Jason pointed to the ring. "You know what that is, slave?" he asked.

"Yes, Master," Lady Moona replied softly, her voice quivering. "It is a whipping ring."

Jason took hold of each of his Mistress's wrists and bound them to the ring. Returning to the side of the room, he slowly pulled on the rope, stretching her arms high above her head, until only her toes touched the floor, before securing the rope to the hook. Then, standing in front of the woman, he pulled her hair forward over her upthrust breasts and tied it in a knot under her chin. The Lady Moona's back was now fully exposed, awaiting its first taste of the lash. Juliette could see her Mistress's eyes wide open and her face white with terror as she watched Jason walk to the end wall and take down the Girl Slave Whip. This whip had a thick handle from which five strips of leather, each a quarter of an inch wide and thick and four feet long, sprayed out. He curled the thongs in his hand and held them in front of Lady Moona's face.

"Kiss the whip," he ordered.

Unable to take her eyes off the dreaded thongs, Lady Moona pursed her lips and placed a long, loving kiss on them then, looking over her shoulder, she watched the youth move to her rear. Then she turned her head forward, closed her eyes tight and clenched her teeth, waiting for the first stroke.

Jason waited, his arm raised until he estimated the woman's nerves were at breaking point. Then his arm sped forward, sending the thongs cracking across the waiting back. Lady Moona's eyes opened wide in utter disbelief as a sheet of agony suddenly seared across her back. The force of the stroke expelled the air from her lungs in a loud 'whoosh' choking off the scream of pain that welled up in her throat. She hardly had time to draw air into her lungs before the youth flayed her back with the second stroke.

Juliette knelt there, utterly spell-bound by the sheer eroticism of the scene. Her own body was responding, as it had been all through the session, and she was frightened that, before the flogging was over, she would be unable to stop herself climaxing. One by one, she watched the twelve strokes applied to her Mistress's bare back. Lady Moona yelled and screamed as she writhed in her bonds. Juliette was astounded that the youth could get such force behind the lashes, which were raising livid weals across the woman's pale back, which was rapidly beginning to match the state of her buttocks. After the last stroke had landed, Lady Moona's legs gave way and her slim arms took her full weight. She opened her eyes just as Jason replaced the whip on the wall. Deliberately and slowly he walked to the end of the divan where the heavy whip had laid for most of the session.

Lady Moona's eyes opened in utter terror and she began to writhe. "Please, master! Not too hard! My poor back is already on fire," she stammered through her sobs.

"Silence, slave," Jason commanded in a thunderous voice.

"Permission to speak, please Master," Lady Moona begged plaintively.

"You may speak, but be quick about it," Jason said as he walked passed her, cracking the long lash on the floor.

"I know you are eager to repay me for the whipping I gave you a while ago," Lady Moona's voice was pleading in desperation. "So I expect you will lash me hard in revenge. I know I dare not beg for mercy but, please Master, order the slave to help me through the punishment."

"You are quite right, slave. I did not deserve that whipping and you are about to suffer my revenge and find out for yourself what a real whipping is like. I fully intend to take my revenge and make the strokes as hard as I can. But, you have been brave, so far, so I will grant your request. But remember, if you come, even after the last stroke, the whipping will start all over again." He signalled Juliette to him.

Obeying his order, Juliette knelt in front of the shaking woman. She reached round and clasped the woman's swollen buttocks and pulled her body towards her and pressed her own face against the woman's mound. As she eased her tongue between the woman's opened sex she felt her body shudder with desire and smelt the woman's musky odour mixed with the smell of her fear. The woman must have head the long lash slither across the floor as Jason shook it out, for her body went rigid.

Crack.

The sound of the of the impact of plaited leather striking bare flesh echoed round the room followed by a shrill scream from the woman. A flood of her juices spilled out of her hard sex lips and on to Juliette's tongue.

Crack.

Juliette found it very difficult to keep hold of the woman's buttocks and her tongue in place as her body writhed in agony under the lash.

Lady Moona screamed and twisted frantically as Jason

applied each of the strokes on her burning back. She writhed in agony, not daring to scream for mercy, struggling to hold on to consciousness. Jason fully intended to reap his full revenge on his Mistress's back, taking full advantage of the opportunity, which would not arise again for a long time, if ever. His Mistress's back and shoulders received the full eighteen lashes, a few of which fell low enough to curl round sending the tip of the lash deep into the soft flesh of her breast.

Jason, a satisfied look on his face, surveyed the woman's back before replacing the whip in its place. He walked to the suspended woman. "You took the whipping well, slave. You now have my permission to satisfy your body," he knelt and whispered in Juliette's ear.

Juliette held the woman's buttocks tight as she sought the depths of the woman's tunnel with her tongue. So advanced was Lady Moona's arousal that it was only a few minutes before her body arched rigid and she screamed with the delicious release. Her juices flowed like a river as her tortured body, at last, succumbed to a series of shattering orgasms, more violent than any Juliette had seen her enjoy before.

Juliette stood back as again, the youth gently bathed his Mistress's face and neck. The woman's back was blazing with the heat of the whipping, red all over where the Girl Slave Whip had laid its foundation and with dark raised ridges showing where Jason had taken his revenge with the heavy whip. Despite the savagery with which he had applied the lash, Juliette was astonished to see that, in no place, had he managed to cut the skin.

As soon as his Mistress had recovered sufficiently, Jason released the rope and, her legs unable to support her, she sank slowly to her knees, her body bent so that her forehead touched the floor. The youth carefully eased her to her feet and guided her to the divan, where she collapsed, face down, moaning and shivering. Juliette, accustomed to the routine, as gently as she could, smoothed the healing cream over the burning back and buttocks. Judging by the hardness of the weals and the heat emanating from them,

76

the youth had certainly administered the flogging with efficiency.

As Juliette worked, she wondered, not for the first time, what drove this woman to subject her young body to such agonies at the hands of her young slave. It was evident that, whilst she feared the pain, she must get pleasure through being put in such a position of submission, beaten and humiliated. She had not failed to orgasm at least twice during each session, and these had been held every day.

The final session, when the whips had been used on her was, apparently, a very special occasion and Juliette wondered if it was her presence that had been the catalyst that brought it about. What surprised Juliette, as she lay on her own bed later, was that, whilst the other slave girls had been well beaten by the youth, she had escaped with a relatively easy time. Again, she, who had become used to being thoroughly flogged for the slightest thing, did not understand why. The riddles in her head were still unresolved as she drifted off into sleep, aware that, in the morning, she was to be returned to Lord Reythal and the whipping that Abaddon had promised her.

CHAPTER 4.

As had been arranged, Abaddon came to collect her the next morning. Lady Moona, now dressed in a concealing gown and not showing any signs of the ordeal she had undergone the previous afternoon and evening, was there to see her off. Just before Abaddon placed the black cloak and hood over, Lady Moona placed a sealed envelope in Juliette's hands, with strict instructions that she was to give it personally to Lord Reythal himself and no other.

It was with trepidation that, after an uncomfortable journey in the cart, Juliette found herself kneeling in front of her Master. She was naked, the cloak and hood having been removed. She held the envelope in her hand, wondering if its contents would be what Abaddon so earnestly desired. Having seen the youth whip Lady Moona the thought of the ogre using a whip on her terrified her. She could almost feel the lash cutting into her soft smooth back. Unlike Jason, there was no doubt in her mind that he would ensure that her pale flesh was well lacerated.

"So! My little slave has returned," Lord Reythal said, looking down on her. "Did you serve the Lady Moona well, slave?"

"I hope I did, Master," Juliette replied dreading the next few minutes. "She ordered me to give you this." She held out the envelope in a trembling hand.

She knelt, trembling with fear, as Lord Reythal opened the envelope and took out the single sheet of paper it contained. He read the contents several times before handing it to Abaddon. It was with relief that Juliette saw the look of disappointment on the ogre's face. Lord Reythal looked at his slave, smiling at the expression of relief on her face.

"You will now tell me all that happened while you were at Lady Moona's house. Leave nothing, I repeat nothing, out. I want to know everything."

Lord Reythal heard her out in silence as she carefully related all that had occurred, omitting nothing except the arousing effect the sessions had had on her body. The telling took the best part of an hour and a half and, when she had finished, a heavy silence fell in the room. Lord Reythal appeared to be considering her account very deeply and carefully until, at last, he began questioning her. Then he ordered her to give him a very detailed description of the Lady Moona, concentrating on her naked appearance. When she had finished, he again fell silent for at least five minutes before turning to Abaddon, who had stood silently by throughout.

"The slave's account seems to confirm all of our suspicions," he said, thoughtfully.

"Yes, my Lord," the major-domo replied. "It most certainly does seem to." Juliette saw, and quailed at the lecherous expression that passed, momentarily across his face. "Do we put your plan into effect?"

"We must not be too hasty," Lord Reythal replied. "We must consider the matter carefully before we act. Everything must be done carefully and according to the law, if the plan is to succeed." Turning to Juliette he continued. "You have done very well, slave. Much better than I had hoped. The Lady Moona speaks highly of you."

"I am grateful if I have pleased you, Master, and the Lady Moona is pleased with my efforts," Juliette replied, relief flowing over her.

"That is as maybe," Lord Reythal said, his voice taking on a stern tone. "I understand that, on the day you left, you greatly insulted Abaddon. In insulting him, you also insulted me! This is a grave matter and cannot be overlooked by your good performance during the last two weeks. Abaddon has advocated a sound lesson with the whip."

Juliette began to shake. So the crafty sadist was determined to get his wish, one way or the other. Visions of Lady Moona's back after Jason had used the whip on her flashed through her mind.

"However, as I have already said, you have served me well and I am inclined to be lenient this time. But, if you ever commit that offence again, nothing will spare your back. You will be taken to the punishment yard this afternoon and receive a public thrashing. Fifteen with the birch."

"My Lord," Abaddon protested. "The slave's offence is very serious and merits a severe taste of the lash. Fifteen strokes of the birch will surely not be a sufficient lesson to her and the other slaves."

Juliette looked up at her Master, terror in her eyes, pleading for him not to give in to the major-domos' wishes.

"Perhaps you are right, Abaddon. You may increase the punishment to thirty strokes if you wish. I am sure you can teach her a lesson in respect for her masters."

"I surely will, My Lord," Abaddon replied, licking his lips.

"No doubt you will," Lord Reythal mused aloud. He was well aware of the major-domo's sadistic streak, but he served him well in other matters. Anyway, the girl was merely a slave! But a pretty one! Too pretty to have her back scarred just to suit the man's wishes!

Abaddon took Juliette from the room before she had collected her thoughts enough to openly plead for leniency. He led her to a small room on the ground floor, overlooking the yard. The room was bare of furniture and the only window was set high in the wall. The time passed slowly. Visions of Abaddon using the birch on Sarita that evening kept recurring in her mind's eye, as did those of her own judicial caning. This time, however, it would not be a select party of strangers who would witness her ordeal but the entire household, including her friends. There was no doubt in her mind that she was going to be severely flogged. Deprived of the chance to use a whip on her, she was sure Abaddon would see to it that her thrashing was as thorough as he could make it. It wasn't fair! He had deliberately goaded her into saying what she had.

Eventually, she heard the sound of a bell being rung in the yard, summoning the household to watch her punishment. She began to shake at the sound. The door opened and, to her surprise, it was Quinell, not Abaddon, who entered. In his hands he held a bundle of chains. He ordered her to hold out her hands and placed manacles, joined by a short chain, round her wrists. Her ankles received similar treatment, although the chain on them was slightly longer. He put a metal collar round her neck and snapped a chain to it. He then instructed her how she was required to conduct herself whilst in the yard. He then made her stand just inside the doorway while he went to see that all was ready. Juliette shivered, more with fear than because she was naked, no clothing having been given her since the cloak and hood had been removed in the Master's study.

Knowing that her time had come, Juliette waited, resignedly, to be summoned forth. Although she had been caned many times but, apart from the introduction with the reins, she had not had any other instrument used on her back. Although, this time, her back had been spared, she was terrified of the birch rods lashing her bottom. She remembered how Sarita, who she now knew could normally take a beating bravely, had screamed that evening. She wondered if she could withstand such pain. Then she remembered the pleasure she had seen Abaddon get out of birching Sarita and she vowed that she would be brave, at no matter what cost, and deprive him of hearing her scream for mercy.

The door opened and Quinell stood there! He had returned for her!

"Remember to behave properly, as a slave should when receiving a public punishment," he said as he picked up the chain and moved through the door.

Juliette was conscious of the audience assembled along one side of the yard. Trying hard to ignore their presence, she kept her head held high as she crossed the yard, her eyes fixed on the 'T' shape ahead of her where her thrashing would take place.

"Be brave, little one," Quinell whispered out of the side of his mouth as they halted in the centre of the yard and he turned her to face the watchers.

Juliette scanned the expressionless faces, seeking out those of her friends. She saw them and tried to smile bravely at them. She saw Abaddon approaching her, a cloth wrapped bundle in his hands. He halted in front of her, his eyes roving over her naked body as a cruel smile spread his mouth. He turned to face the household.

"The slave Juliette is guilty of showing disrespect to me and her Master. She has been sentenced to a public thrashing of thirty strokes of the birch." He turned to face Juliette. "Prepare," he ordered.

Juliette sank to her knees before him and raised her eyes to his. She shuddered at the gleam of triumph that shone in them. She swallowed hard, for, in her mind, what she had to do was worse than any beating.

"Master," she spoke loud, as Quinell had instructed her, striving hard to keep her voice even. "I confess my guilt and humbly beg that I will be soundly punished to teach me to be respectful in the future."

She had feared that the words would stick in her throat and was relieved when she had managed to keep her voice even and loud so that everyone in the yard would hear. She dared not do otherwise than follow the required ritual. She rose to her feet. Quinell made to take hold of her arm but, with a weak smile at him, she shrugged his hand away. Casting a last fleeting look at the watchers, she turned and, taking care not to trip on the chain, walked the few paces to the place where her thrashing would be administered. She felt the round log press against her mound. Taking a deep breath, she bent over, feeling the surface of the log, which has been worn smooth by the writhing of previous victims, cool against her stomach. She felt Quinell spread her legs wide and chain her ankles to rings set in the ground and pull her arms back and clip them to the same rings. She was glad it had been him, and not Abaddon, whose hands had touched her skin. Her back was to the audience, her buttocks stretched very taut, perfectly poised for the beating to come.

Quinell gently pulled her head up by her hair as Abaddon stood in front of her and unravelled the cloth bundle in his hands. She trembled, her resolve to be brave nearly deserted her as the instrument with which she was to be flogged was revealed. The birch was far worse than the one she had seen used on Sarita. This one consisted of perhaps a dozen long thin straight branches from which the outer covering had been removed and she could see the small sharp nodules where the side shoots had been removed. Each rod shone in the sunlight. Abaddon had clearly taken a lot of trouble preparing it!

"Are you ready?" Abaddon's voice was grim yet triumphant.

"Yes, Master," she replied as required. But she had lied! She would never be ready for what was about to be done to her. A sudden surge of revolt came over her at the injustice of the whole affair. "Do your worst, you sadistic bastard," she muttered under her breath.

To her horror, Abaddon crouched down at her side and whispered in her ear. "I heard that, you slut. Next time I will make certain you feel the lash. In the meantime, yes, I will enjoy thrashing your impertinent buttocks."

Abaddon's legs disappeared from her sight as he moved to her side. She tightened the grip of her small hands on the chain that secured her wrists. Somehow, she forced her legs not to shake. She regretted what she had just said. She should have known the ogre would hear them and that she would suffer badly as a consequence.

Thwack.

The birch struck her taut bottom and, immediately a blaze of fire, a wide band as the birch spread on impact, covered the whole of her cheeks.

Thwack.

Thwack.

She had counted three strokes. Her Master had ordered thirty. How could she endure such a beating? Her young and tender bottom was not meant for such savage treatment! She hated the man wielding the birch rods with all her being.

Abaddon lashed the rods across her burning cheeks five more times but, apart from a sharp gasp as each landed, she had managed to remain defiantly silent. How she had done so with eight strokes searing her bottom, she never knew. But her silence was infuriating Abaddon. He liked the girls to scream as he thrashed their buttocks. Her defiant silence was spoiling his pleasure. His frustration grew. Even now, after she had just insulted him again, she was doing her best to ruin his enjoyment.

Swish. Thwack.

This, the ninth stroke, broke Juliette's rigid control. A shrill scream followed the report of the stroke A smile curled the man's mouth. Now he would make her really sing for him!

Ten

Eleven.

Twelve.

Juliette's brain was counting the strokes even as her screams echoed round the yard. Her body was writhing on the log. Quite delightfully, Abaddon thought! Her buttocks felt as if a raging fire had been lit beneath them and the pain became intolerable. She still had another eighteen to come and she wanted to scream for mercy, but her pride would not let her. Better that her poor buttocks suffered any degree of agony that to give him the satisfaction of hearing her do that!

Abaddon was really enjoying thrashing this bitch's arse. She was squirming and screaming delightfully and her body was pouring with sweat. Just how he liked them to be! With mounting satisfaction, he laid on another eight searing strokes and received the added bonus of seeing the weals on her taut cheeks begin to split and thin lines of bright red appear. The sight of these turned the balance of his mind. He paused to wipe the sweat from his own brow as he summoned up his strength to lay on the remainder of the bitch's sentence. He wanted to go on lashing her behind and not stop until he made her scream for mercy. But part of his brain was aware that he had announced thirty strokes and the watchers, particularly Quinell who was standing close by, would be counting to see that he did not exceed that total.

Ten strokes only left to him and he steadied himself, mentally pushing aside the madness that the sight of blood had awakened in his mind. He would make the most of those ten, if only for this time!

Juliette knew that she had been writhing on the log and giving Abaddon the pleasure of seeing the signs of her suffering. She knew, also, that the pressure on her mound, and the movement, was intensifying the arousal that was mounting inside her. She knew she could not avoid this happening and was ashamed that the watchers would have a clear view of the responses of her body. Worse still, the ogre that was thrashing her would see. She must concentrate her hardest as the last ten strokes were laid on to prevent the arousal breaking through her control and climaxing into an undisguisable orgasm.

The twentieth stroke had made her scream even louder as her body arched against the restraints and sapped the last of her strength from her slim body. As the tension passed, she collapsed over the log.

Quinell, seeing this, signalled to Abaddon to hold back the next stroke as he crouched in front of the slave and lifted her head up so he could see her face. Her eyes were open and bleary and her mouth was opening and closing in silent screams. "Hold on, little one," he whispered. "Only ten more and then it will be over…" Reluctantly he straightened up and signalled to Abaddon to continue with the punishment. Truly, the slave deserved the punishment, he thought, but he was sickened by the obvious sadistic delight that Abaddon was enjoying in administering it.

Juliette heard his words faintly through the mist of pain that had engulfed her brain. Ten more to come! Ten more terribly searing strokes of that dreadful birch across her suffering bottom! From some unknown depths, she summoned up the dregs of her courage and concentrated on fighting the arousal that was now almost out of control. Better he heard her screaming than to give him the satisfaction of seeing her orgasm. He would claim that the beating was giving her pleasure and not punishing her and demand that she should still be whipped.

Abaddon, oblivious of anything but the pleasure at the pain he was inflicting and the stimulation it was giving to his libido, determined that these final strokes would be the hardest and most severe yet. He took a couple of steps back and ran forward, lashing the rods with terrible force across the slave's buttocks. He nodded with satisfaction as the slave's body jerked violently against her bonds and a piercing scream echoed round the yard.

How Juliette survived those last ten strokes she would never know. She was using all her remaining strength to fight off the orgasm. Her body jerked violently as each stroke lashed her, rocking her body back and forth on the log, making her situation even harder to control. At last the birch stopped its onslaught and her ordeal was over. She lay collapsed over the log, her moans and mewing loud enough for the watchers to hear. She was to be left there for an hour so that, as the slaves and servants went about their duties, they could see her and be reminder of the fate of anyone who offended the Master or his major domo.

The sun, which was still high in the sky, blazed down, its scorching heat falling directly on the slave's already burning buttocks. Juliette lay over the log, her shadow hiding the damp patches on the ground where her tears and sweat had fallen. It was by far the worst thrashing she had ever received, even worse than the judicial beating that had started her life of slavery. She hated and dreaded the pain that was inflicted on her young body each time she was flogged. Even more, she hated the men who ordered it and those that inflicted it. Yet each time she had been thrashed, and each time she watched other slaves being disciplined, her body reacted the same as it had when she had lain in the arms of a young lover. Those times seemed so far away now and she detested her body for the way it refused to obey her and behaved each time the pain erupted in her bottom.

Maya and Sarita approached her softly on bare feet. Juliette, now slumped motionless over the log, felt them gently release her wrists and ankles. She emitted a low moan as they carefully eased her upright and, with her arms round their necks, led her stumbling from the yard. In their own quarters, they laid her face down on her bed and gently bathed her face and bottom with cold water. As the cold water, and then the cream, seeped into the cuts left by the birch, Juliette could not help flinching and squirming as the sting awakened the pain.

Juliette wanted nothing more than to slip off into a comforting sleep and escape from the pain that burned and throbbed in her bottom. That release was, however, to be denied her! All three slaves were to wait on table that evening and Juliette was to be naked. For once, Sarita and Maya had been ordered to wear a fine shift so that Juliette's nakedness would be more pronounced.

Juliette helped serve the evening meal and, as expected the state of her buttocks did not pass unnoticed, especially by the younger son who made numerous comments that made Juliette cringe with shame and embarrassment. She did have one uneasy moment when serving the older son. She felt his hands slide up her thigh and onto her aching cheeks. His touch was light as he ran his fingers over the weals that still stood out, hard and hot. She gritted her teeth but managed to remain still, even when his fingers strayed between her legs. She felt a slight thrill soar through her as his fingers found her clitoris and pressed it lightly. Under any other circumstances, he being so strong and handsome in her eyes, his attentions would have been enjoyable.

After the meal, Juliette was ordered to attend on the Master in his room. His use of her was fierce and thorough, the friction as she writhed on the bed rekindling the fire in her bottom as she served his pleasure. This time, instead of sending her away with her needs still raging inside her, he permitted her to release her control and she succumbed to several shattering orgasms that left her completely drained but satisfied.

When she was finally dismissed and returned to her quarters, she found her two friends were still awake, waiting for her return. It was the first time they had been alone since her return from the Lady Moona and they were eager to know what had transpired during those two weeks. They listened, astounded, as Juliette related all that had happened. When she told them how the woman had changed places with her slave and submitted to him beating

87

and whipping her, they took a lot of convincing that Juliette was not making the whole thing up. Little did they know that, at sometime in the future, they were to see for themselves. Neither Sarita nor Maya could throw any light on the enigmatic conversation between the Master and Abaddon that had taken place after Juliette had reported to them on her return.

Juliette quickly readjusted to the normal routine following her return and the days drifted into weeks and the weeks into months. Juliette was sent for many times by the Master to serve his pleasure at night but not once, was any further reference made to those two weeks at the Lady Moona's. Due to the strict regime, Juliette received quite a few beatings but Abaddon never had the chance to fulfil his wish and use a whip on her back. On the occasions when he was the one punishing her, the Master had always designated the punishment and either he, or Quinell were present to see that it was correctly applied. This successfully restricted the man's sadistic tendencies. Juliette was not made aware that the Master had ordered specifically that her body was not, on any account, to be permanently marked in any way.

Her twenty-second birthday came and passed unnoticed save for an extra sisterly hug from her two friends. A lot had happened to her since that day, shortly after her twentieth birthday, when she had been flogged and sold into slavery for a crime she did not commit. She, herself, had changed a lot in that time and she had learned many things about herself that would, presumably, otherwise have remained undiscovered.

For about a week the three had been aware of unusual activity in the mansion. The Master and his two sons had been away on a long journey for two months and, to everyone's delight, had taken Abaddon with them. During this period Quinell had been in charge and, although discipline had not been relaxed in any way, the slave's existence had been far more tolerable. Since their return, however, there had been comings and goings that had remained unexplained. One morning, Abaddon came for

Juliette and, having supervised her whilst she bathed and made herself presentable, conducted her, naked, into Lord Reythal's presence. She sank to her knees before her Master, keeping her eyes demurely lowered as she tried to fathom out what she had done wrong to cause this unexpected summons before him. She was conscious of her Master's deep scrutiny. She felt her face redden under his intense gaze, aware of her nakedness. This uncontrollable reaction confused her, considering that she spent all of her time either naked or clothed in revealing transparent garments. Just last night, she had served her Master in his bed and he had used her more thoroughly than was usual.

"Stand, slave," Lord Reythal commanded, breaking into her drifting thoughts.

Juliette rose to her feet and, placing her small hands against the back of her thighs, stood waiting for his next order. Would this be a sentencing to a thrashing or, she shuddered at the thought, was the beast who stood at the Master's side to get his own way at last and take her to be whipped across her back?

Lord Reythal looked his slave up and down. Did she detect a glimmer of regret in his eyes? If so, did this mean she was truly to be whipped? She began to shake with dread at the thought.

"Why are you afraid, slave?" Lord Reythal asked quietly.

"I have been summoned, naked, to the presence of my master," Juliette replied softly, wishing she could hide the fear that seethed within her. It was all she could think of in answer.

"Do you think you are here to be beaten. Have you done something wrong?" Lord Reythal asked.

Juliette trembled even more. Why was he playing cat and mouse with her? If she was to be beaten or whipped, why didn't he get on with it? "I hope I have not been displeasing," she stammered. "But a Master does not require a reason to have his slave beaten."

Juliette was aware that Abaddon was listening to her every word and would jump on the slightest excuse to find fault with her. As much as she had hated speaking the words, she was determined not to give him any excuse to have her punished.

"No! You are not here to be beaten," Lord Reythal said, much to her relief. "My son, Charles, has proved himself to be a man now, during our journey abroad, and it is time he had his own household. I am giving you to him as a house-warming present. You will serve him well. As you have served me. He is now your Master."

"I will do my best to please him, Master," Juliette said quietly. What else could she say? But, in a way, she was glad. The son was young and handsome and, hopefully, Abaddon would not be part of his retinue and she would, therefore, escape from the ogre's clutches at last!

"Abaddon will take you to him, now. He is collecting the last of his belongings from his rooms," Lord Reythal said. He reached out towards her, a sealed envelope in his hands. "This contains the documents transferring the ownership of you to him. You will give it to him."

Juliette, completely stunned by the events, took the envelope from him as he reached down beside his desk. She shuddered as his hand reappeared holding a cane and Girl Slave Whip.

"These are to ensure you do serve him well," Lord Reythal said, holding the instruments out to her.

Juliette took them with a trembling hand. Just the touch of any implement of punishment made her cringe.

"Go now, slave, and present yourself to your new Master."

She felt Abaddon take her arm and lead her from the study. A feeling of relief, and victory, surged through her. She was out of the bastard's clutches! She had won!

"Do not think, not even for a moment, that you have escaped from me for good," Abaddon whispered in her ear as they halted outside a closed door on which he knocked. 'The beast can even read my mind' Juliette thought with horror.

She heard a summons from within and Abaddon opened the door and ushered her inside. The room was empty, except for a packing case or two and the figure of a man standing looking out of the window. The figure turned to face them and Juliette sucked in her breath with surprise. He was certainly the older son of her Master but he had changed since she had last seen him. He seemed to have grown up and, instead of the youth she was accustomed to seeing, he now looked every inch a full-grown man. Also, he seemed more handsome, in a rugged sort of way. She stumbled as Abaddon pushed her forward and ordered her to her knees.

"Thank you, Abaddon. You may leave us," Lord Charles, as Juliette assumed he would now be called, said, dismissing the man. The sound of his voice, so deep and mature, sent shivers of delight down Juliette's spine.

When Abaddon had closed the door behind him, Lord Charles looked down on his kneeling slave. "So, my father kept his promise." He took the envelope from her extended hand and read the contents quickly. "You are now my property," he said looking at her and sending more shivers down her back.

"Yes, Master," Juliette answered, her voice sounding breathless. There was something about him that made her feel uneasy. Not frightened but uneasy! It came as a sudden shock to her that, in appearance and manner, he closely resembled the fictional dream man that she had longed for during those days before she became a slave. Now, it seemed she had found him but he was not the tender ardent lover she had dreamed about. He was her master and she was his property.

"I see my father was thoughtful enough to send a cane and whip with you. Does he think I will need them?"

"I hope not, Master, but that will be your decision," Juliette answered. For the first time since her enslavement, she wanted to feel the cane and whip lashing her body. She couldn't explain this but, for some very strange elusive reason, she wanted this man to completely master her and make her love him as her love master.

Lord Charles took the instruments from her hands and put them on one of the cases. He ordered her to stand and, twisting her arms up behind her back, manacled her wrists together between her shoulder blades. He threw a black hood over her head and secured it round her neck with a metal collar from which dangled a long chain. She was led from the room and out into the yard where she sensed her Master mount a horse. With a jerk on the chain, he set off with Juliette trotting at his side. She felt a tear slip from her eyes and a sudden ache in her heart as she realised she had not even been allowed to say 'goodbye' to her friends. They eventually halted and her master dismounted and led her into a building. The hood was removed and she gasped at the sight that met her eyes. She was in a large hall, newly decorated in a fashion that was completely strange to her. An elderly man and woman stood to one side. They were dressed in strange garments. It was as if she had awoken in a different world.

"This is Mehmet and Aylena, his wife," Lord Charles said, nodding a greeting to the couple. "They run the house and you will obey them as you would me."

Juliette cast a furtive glance to the couple. The woman gave her a warm smile, but the man looked at her with a stern expression on his face, as he surveyed her naked body.

"Go with Aylena and she will see to it that you are cleaned up and give you the garments you are to wear in the house." He turned to the woman. "Bring the slave to my study when she is ready for inspection." He removed the manacles from Juliette's wrists and marched off across the hall to disappear along a passage.

Juliette followed the woman to the back of the building where a bath of hot water already awaited her. Having stood perfectly still while the woman depilated her body she gratefully got into the bath and washed the dust of the journey from her body and hair. The woman allowed her to lie back and enjoy the luxury of a good soak for a few minutes before ordering her out. Having dried herself, she sat on a stool in front of a table while the woman brushed out her long tresses. Then, under the woman's guidance, she applied cosmetics from an array of jars on the table. She was somewhat startled when the woman rubbed rouge over her nipples and outlined her sex lips with black kohl. Then she was ordered to stand in the centre of the room while the woman walked round her, inspecting the finished product closely.

"You are very beautiful, child," the woman said sweetly, the inspection over. "You will surely give your Master much pleasure."

"Thank you …" Juliette hesitated. "Please, what do I call you?"

"When we are alone, you may call me Aylena. If there is anyone else near, you must call me 'madam'. You will always call my husband 'sir'. If you forget you will be in bad trouble, he is very strict."

"Thank you," Juliette responded. "I will try and remember."

"See that you do, child," Aylena said in a very serious tone. "If not, you will find yourself sent to Hassan for a lesson. That would not be very pleasant for you."

Juliette warmed to the woman who seemed to be kind and helpful. Apart from her, and her husband, Juliette had not, so far, seen any other servants about, but who was this Hassan she wondered. Whilst she had escaped the dreaded Abaddon, she realised she was still a slave and no amount of kindness from this older woman would change that. Lord Charles had, whenever she had encountered him, seemed kind and considerate, but she knew, she would still have to be careful if she was to avoid punishment.

"Thank you, Aylena. You are very kind." Juliette hoped that, despite the difference in their ages and status, she had found a friend in this woman.

"Now you must get dressed," Aylena said. "The Master will not expect to be kept waiting too long." She picked up some garments that lay on a chair on one side of the room and handed them to Juliette.

Under Aylena's guidance, Juliette began to dress herself in the garments. A pale diaphanous skirt, that hung on her hips from a soft leather gem studded belt, slit in two places at the front so that, as she moved her shapely legs were exposed to the tops of her thighs. A pair of golden cups covered her breasts, with holes cut in them for her nipples to poke through, kept in place by a golden chain suspended round her neck. Juliette thought that the cups would fall away as she moved but they fitted her orbs too snugly and prevented this happening. Then a fine veil, of the same material and colour as the skirt, was clipped to her ear lobes and hung down, covering the lower half of her face.

Aylena stood back to ensure that this fitted the slave's body perfectly. Then she crouched down and fitted a fine chain round each ankle to which were attached tiny bells that tinkled as she moved. To complete the ensemble, a gold band, in the shake of a coiled snake was put on each upper arm. Juliette looked at her reflection in a long mirror and gasped with surprise. She was not, by nature, vain about her looks but even she had to admit that the image she saw was extremely beautiful and erotic. It reminded her of how Lady Moona had looked on that last night in her house.

"Where do these clothes come from, Aylena?" she asked.

"It is the costume the slave girls wear in my Country," Aylena replied as she stepped back to get a better look at her charge. "You would do credit to any harem, my child. Be proud of yourself. With looks like yours, you could captivate any man's heart. Now a few drops of perfume and we had better get along to the Master for his opinion."

Aylena, smiling with satisfaction, led Juliette into a large room, very strangely decorated and furnished. Her new Master, Lord Charles as she assumed he was now known, reclined on a low sofa. Juliette approached and knelt in front of him.

"Stand, slave, and turn slowly round," Lord Charles commanded.

Juliette obeyed and, having completed the turn, stood facing him, her eyes demurely lowered, awaiting his verdict with trepidation.

"Excellent, Aylena," he said after a short pause. "You have improved her no end. You may now take her and show her around the buildings and grounds and explain her duties to her. She will wait on table during the evening meal. See that she is sent to my room after the evening meal."

"Yes, my Lord," Aylena replied, and then turned to Juliette. "Follow me."

Aylena took Juliette on a tour of the mansion, explaining her duties to her as they went. To Juliette's pleasure her duties were not to be too onerous since, as Aylena told her, her main purpose was to provide pleasure for her Master. Wherever the Master's journey had taken him, he had certainly returned with some strange ideas on furnishing and furniture. The entire mansion was a showpiece to this taste, as was the revealing costume, which she was wearing. Although initially strange to her, Juliette found them quite pleasant and she was enjoying the tour round the mansion and grounds. She did see several other people who, she assumed by their demeanour, were servants and it appeared that, at the time, she was the only slave in the household.

As the tour came to an end, Aylena halted outside a heavily studded wooden door set in a high wall. Giving Juliette a worried sideways look, she opened the door and ushered Juliette inside. Juliette looked round what had turned out to be a large yard, enclosed on three sides by a high wall and on the fourth by the rears of a row of buildings. The things she saw filled her with fear and dread.

"This is the Punishment yard," Aylena whispered. "Where you will be sent if you are silly enough to displease the Master."

Juliette did not need the woman's explanation to inform her of this. Scattered round the yard were various contraptions, obviously designed for the sole purposes of securing a victim in the appropriate position for punishment. On one of the building walls, under a large canopy, was a selection of canes, whips and other instruments for inflicting that punishment. If all these were not enough to strike terror into her, the sight of a man emerging from one of the buildings was. He was huge, both in height and girth, his bare chest and arms thick with bulging muscles. Although naked from the waist up, his attire was strange. He wore a pair of baggy trousers, nipped in at the ankles, and held up by a wide leather belt studded with many coloured stones. A curved sword, which Aylena told her was a scimitar, hung from the belt, as did a small jewelled dagger. All in all, he presented a terrifying if colourful picture.

"He is Hassan," Aylena said, noticing the girl's transfixed gaze. "He is the Master's head groom and blacksmith. He will also act as the Master's executioner and be responsible for disciplining you should you be unfortunate enough to displease the Master."

Juliette had already assumed this last fact and was shaking merely with the thought of being sent to this giant. Even from across the yard, she felt small and vulnerable in his presence. She was grateful and relieved when Aylena ushered her from the yard and closed the door behind them. If for no other reason than to avoid being sent to Hassan, she vowed to do her best to please her new Master.

Juliette kept herself busy during the rest of the day, mainly assisting Aylena in sorting out the kitchen and their rooms. Aylena and Mehmet had their own small suite of rooms in one wing of the building. Juliette was shown to another room in the same wing, which, Aylena said, was hers. It was reasonably comfortably furnished and, to Juliette's surprise, had no lock on the door. The bed looked invitingly soft and comfortable.

"You will be given quite a bit of latitude here," Aylena began to explain as she saw Juliette's startled expression. "The door is not locked, nor is the window barred. You have the freedom to go anywhere in the mansion and grounds in your free time, other than to the west wing, which the Master occupies. You only go there when he sends for you. As you have seen the grounds are pleasant but you must not pick the flowers except with my, or Mehmet's, permission. Do not, on any account, even think of trying to escape. The only gates from the grounds are locked and guarded, night and day, and the wall is far too high to climb. Any attempt to escape would surely fail and be discovered and the punishment that would follow does not bear thinking about."

Juliette assisted Aylena in preparing the evening meal for the Master and the servants. The latter were fed in a large room adjoining the kitchen and it was one of Juliette's tasks to serve them. To her surprise, neither the men nor women paid any attention to her, other than to ask for this or that. By and large, they treated her as one of their own. The only fly in the ointment, as she was to find out, was Mehmet. Whenever he was around, he seemed to spend most of the time ogling her body.

She waited at the Master's table in the evening and was surprised to see how little of the wine he drank. When the meal was over and the dishes cleared, Aylena supervised her preparation for the visit to the Master. She was bathed and made up, just as she had been for the earlier presentation and inspection. Then Aylena led her, naked, to a room in the west wing. As she entered the door, the first thing Juliette noticed was the complete absence of any furniture. Then her eyes lowered and she saw a large thick piled rug in the centre of the room and a number of large cushions scattered about the floor. Her heart missed a beat as she noticed large rings set in the floor at the corners of the rug and chains, which ended on manacles, attached to them.

"Lay down in the centre of the rug," Aylena said softly.

Juliette obeyed. She felt the woman take each of her limbs in turn and attach the manacles to her wrists and ankles. Then, exhibiting strength in one so old and frail looking, she eased Juliette's body up and slid a thick cushion under her buttocks. Then the chains were pulled tight, spread-eagling her body so that she could hardly move.

"Remember, child," Aylena whispered, kneeling at her side. "You are beautiful and have a delightful body. But you are here solely to please your master. You must banish any pleasure your own body may demand from your mind, unless the Master says otherwise. I know he will be pleased with you."

So saying the woman rose and silently went from the

room. Juliette was left alone with her thoughts. It was plain that she had been positioned to be used, and she felt her nipples harden and a warm glow begin to spread through her body. Her sex lips became moist and her love tunnel muscles began to flex in anticipation of the invasion to come. Her apprehension began to increase. She was used to the savage and demanding way in which Lord Reythal used to take his pleasure of her, leaving her exhausted and unsatisfied and she wondered what it would be like with the son. She remembered Aylena's last words to her and, mentally, started to prepare herself for what was to follow. At all costs she must please her master. A visit to Hassan's yard awaited her if she failed.

The silence in the room was broken as a door was opened and closed. She raised her head and saw her Master standing between her spread feet, a smile on his lips and sheer lust in his eyes. He was completely naked. Her eyes opened wide at the sight of his manhood, which, although only half erect, was long and thick that she shivered with fear, doubting whether her small body could accommodate it.

She saw him kneel between her legs and shut her eyes in anticipation of a brutal entry. Much to her surprise, some minutes passed without anything happening. She was about to open her eyes, fearing that, for some reason he was not pleased with her, when she felt fingers lightly stroking the inside of her thighs. Her eyes shot open in surprise, only to look straight into those of her Master.

"Do not move and remain silent," he ordered. "You will not come without permission."

The subtle stroking continued and Juliette felt her body responding. She forced herself to obey his orders although it was nearly impossible to remain silent as his fingers roamed over her thighs, stomach, and finally her vulva making the lips round her opening harden and swell with desire. His hands glided lightly over her body until they closed over her breasts. She felt her nipples being alternately gently rolled and pinched between his strong fingers. Nothing like this had been done to her since her enslavement and she did not understand. It seemed that he was intent on giving her pleasure instead of forcing himself on her. Even if she had wanted to try, she could not stop her body responding to these seductive attentions. Strong needs flooded through her body until, with a deep groan, she tried to thrust up towards him.

"You were ordered to remain still and silent. I will not tolerate disobedience, as you will discover," his deep voice warned her.

"Sorry, Master," Juliette panted as another surge of desire swept through her.

It suddenly dawned on her what he was doing. He was firing the desires in her body and, at the same time, forbidding her to respond. He was training her! Mastering her more thoroughly than any beating ever could! Confusion and panic raged in her mind. Her body wanted him to take her, use her and make her submit to him as her 'love master', but her brain rebelled at the manner in which he was instilling his ownership over her. Love and hate vied for supremacy! Her master continued his attentions to her young body, a smile of satisfaction on his face as he sensed the battle raging within her. This was something quite new to her. When she had been used by his father, her body had merely been the vessel in which he slaked his thirst.

Hard as she tried, her body overcame her brain's caution. She wanted nothing more than to surrender herself to her young master and enjoy the delights he was arousing in her. To call out and acknowledge him as her master and declare her everlasting love for him! She was saved by the sudden cessation of his attentions. She opened her eyes and looked along her body, between her throbbing breasts with their hard erect nipples, and saw him kneeling between her knees. She gasped as she saw his now erect penis and the heavy sac beneath it. A moment of sheer panic shot through her as she saw the size and thickness of his manhood poised, ready to invade her slim body. Surely her small tunnel could not accommodate it and would be ripped apart. She watched, breathless, as he slowly descended on her. She felt the throbbing tip of his lance against her opening.

Slowly, making every nerve of her body scream with her desire, he began to enter her. Deeper and deeper into her body went his manhood, until she began to think there was no end to the depths that she would be penetrated.

His face hovered above her own until his lips met hers in a masterful and savage kiss that took her breath away. Then he began to take her, his heavy sac banging against her as he started to move back and forth inside her, gradually increasing the force and frequency of his thrusts. She felt her own muscles close about him, trying to imprison him inside her. He made no attempt to hurry the process and this merely served to heighten the delicious sensations that were flooding through her, sending her arousal soaring. Then she remembered his warning! But how could she control her responsive body against what he had done and was doing to her? Her body had never been subjected to such erotic and uncontrollable feelings! She felt him increase his momentum and her muscles gripped him tighter raising her arousal to the point of climax. With one final thrust, the most violent and deepest of all, his emission jetted into her. Feeling his hot seed shoot into her was too much for her control. Her small body arched rigid under him, lifting them both clear of the rug, as a cry of jubilation left her lips and she rushed into the most shattering orgasm she had ever experienced.

She became aware of the mist before her eyes beginning to clear as she slowly emerged from the aftermath of her orgasm. Her limbs had been released from their bonds and she felt his hands under her head, lifting her towards him. She opened her eyes and saw him kneeling astride her chest, his manhood close to he face. It was still quite hard and rigid as she leaned forward and took it into her mouth and proceeded to lick it clean, tasting the sharpness of his satisfaction mixed with her sweetness. When she had finished, he thrust her from him. She rose to her knees and, spreading them wide apart, sat back on her heels placing her trembling hands, palm upwards, on her quivering thighs. She looked at her master, the man who had succeeded in mastering her where others had failed. Helpless in her satisfaction, she was on the point of declaring her love and submission to him when she saw him look at her, a strange expression of utter surprise and incredulity on his face.

"Father said you were good," he said quietly, more to himself than to her. "But he seriously underestimated your ability to give satisfaction. I must remember to tease him. You really are extraordinary. He couldn't have realised just how good or he would never have given you away."

"I am happy if my Master found his slave satisfactory," Juliette said in a whisper, her eyes full of the adoration she felt for him. Her jubilation was short lived, however.

"Good? Yes!" he said, turning his hard eyes towards her. "But you are also disobedient. I ordered you to remain still and silent and not to come without permission. Your life here will be pleasant and easy, but I will have unquestioned obedience from you. You are still a slave. You must learn that it is your master's pleasure you are serving, not your own." Juliette shook as she anticipated his next words. "You must be taught to obey at all times. At all times! Tomorrow morning, you will go to Hassan and tell him you have been disobedient and ask him to give you eighteen strokes with his special cane."

"Yes, Master." Juliette could hardly believe her ears. The man, who so recently had been so gentle with her, had just ordered her a severe beating.

"You may leave me now, slave. You will report to me again immediately after your punishment tomorrow," Lord Charles commanded.

"Yes, Master," Juliette replied, rising to her feet.

As she made her way back to her own room, her mind was in a whirl. Her body still glowed from the wonderful things he had done to it, yet tomorrow, at his orders, it was to be soundly beaten. How could he have expected any woman to control herself under such attention? He had deliberately sought out the most sensitive and responsive parts of her and subjected them to stimulation he must have known she could not resist. She hadn't and now she was to suffer for it! She had been on the verge of declaring her undying love for him only to find that he was just as cruel as all men. There was no justice in all this! But then, she was a slave and he had been training her. She had failed the test and now her poor bottom must pay the price.

CHAPTER 5.

As usual, Juliette rose early the next morning. A terrible dread hovered like a dark cloud over her. Fear of the ordeal ahead had driven her protestations of injustice from her mind. Used as she was to being beaten, the prospect of eighteen strokes of a cane from the giant she had seen yesterday filled her with dread. That her master had stipulated she was to ask for it to be done with Hassan's 'special cane', whatever that was, only added to her terror. She helped Aylena prepare the master's breakfast in silence. She didn't want anyone, especially Mehmet, to know too soon of the fate that awaited her. That she would spend the rest of the day naked, the evidence of her thrashing on full display, was bad enough.

After the breakfast dishes had been dealt with, Aylena put her food in front of her. It was not the usual horrid gruel that she was used to. On arriving at Lord Charles' mansion, she had discovered that her diet was to be far nicer and tastier than that! She took one look at the dish and gently pushed it to one side.

"I don't think I can manage anything this morning," she said, trying not to look at the old woman.

"Why ever not?" Alyena asked, concern in her voice. "Are you feeling ill?"

Juliette looked quickly round to ensure that Mehmet had gone and that they were alone. "I disobeyed the Master last evening," she whispered. "I am to report to Hassan this morning and ask for a beating."

"You poor thing," Aylena said, putting a comforting arm round the girl's shoulder. "The worst thing is thinking about it beforehand, so you had better go and get it over with now. Try and be brave, child. Hassan is a fair man but he does not like his victims to yell too much too soon. He thinks they are trying to cheat by making him think it is hurting more than it is."

"Thank you for the warning," Juliette said as she rose and began to walk towards the door.

"Good luck, child!" Aylena called after her. "Come straight to me afterwards, and I will attend to your bruises."

Juliette closed the door on the woman's words, and began the long walk towards the yard, Hassan's yard. The rebellion in her mind that had, so far, been held back, welled up inside her. She was walking to a beating, a bad beating, for something that was not her fault. Admittedly, she had disobeyed her Master, but she defied anyone not to have done so under the circumstances. He had imposed such overpowering urges in her that he must have known she would be unable to control. It just wasn't fair! Would she ever again enjoy the proper protection of justice? No! She told herself, resignedly. You are a slave and will always be one. A slave and justice do not mix together.

She was unable to suppress the shakes that came over her as she opened the heavy door and entered the yard. He had just emerged from one of the buildings on the far side and stood looking at her as she walked towards him. She tried not to look at the various contraptions, over one of which she would soon be bent, as she approached the giant and knelt before him. She felt so small and vulnerable. He was dressed the same as when she had seen him yesterday and the sight of his rippling muscles filled her with terror.

"What is it, girl?" he demanded in a high pitched voice.

"Please Sir," Juliette began, trying to make her voice sound meek and submissive but at the same time hiding her terror from showing through. "I have been disobedient and my Master has ordered me to ask you to punish me. I am to receive eighteen strokes of the cane." Juliette paused for a second to screw up her courage before adding. "Your special cane."

"Stand and strip," Hassan ordered.

As scared as she was, Juliette did not fail to notice the absence of the hint of any pleasure, sadistic or otherwise in his voice. She rose and discarded the flimsy working shift and stood, naked, awaiting his next order.

"Go to the bars and bend over," Hassan ordered, pointing towards the centre of the yard.

Juliette turned and hesitated for a second before walking

towards the place he had indicated. She saw horizontal beams at waist height, set on stout posts. She halted as her mould touched the nearer beam. It was only slightly wider than her hips. Taking a deep breath, she bent over until her shoulders rested on the other beam. This was much longer than the first and, instinctively, she stretched her arms along its length. It was slightly lower than the first and she felt her buttocks stretched taut to present a perfect target. She watched, petrified, as Hassan quickly secured straps round her wrists and upper arms, pinioning her to the beam. He walked behind her and, spreading her legs wide, tied her ankles to rings fixed to the ground. There was a gentle breeze blowing and she felt this between her open buttocks. She was glad there was no audience to see her so shamelessly displayed.

She looked up as Hassan strode to the wall where the canes and whips hung. She nearly uttered a scream as she saw him take down a long thin cane, much longer than any she had seen, or felt before. As he turned and walked towards her, Juliette remembered Aylena's warning and summoned up her courage to take the thrashing as bravely as she could. She saw the giant halt two paces in front of her and to her left. He held the cane out in front of her face. She eased her head forward until her mouth was touching the cane and kissed it.

Hassan took two quick paces forward, spun on his toes and brought the cane whistling down in a wide arc so as to land across the centre of the taut buttocks. Immediately a line of fire, much worse than any other first stroke she had ever received, blazed across the full width of both cheeks. Juliette nearly bit through her lips as she stifled the scream that threatened to erupt from her throat. Hassan peered behind her to survey her bottom, checking that his aim was right and that the stroke had landed correctly. Satisfied, using the same technique, he laid another five searing strokes across her bottom.

Juliette had watched out of the corner of her eye as he had lashed the first stroke across her backside. She was stunned by the manner in which he did it. She was to find

105

out that this was the standard procedure the giant adopted for the first six strokes of a caning, or switching. Her head had jerked up as the second landed and as the third laid its line of fire, she had felt her nipples spring hard and erect. Her body was responding in its usual way, but much sooner than normal. The fourth made her eyes fly open and the tears cascade down her face. A deep groan escaped through her clenched teeth. The fifth and sixth wrung shrill cries from her as the pain began to break the rigid control she was trying to exert.

Again the giant inspected her buttocks. Six livid red weals, already rising into hard ridges decorated her skin, no one overlapping another. The slave had taken the first six well and he was satisfied with the result. She had not yet screamed and had not writhed too much on the beam. He moved silently to stand at the side of the bent girl.

Crack.

Juliette had not sensed the movement he had been making as he took the two paces passed her. This stroke came completely unexpected and caught her off guard. She could not stop the loud scream from surging from her open mouth, nor stop her body writhing violently on the beam. Immediately the movement of her mound on the beam ignited an arousal in her tunnel and she felt her sex lips become moist.

Thwack.

Crack.

Thwack.

Juliette writhed and screamed loudly as each stroke added its share of fuel to the raging fire burning in her bottom. Her body began to sweat profusely. Her tears had already made damp patches on the floor beneath her head and now droplets were beginning to run down her breasts and fall from her nipples to form their own stains on the ground. Her mind informed her that she had taken ten strokes and had another eight to come. The last two strokes had landed across the lower half of her buttocks, the most tender part, and lifted her up on her toes. The giant certainly knew how to thrash a girl's bottom!

Unknown to Juliette, Hassan had received specific instructions from Lord Charles earlier in the morning. After delivering the tenth stroke, he laid the cane down and crouched at the side of the writhing girl. As the Master had foretold, the girl's nipples had engorged. He edged round behind her and looked hard at her vulva. Again the master had been right. The lips were open with the edges hard and he could see her clitoris peering out. Also he saw the droplets of her juices seeping down her thighs. He stood straight and picked up the cane. He bent over near the girl's head.

"The Master has ordered that you are not to come while under punishment," the giant's voice rang in Juliette's ear. "If you disobey the order, a further twelve strokes will be added."

A bucket of ice-cold water thrown over her head could not have shaken Juliette more. The Master must have told the giant how her body reacted to a beating and she felt shame flow over her. She had taken ten strokes so far and there were another eight to come. The prospect of that being increased to twenty sent waves of terror shuddering through her. Whatever happened, what ever the giant did to her, she must avoid earning the extra at all costs! From now on, she must concentrate all her resources on controlling the arousal, not matter how much she screamed or writhed. She gripped the beam with her small hands until her knuckles threatened to burst through the white skin.

Hassan had received his orders! Having given the girl the warning, he stood immediately behind her. He raised the cane high and brought it whistling through the air, up between the sprayed legs to land right on her sex lips. The girl's body shot up off the beam, stretching her legs to the limit, her toes lifting off the ground. She screamed and screamed as the exquisite agony raged through her vulva and into her tunnel.

"You are being beaten because you could not control your body," Hassan's voice penetrated the mist of pain that had engulfed her. "To teach you a lesson in control, you are to be tested to the limit."

Juliette heard the words and shook with terror. Many more strokes like that and she would definitely get the extra penalty strokes! Then she felt the cane slide lightly, back and forth, over the spot where the last stroke had landed.

"Please, no! Please not that, Sir!" Juliette heard her voice pleading. "Beat me but please do not touch me there!"

The slave's pleas went unheeded. His threats ran in her ears as he replaced the cane with his fingers and began to probe just inside her tunnel. This is not fair, her mind screamed. The arousal, which she was fighting to control, began to soar at his touch. It was difficult enough to keep control while being beaten without this added torture. Had her Master instructed the giant to ensure her poor bottom did receive the extra strokes? She tried to clench her cheeks and thighs together to restrict his movement. How she could survive? Just the thought of another dozen strokes with that 'special cane' was beyond her comprehension.

The giant, considering that he had fully obeyed the Master's orders, withdrew his fingers. He was no sadist and the girl had, so far, taken the thrashing well and managed to control her body's natural response. He picked up the cane and, stepping behind her brought the cane up, hard, again between her thighs. The stroke landed full on target, raising her up off her toes and wringing long agonised screams from her mouth. Her body writhed violently with the pain, fine sprays of her sweat forming rainbows in the sunlight. The stroke, whilst hurting terribly had invoked the opposite effect to the one he had anticipated. The rod had struck directly on her clitoris, sending sharp spasms of sheer agony through her tunnel and body. But this intense pain had been as effective as a bucket of ice cold water over her head. It quenched the arousal. Juliette felt the arousal recede and couldn't believe her luck.

Hassan returned to his place at the girl's side. She still had six strokes to come and the Master had told him to ensure these were the hardest of all. Six times he raised his arm high in the air and brought the rattan down with a resounding 'crack' across the slave's buttocks. He aimed so that each stroke was now laid diagonally across her bottom, cutting across the raised weals, and the end of the cane whipping up under her cheeks.

Part of Juliette's mind was still counting the strokes. As the fifth burned a path across the previous weals, her body arched rigid with the pain and a long scream of surrender echoed round the yard. Her strength had finally given out and she collapsed across the beam, moaning and mewing with the pain. Only one more to go, her brain registered, and then she would have survived yet another flogging. Her body jerked violently as Hassan, as was his custom, put his full weight behind the stroke. It was his belief that, no matter how severe a flogging a girl had received, it was always the last stroke that remained in her memory the longest. Once again the slave's body bent backwards in a rigid arc, straining against her bonds as her agonised scream followed the loud report, rebounding from wall to wall.

While Hassan replaced the cane in its place, Juliette lay slumped over the beam, her body sobbing loudly. Hassan allowed her a few minutes before bending behind her and releasing her ankles. He looked at her buttocks and saw that the last three strokes had cut into her skin and thin red lines were forming on the top of the weal. The Master would see that he had carried out his duty properly! He released her wrists and her hands flew behind her and began lightly rubbing her bottom to ease the pain.

"Get up, slave," he ordered.

Ever so slowly, using the beam for support, Juliette eased herself upright, each movement sending streaks of fire through her body. She turned to face the giant

"Go and report to your Master," Hassan ordered. "Immediately!"

"Yes, Sir," Juliette answered, stammering through the sobs that she had not yet managed to fully control. She was about to turn away when she remembered. She sank to her knees and bent forward and placed her lips on the giant's feet. "Thank you, Sir, for my beating."

She was just rising, when the giant reached down and, holding her arms, gently assisted her to her feet. "Go now, little one," he said softly. "And try not to be sent to me again."

Juliette looked up at his face and tried to smile her thanks at this unexpected solicitude for a slave. Then, walking as gingerly as she could, she left the yard and made her way to her Master's study. Several servants turned to stare at her as she passed them and she realised that the sound of the beating and her screams must have been audible throughout the mansion and grounds. None made any comment, or gave any sign except Mehmet who stopped her and, with a lecherous smile on his face, made her turn her back to him while he inspected her bottom. This made her blush with shame and re-ignited her hatred of all men. She just couldn't understand why they got so much pleasure out of seeing a girl hurt! She found Lord Charles in his study and knelt in front of him, moaning as her bottom sank onto her heels.

"Stand and show me your buttocks," he commanded.

Juliette obeyed and stood as still as she could as he lightly ran his fingers over the hard ridges on her cheeks. Even his light touch caused renewed spasms of pain to course through her body, especially when he seemed to press the most painful ones.

"Did the beating hurt?" he asked.

"Yes, Master," she replied meekly. She thought the question totally unnecessary. Couldn't he see for himself the state her poor bottom was in?

"How many strokes did Hassan give you?"

"Eighteen, Master, as you ordered," Juliette replied

"Only eighteen? So you managed to control yourself during the punishment? Better than you did last night, it would seem. Have you learned your lesson, or was it the fear of the extra strokes that enforced your control?"

"I hope I have learned my lesson, Master," Juliette replied. "But the threat of another twelve strokes like that probably helped. I have never felt anything hurt so much as Hassan's special cane." The sheer incongruity of the conversation amazed Juliette. Here she was, in terrible agony, and the man who had ordered the flogging was discussing it quietly with her as if she hadn't been involved

110

at all!

"We shall see the next time you are summoned to serve me. Now go to Aylena. This time you may have the soothing cream on your behind. If you continue to disappoint me, however, it might well be the spirits that are used on you."

"Yes, Master," Juliette said, wondering what he had meant by the spirits. "Thank you, Master for my beating." So saying she hurried from the study.

She found Aylena in the kitchen, preparing the mid-day meal.

"Oh! My goodness!" Aylena exclaimed as Juliette entered the kitchen. She opened her arms wide and took the naked girl into a tender embrace. Juliette, unaccustomed to such tenderness, immediately broke down, sobbing.

"The Master said I may ask you for some cream to put on my bottom," Juliette managed to say.

The old woman immediately became business like. She made Juliette lie down on an old couch at the side of the room and, taking a jar from a shelf, gently smoothed the soothing cream over the bruised buttocks. It immediately began to ease the burning fire in her cheeks. Juliette kept her thighs pressed together. As much as that stroke still hurt, she just couldn't bear for this kindly old woman to know she had been beaten 'there'.

"There," Aylena said, as she stood up and replaced the jar. "Just you lie there for a while and you will soon feel better."

"Thank you, Aylena," Juliette said, with genuine feeling at the woman's tenderness. "You are very kind and gentle." She paused for a moment as the woman brushed aside her thanks. "The Master said that, next time, he might order the spirits instead of the cream. What did he mean?"

"Pray that he does not!" Aylena said, her horror at the very idea clear in her voice. "It is something that is sometimes done in my Country. It is a special spirit that burns and, if the skin is broken, the pain is worse than the thrashing itself. The slave has to be tied tightly down when it is put on and for some time after."

Aylena worked on in silence and insisted that Juliette stay on the couch until she felt well enough to move around. As she lay there, Juliette wondered about the woman. She seemed to accept the thrashing of a slave as a normal thing but her tenderness in creaming her bottom had been in contrast with this image. How did she know so much about it? What was she, back in her own Country?

As usual after a beating, Juliette had to remain naked for the remainder of the day. Once she felt fit enough to move, she got up from the couch and got on with her work. As she went about her tasks, she encountered some of the other servants, but none took any notice of her nakedness nor of the bruises on her bottom. None, that is except Mehmet. He seemed to take delight in making her stop whatever she was doing and bend over and show him her bottom. This made her feel terribly ashamed, especially when she began to notice the bulge in his baggy trousers as he gloated over her naked body and her bruised behind. Fortunately he never touched her, but the idea that an old man like him could desire her body made her feel sick. Fearing the consequences if she offended him, she kept her thoughts well hidden and did as he ordered. The one thought that haunted her was that her Master might, one day, order her to serve and pleasure the old sod. That was one order, she resolved, she would flatly refuse to obey, no matter what the consequences might be. Even a whipping followed by the spirit treatment would be preferable to that!

The memory of that day's flogging was to remain in her memory for a long time. She had learned her lesson! The Master sent for her quite frequently and, after that painful experience, she managed to exert enough control over her body to avoid a repetition of her offence. But under his attentions, she went through mental agony. He was handsome and tender at times and her body loved the things he did to it and, whilst she was under his control, she experienced many wonderful sensations that sent thrills of utter bliss through her. None more so than on the occasions when she was given permission to release her control and surrender to the series of shattering orgasms that he induced in her body. On the other hand, he never let her forget that she was just a slave, worth less than his animals. This callous attitude towards her conflicted with the moments of tenderness and kept her in a permanent quandary.

Other than when attending on her Master, Juliette's duties were not over onerous and she found that she had quite a lot of spare time to herself. Aylena was kept busy for most of the day and, when she wasn't helping her, Juliette wandered around the gardens. As much as the older woman and she had become close, Juliette missed the company of Sarita and Maya considerably. The girls were of her own age and, as much as she tried, Aylena's company did not make up for their absence. After the flogging on her second day, Juliette concentrated on doing her work and serving the Master as best she could and, therefore, she was sent to Hassan's yard for a beating infrequently.

She had been with Lord Charles for about six months when, about the middle of one morning, she heard a lot of unusual commotion in the house. There was a lot of coming and going and everyone she saw wore a very gloomy expression on their faces. The reason for this had not filtered down to the kitchens and it was not until they were all summoned to the main hall that her curiosity was to be satisfied. The whole household had assembled there. After a short time, a hush fell on the gathering as Lord Charles appeared and walked a few steps up the wide staircase. He turned and faced the crowd and Juliette immediately sensed that something terrible had happened by the sad and bewildered expression on his face. He cleared his throat and announced that, earlier in the morning whilst out riding, his father, Lord Reythal had been thrown by his horse and had suffered fatal injuries. The whole household of both estates would observe a month's mourning.

For the next four weeks, Juliette saw nothing of her Master. Bits of news did, however, filter through as Lord Charles set about dealing with his father's affairs. Lady Reythal, whose health had suffered a quick decline at her husband's death, had retired and gone to live with her sister.

113

The younger son had been dispatched to join the army that was gradually being strengthened. As far as Abaddon was concerned, no one knew what happened to him. One day he was there, and the next gone. Juliette felt as if a cloud had been lifted from her life at this piece of news. Lord Charles had decided to remain in his own mansion, rather than move into his father's and he set in motion alterations and additions to accommodate the larger household that he would have to maintain.

One afternoon, just after the period of mourning was over, Juliette was summoned to her Master's study with Aylena and Mehmet. Lord Charles was seated behind his desk and Juliette shivered, wondering if she had done something wrong and was to be sent to Hassan. She was, therefore, relieved when Lord Charles began to announce certain changes. Mehmet was to be promoted as major-domo, responsible for the running of the entire household. A new cook had been engaged and Aylena was to assist her husband, with particular responsibility for the cleanliness of the inside of the mansion and the catering. Lord Charles, having disposed of these and other minor matters, said that he was increasing his personal slaves and that Sarita and Maya were to arrive later that afternoon. Juliette was overjoyed at this news and waited impatiently for the pair to arrive. When they did, there was a joyful reunion. They soon brought each other up to date with their news.

The enlarged household soon settled down to a routine. Having taken over Lord Reythal's business affairs, her master and Quinell, who had been made his personal adviser were kept busy getting the hang of the business and ensuring that it continued to run smoothly. There was one venture that Lord Reythal had pursued and nearly brought to a conclusion just before his demise. Lord Charles, who had been kept closely advised of it lost no time in completing the matter. One afternoon, the three slaves, Aylena and Mehmet were summoned to one of the smaller halls. When they arrived, they found Lord Charles already seated on an ornate chair on a dais at one end of the hall. He looked very imposing in his full regalia. When the arrivals had been ushered to one side and warned to remain silent, Lord Charles nodded to Mehmet who thumped loudly on the floor with his staff of office.

The door at the other end of the hall opened and Quinell entered followed by four men in Lord Charles' livery. Between them they led three naked women and one naked man. Black hoods carefully hid the identities of those. The procession halted in front of the dais and Lord Charles ordered the hoods to be removed. Juliette could hardly believe her eyes as their identity was revealed. It was Lady Moona, Jason, and her two musicians.

"What is the meaning of this?" demanded Lady Moona as she looked round, her face flushed with anger and embarrassment. "Why am I naked? Why have I been brought here and, for that matter, where is here? I demand an explanation."

"Silence, Moona," Lord Charles' harsh tone cut short any further outburst from the girl. "You allowed your finances to get into a serious mess and your debts mounted too high. Your creditors demanded payment, which you could not possibly meet. Instead, I met their demands and, in accordance with the Law, you and your remaining possessions, that have not been sold, are now mine."

"That can not be!" Lady Moona shouted indignantly. "I was told nothing of this."

"Oh it can be and is!" Lord Charles replied. "You were warned by the magistrates on a number of occasions but chose to ignore both their warning and advice." He paused to look at the girl, whose face was a mixture of disbelief and anger.

"Then I expect to be properly treated by you as a guest should be. Not dragged naked into your presence with all your staff looking on." Lady Moona shook back her long hair and stared at him haughtily, interrupting his flow.

"I have just said that you are now mine. My possession! My slave! According to the Law. Here are the documents." He waved a bunch of papers in the air. "It is all legal and final. If you speak again without permission, or fail to address me as 'Master', I will have you thrashed." He looked into the girl's face that had suddenly gone whiter as the truth of what he had said dawned on her. "I understand that you enjoy that sort of thing. I am sure you will have plenty of enjoyment in the future now."

"I don't know where you got such a stupid idea from?" Lady Moona shouted. "I demand to see a magistrate. This is all just a terrible sick joke."

"Juliette. Step forward," Lord Charles commanded.

Juliette obeyed and the lady Moona turned her head and saw her for the first time since entering the hall. Her face, which had returned to being red with indignation, suddenly turned white again and her legs began to shake.

"This is where I, or rather my father, got the idea from. You remember Juliette, I am sure."

"Yes. I remember her," Lady Moona whispered.

Lord Charles leaned back in his chair, a smile spreading his mouth wide at the girl's obvious discomfort. Then his expression suddenly hardened as he leaned forward towards the naked girl.

"As I said you are now my slave." Lord Charles turned his head towards Quinell. "The slave has, on a number of occasions, spoken without permission. Also she had failed to address me correctly. She needs to be taught a lesson and learn her place. Take her to Hassan immediately. In addition to the customary ten lashes with the leathers across her back, she is to get twenty strokes of the cane across that delightful backside."

"You can't do this to me," the Lady Moona yelled as two of the men grabbed her arms. "I am a free woman!"

"Quinell," Lord Charles called out. "Add another five strokes with the cane. Take her out of my sight and see that it is done. Then bring her back here and I will see if she has learned her place."

Yelling and struggling, her face suddenly petrified with fear, Lady Moona, or just Moona as she should now be called, was dragged from the hall. A heavy silence ensued as the door closed behind them. Juliette knew that Hassan's yard was not far away, for she had been taken there many times herself, and she had been told by Aylena that the sound of her floggings could be clearly heard anywhere in the mansion and grounds. She winced as the first 'crack' sounded in the hall, signifying that the slave's beating had begun. She counted three strokes before the report was followed by a shrill scream. There was a short hiatus after the tenth report, and Juliette mentally saw the girl taken from the post and bent over the beams. Then the reports started up again, each followed by an agonised scream.

The people in the hall listened in silence, their faces expressionless, as the girl's sentence was meted out. One by one, the reports of Hassan's cane striking bare flesh sounded in the hall. Moona's screams became shriller as the thrashing progressed and she felt the full force of a cane wielded by the strength of a man's arm for the first time. Some minutes later, Quinell returned, his men dragging a much dishevelled and weeping Moona between them. They led her to the dais and turned her round so that her Master could see the girl's buttocks. Heavy dark red and swollen weals on her buttocks, and the lighter red bands across her back, signified that the thrashing had been well administered. She was turned to face her Master and forced to her knees which one of the men kicked wide apart. The slave's sex lips were dripping and her nipples stood out, erect and proud, from the soft mounds of her succulent breasts. Clear signs of the arousal the beating had caused, which were not missed either by her master or the others in the hall.

"So, it is true," Lord Charles mused to himself. He then addressed the weeping slave. "I suspect a flogging from the arm of a man is far worse than what you are used to from your boy, eh?"

"Yes, Master," Moona's soft and meek reply, uttered between the sobs that still made her body shudder, showed just how quickly she had learned her new status.

"Yet even a severe beating still arouses your body. That is most curious. Now I have two slaves who are stimulated by a thrashing in this manner."

Juliette could not help her face turning bright red at this open reference to herself.

"I trust, slave," Lord Charles continued. "That you have now learned your place in this household."

"Yes, Master," Moona replied, a shudder passing through her body. She had very quickly, and thoroughly, learned her new status. The hard way! Her session with Hassan had certainly dispelled her earlier arrogance.

"I understand that you consider yourself an accomplished dancer. I will express my opinion on that later. In the meantime, I believe you know of a cream, which has some strange quality my physician can not understand, that removes all traces of a beating very quickly. You will give the recipe for the cream to Aylena. She will see to it that your back and buttocks are treated with it. I want them clear of the weals as soon as possible."

There was a short paused as Lord Charles looked over the head of the kneeling girl and considered the other three naked slaves.

"Right, Quinell. Take Jason to the stables. He will work under Hassan." He turned to look at Aylena. "Take this." He pointed at the kneeling girl. "And see to her. She will, for the time being help Juliette in assisting you. The other two slaves will work in the kitchens, but they also will continue in their role as musicians. They rest of you will go and continue with your work."

Juliette followed Aylena, who led the still trembling Moona, to the kitchens, the other two slave girls in tow. The faces of her two charges betrayed the shock of seeing their previous mistress flogged so severely. It was a sharp eye opener to them and a warning of the severity of the treatment they could expect if they were found wanting in any way. When the small procession reached the kitchens, Aylena made Moona lie on the couch while she spread the cream over her back and buttocks. Juliette knelt near the girl's head.

Moona looked at her through eyes that were red from her weeping. "Your Master is a strict one, Juliette. I have never dreamed that a beating could hurt so much."

"That is because you were only playing at being a slave before, and Jason is only a boy and it was on your orders that he acted. Now your beatings will be for real. You will have no control over how severe they are. You will find your life very different here. The master is strict, so you had better learn quickly if you do not want your back and bottom to suffer too much."

Moona shuddered as the truth of her predicament was hammered home to her. Aylena had finished applying the cream and Moona eased herself from the couch.

"Am I to be given any clothing?" she asked.

"It is the rule that a flogged slave remains naked for the remainder of the day," Juliette answered. "Tomorrow, you will be given clothing, the same as Sarita, Maya and myself." She saw Moona look at the filmy working shift she was wearing. "Yes! Even these do little to conceal our bodies. The Master likes to be able to see his possessions. Now I had better show you around and explain your duties, or we will both be sent to Hassan for being dilatory."

Juliette conducted Moona around the mansion and grounds, explaining her duties and the best way to avoid being punished. As the tour progressed, Juliette took the opportunity to quiz the girl on her past and resolve the questions that had been lurking at the back of her mind ever since those two weeks when she had been sent to the girl's house. She learned that Moona was, as she had expected, only two years older than herself and had inherited the house and a large sum of money on the death of her parents. Her parents had been strict and kept her away from men. Being so young she had mismanaged her affairs and got into debt. Hence her present predicament!

Later that day, after the girls had served at table for the evening meal, they, along with Aylena, were summoned to Lord Charles' study. He informed them that Juliette was appointed 'First Girl' and would be responsible, under Aylena, for supervising them, allotting the work and ensuring that they carried out their duties properly. She would convey his orders to them and they were to obey her as they would him. She would be responsible for their conduct. At this point he handed a short thick leather strap and a book to Juliette. He informed her that she would be

119

responsible for dealing with the very minor breaches of discipline by applying up to six strokes of the strap across their bare bottoms. She must keep a record of all such incidents in the book. Juliette gasped in horror when he said that any other offences would mean the offender, and her, being sent to Hassan for punishment. She thought that she suffered enough at the giant's hands for her own offences, now she was to be beaten for theirs as well!

Lord Charles ordered that the two musicians were to practice regularly. That Moona was to keep up with her dancing, and she was also to teach Juliette to dance. He said that Aylena would supervise and assist in the lessons.

The following days and weeks passed uneventfully. Juliette was kept busy, the mornings doing her own work and supervising the others and the afternoon with Aylena and Moona learning to dance. This had not turned out to be as easy as she had thought. At first she spent many hours doing exercise after exercise to make her body supple enough to perform the dances properly and seductively and, when she eventually went to bed at night, she was utterly exhausted. Lord Charles, during this period did not send for her at night very often. It was Sarita and Maya that he usually summoned to his bed. As much as Juliette was grateful for the respite, it meant that her body was denied the usage that it needed and her nerves and temper began to suffer. Lord Charles spent a lot of time away from the mansion and Mehmet usually went with him. This meant that discipline was not as strongly enforced and Juliette did not even have the sessions with Hassan to bring on arousal and quench her needs.

She was by no means jealous that, when he was at home, Lord Charles sent for Sarita and Maya, much more frequently than he did her, but she would not have been human if she did not resent the attentions he paid to them a little. One morning her frustration boiled over, The previous day, Aylena and Moona had worked exceptionally hard and she had gone to bed more exhausted than usual. Normally she slept well but, that night, she had been restless and awoke in the morning with a headache. The crunch came when Sarita, in Mehmet's presence, chose that particular day to question an order. It did not help matters that it had been her that had spent the previous night in the master's bed.

"Sarita. Come here this instant," Juliette shouted, anger, and frustration, mounting inside her. "It is not permitted for you to question my orders. The Master made that plain! Turn round, bare your bottom and bend over. Hold your ankles and do not move."

Sarita, taken utterly by surprise at Juliette's outburst, turned round. She lifted her working shift clear of her bottom, bent over and grasped her ankles. Juliette, anger blinding her to what she was doing, lashed the strap across her friend's taut buttocks for the full six strokes. Sarita, well accustomed to being thrashed by a man, only let out a quick gasp of shock as the first landed and then remained silent as the following five curled round her cheeks. Mehmet, who had stayed to watch, left the room smiling. It was unusual for him to see one girl beating another!

"You will obey me in future, slave," Juliette shouted after laying the last stroke across her friend's buttocks. "Now get up and do as I ordered."

Slowly Sarita straightened up and turned to look at Juliette. There was a strangeness about her eyes and her face showed her surprise and sadness at the sudden unexpected turn of events. Looking into her friend's face, Juliette was overtaken by remorse at what she had done. She flung herself into her friend's arms, sobbing and begging her forgiveness.

"It's alright," Sarita whispered, hugging her friend tightly. "I asked for it and you were quite right to beat me. Anyhow, you had no choice. Mehmet was there and would have reported us both if you had not acted as you did. Both of us would then have been sent to Hassan."

"But I hurt you," Juliette muttered through her tears. "You are my friend and I should not have taken the strap to your poor bottom."

"You are First Girl and it was your duty," Sarita reminded her sweetly. "Don't worry. It didn't really hurt that much, only stung a bit. I have had far worse! Your arm is nowhere as strong as a man's."

The sincerity behind these words mollified Juliette. It had been the first time she had used the strap on any of the girls and she vowed that, whatever the consequences, it would be the last. Fortunately for her, the girls took care to behave in the future, especially when Mehmet was around. At other times, Juliette turned a blind eye to any minor transgressions. Consequently, Sarita's beating was the only entry to go into the book. This pleased Juliette at the time but was to be the cause of a most unpleasant experience in the future.

CHAPTER 6.

Once her body had become supple enough for the need for the exercises to be discontinued, Aylena and Maya proceeded to teach her to dance. To her surprise, Juliette enjoyed herself and quickly became quite proficient. Moona also learned a lot from Aylena's instruction and it was not long before both girls were earning her praises.

Juliette was puzzled by the woman's knowledge. The things, and methods, she used to teach them were most strange coming from someone of her years. One day, when she and Aylena were alone, she dared to ask the woman how this was. Aylena, far from taking offence as Juliette had feared, was only too happy to explain. It transpired that, until Lord Charles had found and bought her and Mehmet, she had been a slave girl herself in an Arab Prince's harem. She had been trained from an early age as a dancer and had become quite famous in that country for the fine performances she provided. That, she explained, was how she was able to teach them so many erotic and seductive dances. It also explained, Juliette thought to herself, why the woman was so kind and tender to the slaves, especially when they had been flogged. She must have, at times, suffered the same fate herself!

Lord Charles, having at last come to grips with his father's business matters, decided that he had time to devote to his own amusements. He had been receiving good reports from Aylena on the girls' progress and decided that he would assess their performance himself. He was intending inviting his business associates to visit his domain, now that everything was in order, and he wanted to see if the girls were good enough to pass their critical inspection. There was also something else that he had intended to satisfy himself about and he could take the opportunity to do this as well. One morning he called Aylena, Mehmet, Quinell and Hassan to his study and, having advised them off his special requirements, sent them off to make the necessary preparations. He had designated that evening for the performance.

His six personal slave girls were summoned by Mehmet and, under his supervision were depilated, bathed and their faces and bodies made up with cosmetics and perfumes. Their long tresses were brushed until they shone and they were then ordered to rest until Aylena came to dress them. The girls waited around, reclining on couches or cushions, until Aylena came to see to their final preparation. Mehmet had informed them that Juliette and Moona were to dance for their Master and have their prowess assessed by him. Consequently, they were both very nervous and apprehensive. Lord Charles had ordered his evening meal to be served early and, as soon as it was over, Aylena came to the room where they waited.

The two musicians, Sara and Carla, were dressed in long flowing transparent tunics, secured on each shoulder by a large brooch and a silver belt round their waists. Sarita and Maya were made to wear shorter skirts and brief boleros. Beneath these flimsy garments, all four were naked and their appearance was most seductive. Juliette and Moona were dressed in filmy red skirts, hung from gem studded bands at their hips, golden breast cups that were held in place by fine gold chains round their necks and backs, and a fine yashmak over the lower half of their faces. Unlike the other four, they were the only ones to wear items of jewellery.

At the appointed time Mehmet took the six slaves to the hall where their Master waited. As they entered, Juliette trembled with excitement and fear at what she saw. Lord Charles, dressed in a long richly embroidered caftan, sat on a throne like chair on a raised dais at one end of the hall. Otherwise the room was devoid of furniture save for a low divan with posts at each corner, a long padded bench and heavy stool and a thick tall wooden post bolted to the floor. It reminded her of the room in which Lady Moona, as she had been then, had staged her evening pleasures. Hassan and the Jason, now almost grown to the stature of a man, each wearing a turban and long baggy trousers, stood with their arms folded across their chests on the dais behind their

Master. They looked most impressive and, Juliette thought, very threatening, especially Hassan, whose shining muscular arms sent shivers down her spine.

Juliette, who had been under the impression that she was only to dance for her master, caught her breath as she saw, arranged on the floor in front of the dais, a variety of canes and whips. The Master would not have them there unless he intended them to be used. The very sight of them, and the knowledge that, before the evening was out, some or all of them would have left their mark on her soft flesh, set her body alive. Her nipples began to harden, she felt tingling in her vagina and her buttocks quivered in anticipation. Out of the corner of her eye, she saw Moona's mouth drop open in alarm. She looked again at the floor and saw what she had, at first, missed. Lying with the canes and whips, was the phallus contraption! The two musicians were led to the side of the room and settled down with their various instruments and Maya and Sarita were ordered to kneel either side of their Master. Juliette and Moona were ordered to kneel to one side of, and in front of, the dais. They did so, their eyes looking with dread at the array of instruments on the floor, which, they did not doubt, would soon be placing their marks on their soft bodies.

"Aylena has advised me that you, Juliette, have become quite a good dancer. You will perform for me first. Moona then, having had more experience, will then try and better your performance. Prepare."

Lord Charles gave the signal for them to begin the evening's entertainment.

Juliette, casting a frightened look at the canes and whips, rose and moved to the centre of the floor. She stood perfectly still, her left leg slightly bent and her hands raised, back-to-back, high above her head. Jason, who had picked up a drum and sat with the two musicians, gave a roll on the instrument and the girls began to play. Slowly and as seductively as she could, she began to sway to the sensuous rhythm that filled the hall. As the tempo gradually increased so did her movements. Trying to remember all that she had been taught, she let her body respond to the barbaric strains and, to her surprise, she felt strange forces taking over her body in a way that had not happened during her training. Was it because she was dancing before a man, or the fear of the whip if she did not perform to his satisfaction?

As the dance progressed, she did not fail to notice the lascivious look that appeared on her Master's face. This spurned her on to greater effort and she concentrated on seducing him with the graceful yet erotic movements of her body to the rhythm. She became quite lost in the dance excited by the knowledge that she was performing well, or so she thought, and the effect the dancing was having on her body, which was gradually becoming aroused. She was quite disappointed when with a final roll on the drum and a clash of cymbals, the dance came to an end and she sank, panting heavily, to the floor in front of the dais.

There was a heavy silence in the hall for a minute or so then Lord Charles spoke. "Very good, slave, return to your position. Now it's your turn Moona."

Moona knelt in the centre of the floor and, as the music started, began to sway back and forth on her knees. Then she gracefully rose to her feet and rising up on her toes, began to dance for her Master. Juliette watched, fascinated, as Moona moved round the hall. She had never seen her dance to seductively before, her eyes flashed as she stole secretive glances in the direction of her Master and her mouth opened slightly as she became aroused. Suddenly there was a change in the tempo and she stopped facing her Master, perfectly motionless except for her stomach, which undulated rapidly to the increased beat. Juliette saw her Master whisper to Maya. The girl rose and knelt in front of him and her head disappeared under his caftan. The movements under the material left no doubt to what she was doing! Moona's dance ended and she sank to the floor in front of the dais, her forehead touching the floor.

"That was very good, also," Lord Charles announced after a minute's silence. "Stand before me, both of you."

Juliette and Moona stood, trembling, before him awaiting his verdict on their performance.

"You are both quite good," he announced. "But I do

detect room for improvement. Aylena will intensify your lessons. I will be inviting some guests here shortly and you will be required to entertain them. They are all used to slaves dancing for them and are likely to judge you very strictly. I want them not to be too critical of your performances." Then, ignoring the girl between his knees, he reached out and touched each of them, first on the nipple and then on their sex lips.

"You are both showing signs of being aroused," he said. "But not yet sufficient for the next item on the agenda. Strip."

Juliette and Moona quickly removed their garments and jewels and handed them to Sarita. They stood naked, wondering what was to come next. They had both been praised for their dancing and were unprepared for the next order.

"Jason. Juliette first." His voice was sharp and menacing.

Jason put down the drum and rose. He grasped Juliette by the arm and led her to the far side of the stool, facing her Master.

"Bend over, slave," Jason ordered and, when she had obeyed, he pulled her wrists and ankles out from her body and secured them to rings in the floor.

"Look straight into your Master's eyes. Do not look away under any circumstances," Jason ordered and then stepped back to the side of the room.

Juliette raised her eyes and looked at her Master. She saw Hassan move to the front of the dais as Lord Charles pointed to the floor. Hassan crouched down and, when he straightened up, she saw that he held a long thin cane in his hand. She felt her legs begin to shake and her buttocks clench. She looked into her Master's eyes, seeking some sign of mercy, but there was none.

"Ten strokes," she heard Lord Charles pronounce.

Hassan walked towards her and passed out of her vision. Even with her eyes on her Master's she could still just see Maya under the caftan. She cringed as she realised the girl was to continue pleasuring him while she was beaten.

127

Crack.

Juliette's body jerked as the rattan struck without warning. A line of fire spread across her cheeks.

Swish. Crack.

This time she heard the sound of the cane approaching and was prepared for the second line of fire it left behind it. She could feel the cane curling round both cheeks, showing that Hassan was laying the strokes on with force.

Swish. Thwack.

A gasp of agony hissed between her clenched teeth as the cane added to her suffering. Tears began to fill her eyes and cloud her vision but she managed to keep his gaze fixed on her Master's eyes.

Crack.

Thwack.

Two strokes in quick succession added their fire to the blaze that had been ignited in her cheeks. She felt her arousal begin to rise. Five separate lines seared her bottom and she had five more to come. She had, so far, managed not to yell nor take her eyes away from her Master's.

Crack.

Thwack.

Shrill cries of pain followed the report of the rattan on her bottom. Only three to come now. As a beating it was a light one but it was having the desired effect on her body. Her nipples had hardened so much that her breasts were beginning to ache and she could feel the moisture on her sex lips. Tears flowed freely from her eyes, falling to the floor beneath her head. Despite the exquisite sensations rising in her body, she felt hatred for the man who had ordered the beating. That he was watching her intently, while Maya still serviced him, added to her hatred. She devoutly wished that, at times, he didn't cause feelings of love for him to find a place in her heart. That he could make her feel love for him at times, and then be so cruel to her at others, confused her too much.

The last three strokes seared a burning path across her buttocks, drawing loud screams from her lungs. She writhed on the stool, the movement intensifying her arousal, which she was beginning to have to exert an effort to control. She felt Jason release her bonds and pull her upright. He marched her to stand before her Master. Again his hand reached out for the breasts and between her thighs, his touch inflaming her desires.

"Good. That's better!" Lord Charles said as he rubbed her sex lips. "Kneel there." He pointed to the floor at his side and turned his head to Jason. "Now the slave Moona."

Juliette knelt as ordered and watched as Moona was secured over the stool. Hassan raised the cane and the slave's beating began. She yelled on the second stroke and screamed loudly from the fourth onwards as her body jerked and writhed as the cane lashed her bottom. The spectacle added fuel to Juliette's arousal, as she knew it would. Moona writhed delightfully as the ten strokes were applied to her buttocks and this seemed, to Juliette, to make the scene even more erotic. After the girl's last stroke, Jason released her and led her to the front of the dais, signalling Juliette to stand at her side.

Lord Charles tapped Maya on the head and she withdrew from under the caftan and resumed her place. Juliette noticed that the girl's face was heavily flushed and her eyes seemed glazed.

"Juliette," Lord Charles' voice broke into her thoughts. "You looked away on three strokes. Later you will receive another ten, but with the switch." He looked at Moona. "Moona, you lost the contest. You looked away five times. Later, you will receive fifteen lashes with the Girl Slave Whip."

Juliette was stunned at her own sentence. She had not been aware that she was in any form of contest. She heard Moona, at her side, gasp at her fate. But neither slave dared to question their Master's decision.

"Jason," she heard Lord Charles say. "Continue with the performance."

Juliette heard movements behind her for a few moments, then Jason turned her to face into the hall. The bench had been put onto the divan and Jason led her to it. He strapped the phallus in place and ordered her to lie down on the bench. He tied her ankles to the bench then, pulling her arms apart, secured her wrists to the corner posts. Moona was then ordered to mount the divan, straddle Juliette's body so that the phallus just touched her sex lips and lean forward and hold on to the two posts to which Juliette was secured. It was just as it had been during her two weeks at Moona's house!

"Do not lower yourself until given permission," Juliette heard Jason order.

Juliette looked up into the girl's face, just in time to see a look of terror spread across her features. The cause of this was soon apparent to her as she saw Hassan walk passed, a wicked looking switch in his hand. By turning her head slightly, she saw him take up his position to the side, level with Moona's buttocks, and felt the girl begin to shake as he laid the switch lightly against her cheeks as he measured his distance. Three times she watched as Hassan's arm rose bringing the cruel switch lashing down across Moona's taut bottom. Each stroke wrung a loud scream from the girl, the force of each rocking her body forward making the phallus rub against her open sex lips. She saw the girl's breasts swaying above her, the nipples hard and prominent in their brown aureoles. Twice more the switch cut across the girl's throbbing bottom, each wringing a loud scream from her lungs as the fire in her cheeks, and the arousal in her sex tunnel, built up.

"You will impale yourself on the next stroke," the voice of Jason sounded above Moona's sobbing. "You will ride the leather without cheating. You are not permitted to come until given permission."

Moona groaned as the order registered in her mind. Her body suddenly jerked as Hassan lashed the switch across her heaving buttocks. Juliette looked along her own body as the stroke landed, saw the girl's body arch backwards and then descend with a savage thrust onto the phallus, which disappeared inside her body. Jason quickly grasped her ankles and, spreading her legs wide, tied them to the corner posts. Moona was not heavy by any means but, as the next six strokes were lashed across her bottom as she rode the invader, Juliette felt the air forced out of her lungs, making it nearly impossible for her to breath. Juliette gasped for breath as the girl above her rode the invader as hard as she could. So erratic were her movements that two of the next six strokes laced across the backs of her tender thighs. Her screams echoed round the hall. Her tears flowed from her eyes, falling onto the girl beneath her. Her arousal was verging on an orgasm and her juices were flowing freely down the leather and running over Juliette's mound and down between her thighs. On the fourth of these six strokes, Moona's hands had slid down the posts, which she had been gripping as tight as she could, and her mouth descended on Juliette's in a burning kiss.

Juliette had been counting the strokes and was amazed that the girl had, so far, held out, as eighteen livid weals were raised on her young buttocks and thighs. The pain, and consequently the arousal it was causing, must have reached intolerable heights and taxed her to the limit to keep the latter under control. Her body was streaming with sweat which, together with her tears and juices, were soaking Juliette and making their two bodies slide about on each other.

Jason gripped a bundle of Moona's hair and pulled her face up off Juliette's. "You will take another six strokes. You will look at your Master as they are applied. If you look away the stroke will not count. When you hear me call out 'six' you may then release your control and come. If you come before then, Hassan has been instructed to flog your backside with twenty strokes. Do you understand?"

"Yes, Sir," Moona replied between her clenched teeth and gripped the posts even tighter.

Juliette had heard Jason's orders with utter shock. The girl had already taken eighteen strokes of that wicked switch, and from Hassan, and was now expected to take another six and, at the same time, keep her eyes fixed on those of her Master. As the girl's body continued to pump up and down on the phallus, Hassan lashed the switch across her heaving buttocks. Juliette, listening to the report of each and listening to Jason count, was astounded that the number of reports had only reached nine when Jason called out 'six'. The pain-wracked girl had managed to only drop her gaze three times as the switch cut into her bottom and thighs. After the count had been completed, Hassan continued to apply the switch to the swollen buttocks as Moona thrust herself up and down on the phallus frantically, screaming and moaning, and begging the orgasm to explode within her and stop the giant from lashing her blazing backside. To Juliette's utter astonishment, the switch lashed another eight searing strokes across Moona's bottom before her body arched backwards, her hands flying behind her and clutching her swollen cheeks, as her body surrendered to a shattering orgasm. The girl's final scream of pain and release had hardly died away before her unconscious body relaxed and fell onto Juliette's driving the air from her lungs in a loud 'whoosh'.

Moona's ankles were released and her limp body lifted off the bench. Juliette was released next and climbed off the divan gasping to draw air into her starved lungs. The weight of Moona's body, and the arousing effect the flogging had had on her, had stifled her. Maya had stepped quickly forward as soon as Moona had been lowered to the floor and bathed her face in cold water. The girl regained consciousness and looked round, still in a daze as Jason led both girls back to stand in front of the dais.

"Most entertaining," Lord Charles mused as his eyes roved over the two sweating and dishevelled slaves. "When my father told me about this I thought he was teasing me. Turn round, slaves," he said aloud.

Both girls turned and presented their backs to him. His eyes studied their buttocks carefully. Moona's were, by far, in the worst state, but Hassan had obeyed his orders perfectly and in no place had he drawn blood with the switch.

"Turn and face me," he ordered and, when they had obeyed, he turned to Jason. "Prepare for the final part of the entertainment."

Juliette and Moona stood facing him, wondering what

ordeal was next on his agenda. They saw him give signals and heard movements behind them. Then Sarita rose and walked passed them and disappeared from view.

"Turn and face down the hall," Lord Charles ordered.

Both girls obeyed and gasped. Juliette could not believe her eyes. The divan had been turned head on to the stool and post. Sarita, now stark naked, was secured on the divan, a large cushion under her buttocks and her limbs spread wide and tied to the posts. Lord Charles pushed between them and walked to the divan. He had shed the caftan and was also naked. They watched as he knelt between Saritas' spread legs, facing the stool and post. His massive penis was already erect.

"Jason. Hassan. You have your orders." Lord Charles' voice broke the silence in an ominous tone that made Juliette shudder. It came to her in a flash what was about to happen and the thought revolted her.

Her worst fears were realised as they led a still shaken Moona and tied her wrists high above her head to the post. Jason parted her hair and draped it forward over her upthrust breasts. Then they came for her and marched her to the stool and bent her over, spreading her legs wide and tying her wrists and ankles to rings in the floor. Looking through her legs, Juliette saw that her Master would have a prefect view of her and Moona as they were flogged while he enjoyed Sarita's body. Looking over her shoulder, she saw Hassan standing between her and Moona and Jason approaching, the switch and Girl Slave Whip in his hands.

"Juliette, you will now have your ten strokes of the switch," Lord Charles said. "Moona you will now have fifteen lashes with the Girl Slave Whip. Proceed, Hassan."

Thwack.

Juliette had closed her eyes tight and clamped her teeth together. Her body jerked as a sharp report echoed round the room followed by a deep groan. But it was not her that had been struck! She opened her eyes and looked between her legs in time to see Hassan raise the whip again. She also saw her Master looking forwards at the post and Sarita's body fully impaled by his manhood as he began taking his pleasure of her. Juliette winced as another four loud reports echoed through the hall, this time followed by loud screams from the girl tied at the post beside her. The high pitched screams testified to the force Hassan was putting behind the strokes.

Juliette looked behind her again, Lord Charles, without taking his eyes off the scene being enacted before him, was pumping up and down on Sarita's prone body, making his slave gasp with the pleasure that was flooding through her. Such was the depth of her ecstasy that she was now totally oblivious of the suffering of her sister slave. She shuddered as she saw Hassan hand the whip to Jason and take the switch from him. She shut her eyes and braced herself for her ordeal to start.

Thwack.

This time her body jumped for real as the leather covered switch cut a flaming trail across her taut buttocks and the weals that already decorated her bottom. She just managed to hold back the scream that erupted in he throat.

Crack.

Again her body jerked against her bonds as the switch lashed her bottom for her second stroke. A shrill scream echoed round the room as her eyes filled with tears. She felt her nipples begin to grow hard and a dampness seep from her sex lips as her body's arousal was rekindled.

Thwack.

Crack.

Thwack.

Juliette's body was now running in sweat and droplets were falling from her nipples to the floor to join the pool made by her tears. Her full-bloodied screams followed each report of the switch on her throbbing buttocks

Her burning bottom had now taken half of her punishment. Hassan was allowing a half-minute interval between the strokes that blazed across her cheeks and she had no longer been able to hold back her screams which followed the reports round the hall. Trying to hold herself in control was difficult enough, due to the intervals between the strokes, and she didn't know which was worse, the waiting or the line of agony when the stroke eventually landed.

Thwack.

Juliette's body jerked but it was Moona that screamed as the Girl Slave Whip recommenced its onslaught on her back. For the first time since the floggings had started, Juliette turned her head and looked at the girl tied to the post. Moona was hanging from her wrists, her legs having given way under her pain wracked body. Four more screams echoed round the hall, heralding the strokes of the blades across her back. In the intervals between the strokes, the sound of pleasurable moans from Sarita could be heard above the pained moaning of the punished slaves. Lord Charles was making his enjoyment of her body last as long as possible and causing his slave to achieve extreme lengths of control.

Crack.

Now it was again Juliette's turn to scream as the switch cut across her taut buttocks. Her body bucked and writhed as Hassan laid three more strokes on the slave's swollen cheeks. Juliette was aware that she only had one more stroke to come but the arousal the pain and domination the beating was causing was almost out of control. No matter what the next stroke might do to her, she must, on no account, lose control. She braced herself, fighting to contain her arousal, conscious that, due to the way her legs were spread, her Master could see the juices running from her sex, testifying to the closeness of her orgasm.

Thwack.

Juliette's scream was a mixture of pain and relief as she realised that she had survived her ten strokes and had succeeded in keeping the orgasm at bay. She allowed her pain-wracked body to collapse over the stool, mewing and moaning. Her ordeal may have been over, but the girl at the post still had five lashes to come. The sound of the leather blades striking her back echoed round the room. Moona no longer had the strength to scream, only a loud moaning escaped her clenched teeth as she, in turn, fought against the orgasm the whipping was sending soaring through her body. Like Juliette, she just managed to keep it under control.

The sound of the lashes landing across Moona's back for the last time, was followed by a shout of triumph from Lord Charles and a scream of intense satisfaction from the slave under him. So excited was Lord Charles by the eroticism of the scene being enacted in front of him that he had given Sarita permission to surrender to her orgasm as he climaxed deep inside her vagina.

Moona's wrists were released and the whipped slave slid slowly down the post to collapse in a heap on the floor. Then the bonds securing Juliette were removed. She eased her pain filled body upright and turned round, just in time to see Sarita and her Master emerged from the delicious mist of fulfilment into which they had sunk. As they rose from the divan, she could see that both of their bodies were running in sweat. Lord Charles replaced the caftan and made his way back to his chair. Sarita, Moona and Juliette were ushered by Jason to the front of the dais and made to kneel.

Juliette dared to look up through her eyelashes at her Master's face and could see from his expression that he had been more than satisfied by the evening's performance. It had, it seemed, awakened a latent streak of perverted cruelty in him and she feared that, if that were so, there would be many repetitions of the evening in the future. She cringed as she thought that, sometimes, it might be her back that the Girl Slave Whip lashed. She had, until then, begun grudgingly to respect her Master for his fairness, but the events of this evening had killed that, and any feelings of love for him that had, on occasions, entered her head.

Lord Charles ordered Hassan to remove the musicians and Sarita and return them to their quarters and to take Moona to Aylena for her back and buttocks to be treated. Juliette was left kneeling before him and, once the others had left the hall, he ordered Jason to take her to the divan and tie her there.

In a daze, Juliette lay, face up, on the divan as Jason spread her limbs and secured her to the post. She shivered as she felt the dampness under her body and her nose detected the scent of her Master and the girl's earlier pleasure. She waited in dreadful anticipation, wondering to what further torments her young body was to be subjected. She could hardly believe her eyes as she saw her Master, the caftan discarded, kneel on the end of the divan. His manhood was again erect with the tip purple with desire. He slowly lowered himself onto her and, despite the hatred seething inside her, she felt her sex lips harden and open, ready to receive him.

He took his pleasure of her slowly and thoroughly. His weight pressed her sore buttocks hard down on the divan, sending fresh waves of pain through her cheeks. This, to her shame, only seemed to make her body's acceptance of him more willing. She felt her muscles contract tight about him as he thrust back and forth inside her. Her hatred of the man, who so recently had pleasured himself in Sarita's body as he watched her flogged, slowly evaporated as her own desires increased. She began to utter low moans of desire as her arousal reached delicious heights. She fought hard to contain this with all her concentration, as to succumb to an orgasm without permission would surly incur a sound whipping for her back.

Suddenly, her Master increased his momentum, His mouth descending on hers in a savage kiss that bruised her mouth. His rough hands sought and found her breasts, squeezing them hard, as he emphasised his ownership of her. She cried out as she felt her nipples pinched hard between his fingers. With a shout of satisfaction, his body arched above her and she felt his pleasure ejaculated as his weapon thrust deep inside her. As he began to withdraw, she felt her muscles tighten about him, milking the last of his seed from him. She felt him rise above her and saw his hard and dripping penis before her eyes. She raised her head and took it in her mouth, licking and sucking him until it was clean.

It had been over all too soon for Juliette. She hated the man and she hated her body, which betrayed her with its needs. She had not come, and had escaped punishment, but

137

her pleasure was only slightly marred by this restriction. The usual conflict raged within her. Whether to hate him for the cruelty to which he subjected her young body, or to love him for the delights he bestowed on it. Paradoxically, she longed to be back with his father. At least she had known where she was with him!

She opened her eyes and looked up into the face of her Master who, again dressed in the caftan, was standing over her.

"You have served me well, this evening, slave," he said, surprising her. Usually he was critical of a slave's performance, even when she knew she had pleased him.

"I try to please you, my Master," she stammered

"Yes, but it takes a sore bottom to bring out the best in you. Doesn't it?"

"Yes, Master," Juliette said, feeling her face redden with shame.

"You did not come while being used. You obeyed the orders. You deserve a reward. Would you like a reward, slave?" he asked.

"If it pleases you, Master," Juliette replied, knowing that a sound thrashing across her bottom would be the price she would surly have to pay.

"It does please me, and you shall be rewarded," Lord Charles said. He called Jason to him and whispered in the youth's ear.

To Juliette's astonishment her Master left the room. Was he not even going to wait and see her orgasm as the youth flogged her? She was further astonished when Jason did not release her and bend her over the stool. She heard him moving about out of her sight then, as he reappeared she let out a sharp cry of disgust. He was carrying the phallus! She writhed and squirmed in disgust as, crouching between her legs, he forced the object between her sex lips and into her tunnel. Sickened though she was, she could not help her body responding to the intrusion. Slowly at first, then gradually gaining momentum, he moved the phallus back and forth inside her.

"The Master said you may come when you wish," Jason

said.

Juliette, to her disgust, felt her arousal reawakened as her muscles gripped the leather invader. There was nothing she could do to stop her body responding. As the youth thrust the thing back and forth she felt her nipples harden and her juices begin to flow. Higher and higher her arousal soared and her body started to thrust upwards, driving the thing even deeper into her. Soon sweat was pouring from her skin as she writhed on the divan, the movement sending spasms of pain through her buttocks, driving the arousal even higher.

Then, as she cried out in ecstasy, her body arched rigid as a series of shattering orgasms thundered inside her. Slowly the mist into which she had descended began to clear and, as consciousness returned, so did the memory of her shame at what had just been done to her by the youth. Without a word, he released her bonds and, grasping a handful of her hair, dragged her to her feet. Still in silence, his grip tightening in her hair, he led her, half stooped over, back to her quarters. Shame and humiliation kept her silent as Aylena made her lie down while she spread cream over the slave's still throbbing buttocks. Her three sister slaves, Moona still nursing her battered and bruised body, must have guessed something terrible had happened to her by the expression on their faces, and tactfully refrained from asking any questions.

As soon as Aylena had finished, Juliette went to her own bed and, turning her face to the wall, wept silently with shame. Until then, she had come to terms with the way her body reacted to pain and domination. Part of her had actually accepted that being sold into slavery had opened doors of pleasure that she would not, otherwise, have known. With Lord Reythal her situation had been acceptable. He was strict, but fair, and took his pleasure of her body as a Master should, without any consideration for the slave's feelings or needs. The son, on the other hand, had deliberately set out to upset her mind with his mixture of gentleness and cruelty. Making her love him and hate him alternately, until she didn't know whether she was coming or going.

There was no going back to Lord Reythal, now that he was dead. All she had to look forward to was a life of continual confusion that would in time, she thought, drive her mad. As tiredness eventually overcame her misery and sleep wrapped her in its comforting arms, a strange thought crossed her mind. Had she not been arrested that day, would one of her men friends have discovered the latent need in her body and made her his love slave?

CHAPTER 7.

As Lord Charles had mentioned, now that the building alterations had been completed and the place decorated and furnished to his satisfaction, he began receiving guests at his mansion. These were, in the main, business contacts from abroad with whom he either already dealt, or prospects that he wished to persuade to trade with him. Since taking over from his father, he was rapidly expanding the business and his empire. His four personal slaves were always required to serve at table when the guests were present and their Master received many compliments on his scantily clad possessions. Not only on table, but frequently in the guests' beds, the slaves were required to entertain and, threats of a sound whipping from Hassan ensured that they always gave full satisfaction.

One afternoon three guests arrived. Unlike the previous ones, these came dressed in their national clothes and Juliette, as well as the others, was greatly intrigued by their appearance. They had light olive coloured skins, their faces darker and weather-beaten. They looked very fierce with their dark expressionless eyes and hooked noses. They were dressed in long white luxurious flowing robes with jewel studded belts round their waists from which hung wicked looking curved swords in magnificent scabbards. Their heads were covered by white sheets held in place by, what looked like, crowns of black rope threaded through oval black wooden balls. Lord Charles already knew them well, having visited them on his trip abroad with his father, and treated them with unusual respect.

Aylena informed the girls that these men were from her own country where they were either chieftains or princes of one tribe or another. They would be very rich and have many slaves of their own, including expert dancers. With them travelled several important looking servants, all male. During the meal times, these guests paid little or no notice of the near naked girls that served them and, when Moona and Juliette danced for them, their performance was practically ignored. The girls were very annoyed at this until Aylena explained that this was totally in keeping with the men's attitude to slaves.

The first night of their visit, the men retired early pleading fatigue from the long journey. On the second night, however, the girls were sent to them for their pleasure. Juliette was not chosen on the first night, and she was called to serve her Master instead. She was shocked at her friends' appearance when she met her sister slaves the following morning. They looked thoroughly exhausted. They each told her of their experience the previous night and of how the men seemed utterly insatiable, using them most of the night so great was their appetite. The two blondes always seemed worse than Moona, and Aylena explained that blondes were rare in the men's country and blonde slaves were highly prized. On the following three nights, Juliette was chosen and serviced each of the men in turn. She tried her best to satisfy them and quickly learned their needs, adapting herself to some of the strange things they demanded of her. She learned many new ways in which a woman could please a man and, she too, returned to her quarters the next morning utterly drained.

When these guests departed, nothing was said to the girls about their service to the men and they assumed that they had been found satisfactory. The only reference the Master made about the guest's stay, was to quiz the slaves on the men's requirements and get them to demonstrate these to him when they attended him at night.

Juliette continued her duties as First Girl but, after the episode with Sarita, the strap remained firmly out of sight. To her relief, neither Lord Charles nor Mehmet asked to inspect the book she had been given. Also, because of the demands of the business, the slaves saw little or nothing of Mehmet during the weeks that followed. It was, therefore, an unwelcome surprise when, one morning Juliette was summoned to him. She knelt in front of the old man, who was clearly in a terrible rage, wondering what the cause of it could be.

"The Master's riding boots have not been cleaned," he

stormed at her. "Neither have his riding clothes been pressed and laid out ready. He is not pleased. You are First Girl and should have checked to see that these things were done. Whose tasks were they?" he demanded.

Juliette trembled with terror at the man's rage. It had been Moona's turn that day but the girl had been in a terrible sulk for a couple of days because the Master had praised Juliette's dancing and not hers when they had performed for him. Juliette knew she had no option but to tell the truth.

"It was Moona's turn today, Sir," she replied, the shadow of doom getting steadily darker.

"Fetch her," Mehmet commanded.

Juliette hurried to do his bidding. He might be an old sod, but he now wielded considerable power in the household. She found Moona and, having quickly berated her for her negligence, returned with her to Mehmet. The two slaves, dressed in their flimsy working shifts, knelt before the major domo, trembling visibly.

"Moona," he said, his voice full of anger. "You have failed to carry out your duties this morning and you, Juliette have failed to see that she did so. You will both follow me."

The two slaves rose to their feet and followed the man as he stormed his way to Hassan's yard.

"Hassan, my friend," Mehmet said as he approached the giant. "I have work for you. These two slaves are to be punished. The slave Moona is to get fifteen strokes and Juliette twenty, both with the long switch."

The two slaves, who had fallen to their knees, shook and their faces turned white as they heard his words, especially at the lecherous tone in his voice.

Hassan looked at the two kneeling slaves for a moment. "Stand and strip," he ordered.

The two rose and unhooking the shoulder clasps on their shifts, let them slide down their bodies to the ground.

"Which first?" Hassan asked, looking at Mehmet.

The old man looked hard at the two naked girls, the tip of his tongue sliding over his whiskered lips. "Moona," he said. "Go to the bars."

As Moona walked shakily towards the bars, Mehmet grabbed Juliette by the arm and led her to the rear of where Moona had now draped her body over the narrow bar. They watched as Hassan secured Moona's wrists, upper arms and ankles in place. He then walked sedately to the wall and took down the switch. As the giant took up his position to the side of the bent girl, Juliette sensed movement at her side. She glanced sideways and nearly cried out with disgust as she saw the man slide his hand down inside the front of his baggy trousers.

"Look to the front," Mehmet shouted at her. "Do not take your eyes of her behind. It is because of you that she is to be flogged."

"This will teach you to neglect your duties, Moona," Mehmet called out as Hassan raised the switch.

Juliette watched as the switch sped through the air and curled round Moona's pale buttocks. A livid weal quickly appeared, turning from white to red in seconds. When three stripes had decorated her behind, Moona had not made a sound, other than a sharp gasp each time the rod struck. Her bravery, or stubbornness as Mehmet insisted on calling it, could not last and she let out a shrill scream on the next stroke. From then on, Moona screamed as each time the switch laced across her behind, the screams getting louder and shriller with each stroke. She was writhing frantically as the pain in her bottom escalated, and Juliette could see the tell tale signs of the arousal that was building up inside her body.

Having absorbed the fifteen strokes of her punishment, Hassan released her bonds and she eased her body upright and turned and knelt, lowering her head.

"Thank you, Sir, for my beating," she stammered through the sobs.

Having performed the ritual, Moona rose and walked gingerly to where Juliette and Mehmet stood. As she approached, Juliette could clearly see her hard erect nipples and the stains down the inside of her thighs.

"Next!" Hassan's high-pitched voice sounded ominously, summoning Juliette to her ordeal.

Casting a fleeting look at Moona, that lacked any signs of sympathy, Juliette approached the bars. She bent over, stretched her arms along the front one and gripped it tight. Hassan tightened the straps, securing her in place.

"This will teach you to be more diligent in your duties as First Girl," Mehmet called to her.

The last word had hardly left his mouth when Juliette heard the dreaded 'swish' as the leather-covered rod descended. She gripped the bar even tighter just as the first stroke curled round her buttocks. The sound of the impact echoed round the yard as a line of intense heat erupted in her cheeks.

She turned her head to look over her shoulder at Mehmet, hate blazing in her eyes, knowing full well what she would see. Sure enough, his hand was down the front of his baggy trousers, pleasuring himself as he watched her being beaten. She turned her head away and stared at the ground in front of her just as the switch thrashed across her bottom.

She managed to stay defiantly silent until the sixth stroke had added its quota of agony. The seventh broke her control and her first scream followed the echo of the impact round the yard. Hassan laid three more strokes across her throbbing cheeks. She was writhing on the bar, the movement aggravating the arousal rising in her belly, as she tried to avoid the switch. Halfway through her punishment! This time, she had to admit, she deserved to be flogged. She had neglected her duties and should pay the penalty. But why did that pervert, Mehmet, have to be there and pleasure himself as he watched? It wasn't fair!

She screamed loud and shrill, and writhed on the bar, as Hassan lashed the remaining ten strokes of her punishment across her writhing buttocks. At last her ordeal was over and her bonds released. Slowly she straightened up, turned to face the giant and fell to her knees and thanked him in the approved manner. She returned to her place beside Mehmet, thankful to see that he had removed his hand from his crotch.

"I trust that you have both learned your lesson," he said.

"Yes, Sir," they replied in unison.

"Collect your shifts and continue with your duties. Remember you will both remain naked for the rest of the day."

The two beaten slaves returned to the house and, as required after a beating, reported to Aylena who applied cream to their buttocks. Their cheeks were badly bruised, dark red ridges criss-crossing each other where the switch had left its mark. The cream that was now being used on their weals was a new type of salve, based on the formula given to Aylena by Moona. Whilst this ensured a rapid disappearance of the marks and swelling it did not, as the other had, make the pain disappear. Consequently, when after the evidence had completely disappeared after a few days, it was still uncomfortable to sit down. Thus, if the slave received another beating quite soon afterwards, whilst her buttocks presented a clean canvas, the beating was all the more painful.

The sight of a slave going about her tasks, naked after a beating, was commonplace and very few of the servants or other slaves took any notice. The exception to this was Mehmet. He seemed to appear much more frequently and insisted that the slave must stop whatever she was doing and bend over in front of him, while he gloated at her striped buttocks. Later that day, Juliette, having managed to avoid Mehmet for some time, was walking gingerly along a corridor when she saw her Master approaching. She stepped to one side and knelt to allow him to pass. Instead of doing so, he stopped in front of her

"Stand," he commanded.

Juliette obeyed, keeping her eyes demurely lowered.

"Look at me, slave."

Juliette raised her eyes and looked into his face. As usual his eyes gave away nothing of his thoughts.

"So. You have been negligent in your duties as First Girl," he said, quietly. "I had hoped better of you. I trust your thrashing was sufficient to ensure a higher standard from you in future."

"I am sorry I failed you, Master," Juliette said. "I will

try and do better in future. Whether the beating was sufficient is for you to judge."

"Quite so!" Lord Charles said. "I have just inspected the book I gave you. I see only one entry there. I do not believe the slaves have been that good. Perhaps another would do the job better than you."

Juliette shivered, and not from the cool breeze wafting down the corridor. She had hoped he had forgotten about the book. She did not want to lose her position as First Girl and have to take orders from one of the others, as much as she liked them. She had to salvage her position quickly. There was only one course she could take.

"Master," she said softly, unable to hide the tremor in her voice. "I was punished for not doing my duty. I was not told I was also being punished for betraying your trust."

"You think you should be beaten again as punishment for betraying my thrust then?" her Master asked.

"That, also is for you to decide, Master. I did betray you," Juliette answered, aware that she had probably sentenced herself to another beating, and a severe one at that.

Lord Charles thought for a few minutes in silence. "Yes, you should be punished for letting me down," he said. "However, I will give you the chance to atone and, at the same time, prove that you are no longer being inattentive to your duty. As proof, I want you to ensure that each of the other slaves gets at least two thrashings from Hassan during the next two weeks. Also, your strap will no longer be idle."

"Oh no! Master," Juliette blurted out, astounded by his decision. "They are my friends. Please do not make me do that."

"I have spoken, slave. The matter is closed. Except to warn you that, if you fail me this time, I will send you to Hassan for thirty lashes of the heavy whip." So saying, he continued on his way.

He left Juliette looking after him, stunned by his order. She had to agree that she had not pursued her duties efficiently and, she supposed, deserved to be punished. The one thing that terrified her more than anything else was the heavy whip. She sometimes had nightmares, in which she was tied to a post and a masked man was lashing her back with a terrible whip, cutting through her soft flesh until the blood flowed over her buttocks and down her legs. She always woke up, drenched in seat and shaking like a leaf. The only way, it seemed, to avoid this was to ensure that her three friends were sent to Hassan and beaten and to use the strap on their bottoms herself. It was a terrible dilemma! Should she tell the others of the Master's order, and hope for their understanding, or keep the matter to herself and let them think that the morning's flogging was the cause?

After a good deal of thought, she decided on the latter course. Rather let them think she had suddenly become officious rather than brand herself a coward. Cowardice for which they would be suffering! Finally she decided on the former. In doing so, she realised, she had sentenced her own bottom to a flogging each time they were beaten. Not only that, she had to beat them as well. During the next two weeks, she kept a very close watch on the others. At first it was not difficult to find genuine faults. But the other soon realised what was afoot and pulled their socks up. Consequently, during the second week, she had to 'manufacture' transgressions in order to fulfil the Master's quota. She willingly accepted the thrashings she also received but what sickened her about the whole affair was Mehmet's insistence that he witness every punishment. She was forced to stand by as her friends writhed and screamed under Hassan's cane, knowing that the old sod was standing at her side, playing with himself. All of the girls were aware of this and it made their ordeals all the worse.

One evening, after the two weeks had elapsed, Juliette was summoned to dance for her Master. When the dance finally came to an end, she knelt panting in front of him. She looked up at him covertly through her eyelashes and breathed a sigh of relief as she saw the smile of approval on his face.

"That was very good," he said to her.

"I am grateful if my Master is pleased with my poor effort," she responded happily.

"I am not only pleased with your dancing," Lord Charles continued. "I am also pleased with the way you are improving as First Girl and making the others perform better. It is always a puzzle that it takes a few thrashings to make them attend properly to their duties."

The glow of happiness that was flowing through her was immediately dispelled by this last compliment. Visions of her friends' tender bottoms suffering under the cane, and the disgrace they felt about Mehmet's antics at their expense, flashed through her mind. That they may have deserved the earlier beatings was no consolation to her conscience. That she had deliberately made false accusations to get them beaten, had made the matter even more terrible. All through the two weeks she had regretted her decision and had been unable to look her friends in the face. This had, eventually turned them against her. She was miserable and had thought hard to find a way to atone and win them back. In a flash, a way became clear to her. It was a terrible decision to make and she was terrified at what it entailed for her. But, she decided, any price was worth paying to put right the wrong she had done to them. But she needed her Master's co-operation.

"Indeed, Master," she said demurely, taking the first step along the path she had just chosen. "I can not help thinking that their suffering was unfair as this was caused solely by my neglect. If I had been more diligent, it would not have been necessary for them to be punished."

"But you were given the same punishments as they, weren't you?" he asked.

"Yes, Master," she replied. Now must come the dreadful confession if she was to get his assistance for her plan. "But that did not alter the fact that they were beaten because of me, especially when I had to invent faults to meet the target you had set. I feel that I let them and you down very badly." There! The confession had been made and now she must suffer whatever fate she had brought down around her own shoulders. She dared not look into his eyes, for fear of what she might see there.

"Have you told the others of this?" Lord Charles asked.

His voice had changed and now there was a hint of anger in his tone.

"No, Master," Juliette replied. "For one thing I was too ashamed of what I had done and secondly, I feared they might not believe my expressions of regrets. They might well think that words come too easily, even if I had been able to make them listen to me."

"Then we must find a way to convince them, mustn't we? I will not have undercurrents of discord in my household," Lord Charles said.

"I think there may be a way, Master. If you approve and will give your assistance." Juliette spoke softly, nearly in a whisper. This was the moment! It was hard enough to just speak about her plan. Would she have enough courage to go through with it when the time came?

"I am listening," Lord Charles said, thoughtfully, not wishing to commit himself until he had heard what she had to say.

With slightly halting voice, Juliette told him of the scheme that had sprung into her mind. He heard her out in silence, an expression of disbelief spreading across his face by the minute.

"Are you asking me to have you whipped?" he asked, when she had finished. "But you enjoy being flogged and, I suspect, your friends are also aware of this."

"Master, I do not enjoy being beaten." She dared to contradict him then, before he could speak, carried on. "I hate the pain and dread every stroke. Unfortunately, something, I think it is the total domination I am put under at the time, makes my body react the way it does. They know this and they also know that I am terrified of my back being hit even with a strap, let alone the whip."

Lord Charles considered the matter in silence for a few minutes. He did not fully believe what the slave had said. He was still of the opinion that she enjoyed the pain. After all, he had seen the effect a beating had on her for himself! Perhaps this was an opportunity to cure her of this! He had an idea. He would agree to her request but, unknown to her until the time came, he would add his own refinement.

"I agree," he said eventually. "You will report to me in my study at ten thirty tomorrow morning, dressed and made up as you are now. In the meantime, you will say nothing of this discussion to anyone."

"Thank you, Master," Juliette said, fear already making her voice sound slightly husky.

"Don't thank me until you have felt the lash," Lord Charles said sternly. "Now go and report to me tomorrow as ordered."

Juliette spent a troubled night, knowing what awaited her in the morning. The other girls avoided her, as they had been doing and she was left with just her own thoughts to torment her until it was time to prepare. At ten thirty prompt, Juliette presented herself to her Master's study. She was filled with dread of what lay ahead for her and her legs already felt weak. She just prayed that she would have the courage to go through with it bravely and that, at the end, her friends would forgive her. She had convinced herself that what she was doing was right. She had to do penance for the agonies her friends had suffered because of her, and they must see her penance in order to earn their forgiveness.

Lord Charles had, in the meantime, been busy. He had spoken with certain of his servants, making arrangements, not only for the performance Juliette had explained to him but also for the refinement he had planned without her awareness. He looked hard at the slave kneeling before him. Even through the almost transparent costume she wore, her delectable body sent delicious sensations coursing through his loins. It was a shame that her softness would soon squirm under the lash but if she truly wished to be whipped, he was happy to oblige, and see that it was done properly. It might just, he hoped, cure her body of reacting the way it did during a beating and thus make the punishment more effective. When he was satisfied with her appearance, he rose and ordered her to follow him.

Juliette, forcing her legs and body not to shake, followed her Master into Hassan's courtyard. She nearly stumbled when she saw that the entire household had been summoned to watch her penance. She had only asked that

151

her three friends were there! Her ordeal was going to be much worse than she suspected. The next thing she noticed was that the whipping post, to which she expected to stand, had been removed and a strange contraption put in its place. What was it? What was it there for? She felt panic grip her stomach. She was relieved when Lord Charles reached the dais at the end of the yard and she could drop to her knees in front of him.

Lord Charles rose and addressed the gathering as silence filled the yard. "The slave, Juliette, has something she wishes to say," he announced, and then looked down at the kneeling figure. "You may now speak, slave."

Juliette rose and turned to face the spectators. She saw her three friends in the front, looking at her with a mixture of dislike and puzzlement on their faces. She took a deep breath and began the speech she had been considering all morning.

"My Master has graciously given me permission to speak to you," she began, looking over the top of her veil at her friends and trying to speak clearly and loud and stop her voice from trembling. "I am guilty of a very serious offence, not against my Master, but against my sister slaves."

A murmur of surprise buzzed through the gathering as the slave paused to gather her nerve.

"During the last two weeks, as you must know, my sister slaves had been summoned to this yard for punishment. Because I had previously been negligent in my duties as First Girl, I had allowed them to become lax and was ordered by my Master to tighten up on them. Had I been as diligent as I should have been, this would have not been necessary. The order was given by my Master instead of punishing me for my negligence, and I carried it out, even to the extent of inventing faults so that they would be punished."

Again Juliette paused for breath and to collect her thoughts. It wasn't sounding as she had meant it to be and she shivered at the murmur of anger that had come from her audience.

"My friends have suffered greatly because of my failure and the falsehoods I told against them. For this I am truly sorry. As a sign of the sincerity of my repentance and deep regret at the suffering I have caused my friends, I have asked my Master to have me soundly whipped. He has graciously agreed to this and also to my request that my atonement be done in public. I humbly beg my friends' forgiveness." She turned to look at Lord Charles and dropped to her knees. "Master. Please give the necessary orders."

"Stand and face the gathering, and strip," growled Lord Charles.

The die was cast! There was now no going back! Juliette rose and faced the audience. Slowly, striving to control her trembling fingers she discarded the costume and jewellery. She stood naked, struggling to conceal any sign of the terror that had enwrapped her now that the time had come.

Lord Charles rose and stood at her side. "To dispel any doubts in your minds." His voice carried clear to all in the yard. "I confirm that what is to happen now is done entirely at the slave's request." He paused for a moment to let this sink in. "The slave has asked for thirty lashes of the whip." He looked round until he saw his head groom. "Quinell, proceed with my instructions."

"Yes my Lord," Quinell said, stepping forward and taking hold of Juliette's arm.

Juliette was marched to the centre of the yard and, able to get a good view, she saw that the strange object she had seen earlier was, in fact a very large wheel. Quinell ordered her to stand on the rim, her feet wide apart. He tied her ankles to the rim and to a spoke. Not waiting for the expected order, Juliette stretched her arms up and outwards and gripped the rim. Quinell bound her wrists to the rim and a spoke. The slave's pale white body was well spread on the wheel. Her hair was pulled forward over her breasts and quickly twisted into two plaits and tied in a knot under her chin. Juliette was wondering why the whipping post had been replaced by the wheel when her nerves received another shock. Taking care to ensure it was securely fixed, Quinell attached a thick leather band to the wheel so that it covered her from her waist to the middle of her thighs. Juliette wondered why this was necessary since she was to be whipped across her back. The mystery deepened when a similar band was attached to the wheel, covering her head and neck. She felt her body begin to shake violently as she saw Hassan approach. In his hand was not the Girl Slave Whip that she had asked to be used but a much more terrifying one. She saw that it consisted of a heavy handle from which hung several plaited lashes, each some four feet long. Hassan was shaking the thongs loose as he approached.

The giant passed behind her and out of her sight. She heard a gasp from the audience. It was fortunate for her that she could not see behind her. Hassan had stopped and carefully judged his position and stared hard at the girl strapped to the wheel. He nodded his head and Quinell tied a cloth over his eyes, blindfolding him. Quinell nodded to two hefty men who were standing nearby. They walked to the contraption on the far side of the wheel and took hold of two handles. To Juliette's horror the wheel began to rotate slowly, a sharp creaking sound breaking the silence that had fallen in the yard.

"Proceed, Hassan," she heard Quinell command. "Thirty lashes, laid on hard, as the Master ordered."

Due to the creaking of the wheel, Juliette did not hear the sound of the thongs approaching. The first stroke landed across the centre of her back and shoulders, driving the air from her lungs in a loud 'whoosh' choking back the scream that formed in her throat. The second came as she was upside down, the thongs lashing across her thighs and some of the ends curling under and landing on her sex lips. A loud agonised scream followed the report of the stroke round the yard. Juliette struggled against her bonds as lines of fire erupted in her thighs and between her wide spread legs.

Allowing a short pause between each stroke as he shook the thongs loose. Hassan rained stroke after stroke down on the spinning girl. He was used to the slaves screaming under punishment but he was a little startled that this one had begun to scream so soon. Nevertheless, he continued to apply the whip as the Master had ordered.

Although she was aware that the wheel was spinning slowly, Juliette had not given much significance to this, especially when the first stroke landed, as expected, on her back. She was stunned, however, when the second stroke landed on her thighs and sex. The excruciating pain sent her into a blind panic making her lose the control she had fought so hard to summon up. Due to the cover over her head, she was unable to see Hassan, so she was oblivious to the fact that he could not see where the strokes were landing. Other than her buttocks and head, no part of the slave escaped the thongs. Her back and thighs bore most of the strokes although some landed on her arms, hands, legs and feet. Her whole body was on fire! Several times the thongs sought out, and found, her sex lips wringing an even louder and shriller scream from her open mouth. Her young body twisted and writhed on the wheel, so much so that, half way through the flogging the wheel had to be stopped and her waist tied to the spokes.

Juliette had asked for thirty lashes, but she hadn't realised the unbearable torment to which she had sentenced her soft body. The one thing she was determined she must, on no account, do was to scream for mercy. Come what may, she must endure the full flogging. So great was her concentration on this, and the terrible pain, that she lost count of the strokes after the tenth. Neither was she aware that, twice during the flogging, Quinell had to halt the proceedings while a bucket of cold water was thrown over her head to bring her back to consciousness. Her whole body seemed to be on fire, wave after wave of exquisite agony soaring through her. The arousal that had been lurking around during the morning and which had come to life as she entered the yard, had soared, time and time again, only just being held in check by her determination that she would not allow herself to orgasm during this particular beating. The tips of the thongs cutting across her open sex and breasts had not helped!

At last, through the fog of pain that had engulfed her, Juliette realised that the wheel had stopped spinning. The metal plates were removed first, then the straps that had held her ankles in place. Then her wrists were released and she sank to the ground, a writhing sobbing heap, mewing her agony to the sand that was wet where her sweat and tears had fallen. She felt Quinell gently take her arms and raise her to her feet and guide her to where her Master sat. He took his hands away and, somehow, she stood, bent over in pain and looked up at her Master through tear filled eyes. She saw him nod his head and slowly turned to face the stunned spectators.

"I thank my Master for my whipping." She concentrated all her remaining strength and courage to keep on her feet and make her voice loud enough to be heard. But she could not stop the stammering and wincing as wave after wave of pain still shot through her body. "I hope that, should he see fit to keep me as Fist Girl, I will fulfil my duties properly in future. Most of all, I hope that the whipping I have just received will suffice to earn the forgiveness of those who suffered because of my negligence."

She just managed to utter the final words before she crumpled to the floor. At a signal from Lord Charles, Aylena stepped forward and held some pungent substance under nose and wiped her face with a cold cloth. Gradually she managed to pull herself together and turned and knelt before her master.

She hoped he would allow her to leave the yard quickly. She urgently needed Aylena's attention to make it possible for her to move more easily before continuing with her duties. For once she would not mind being naked, as even the touch of the flimsy working shift on her body would, she was sure, be agony.

Lord Charles had watched the whipping intently. He had seldom seen a young girl take such a severe whipping and make such a quick recovery. He looked down on his kneeling slave with a feeling of pride that he owned such a creature. Strangely, he felt a tinge of pity for this young tender body that he had enjoyed so often. He had not failed to see that she had still been aroused, even under such a hard ordeal, yet had managed to control the orgasm even through pain that must have numbed her brain. He mentally pulled himself together. This would not do! Feeling sympathy for a slave! She was, after all, only an animal! He pulled his mind back to the matter in hand. He still had his plan to cure her from enjoying being beaten. He rose and addressed the audience, who were expecting to be dismissed.

"You have all seen the slave receive the whipping she requested." His voice stilled the gathering. "Whether this was sufficient to earn the forgiveness of the other slaves, I leave it to those concerned to decide." He paused for a second or two. "She will continue to be First Girl but, by her own admission she not only abused that position but also brought false accusations to me, causing me to make unfair judgements. She must be taught that lying to her Master is a very serious offence and will not be tolerated. As a lesson to her, and to you all, she will now be punished for that offence." He looked down at the kneeling girl, who was shaking visibly, her eyes open in utter disbelief that she was to be punished further. "For her offence, she is to receive the spirit treatment, her buttocks having first been prepared by twenty strokes of the switch. This punishment will be carried out immediately. Proceed, Quinell."

Juliette knelt, rooted to the spot in terror. That she was to be flogged again was bad enough, but he had mentioned the spirits. What was it that Aylena had said in answer to her question? 'Pray that he does not!' She had not believed the answer to the question, believing that no man could inflict such cruelty on the soft body of a young girl, even if she was just a slave. Now she was to find out that she was wrong, the hard way! And it was her young tender body that was to prove her wrong! Out of the corner of her eye, she saw Aylena leave the yard, a very concerned expression on her face. Her mind was in a terrible turmoil. Her body blazed with the weals left by the thongs. She had asked for the whipping both to earn the forgiveness of her friends and

157

to pay for her failure to serve her Master properly. He had agreed to this, as she had thought, but he had played her false. The whipping had not, as she had thought, also atoned for her offence against him. Now she was to receive yet another thrashing, followed by the spirits, as he said, for lying to him. It was not fair! Not justice!

She felt her arms seized and she was pulled to her feet, shaking and facing her Master. Aylena, who had returned, held a goblet out to her.

"Drink this, child," the woman said softly.

"What is it?" Juliette asked, no longer caring that she had spoken without permission.

"It is a potion that will ensure that you remain conscious and will hold back any sexual stimulation the pain may arouse," Aylena said. "Drink it down quickly. I am sorry my child." She added the last in a whisper that only Juliette heard.

Not only was she to be beaten again, but her Master was ensuring that she had no distractions or unconsciousness to detract from the pain that would be inflicted on her! And she had, at times, thought of him as a fair and tender man! How mistaken she had been! No longer caring what happened to her, she took the goblet and drank down the potion.

"Proceed with the punishment," Lord Charles commanded.

Quinell turned her to face the centre of the yard. Hassan stood there waiting for her, the longest and thinnest switch she had ever seen in his hand. She felt her legs go weak with terror. She felt Quinell's hand on her arm and shrugged it off. She turned her head and looked at her Master, sheer hatred blazing in her eyes, then turned back to face the beams. She could not avoid what was about to be done to her, but she would not let him have the satisfaction of hearing her beg for mercy. Slowly, Quinell following a pace or two behind her, the doomed girl walked to the beams. She halted when the narrow one pressed against her mound and slowly bent over, laying her shoulders and arms along the longer one.

"No! Bend over double, slave!" she heard Quinell order.

She hesitated, unable to believe what she had heard. In doing so she would stretch her poor buttocks to the limit and the thin switch that Hassan held would cut into her like a knife!

"Bend, child," she heard Quinell whisper gently in her ear. "Get it over with quickly."

Shaking her head in utter disbelief that she had heard right, Juliette ducked under the beam and reached backwards until her face was almost touching the upright over which she was bent. Her legs were pulled wide apart and roped to the iron rings, then her wrists were tied to the same rings. The position made the weals on her body hurt more than ever as they were put under the tension of her strained muscles. She tried to stop her legs shaking, and failed. Doubled as she was, her buttocks were stretched extra taut. In her mind's eye, she saw the switch, with which she was to be beaten. It would cut, she thought, leaving lines of raw flesh for the spirits to enter and do their worst. She no longer had any doubt in her mind as what the spirits were and their purpose. She nearly let out a terrible scream of terror.

Crack.

The report of the switch striking her bottom was followed immediately by a terrible scream from the bent slave. Nine more times Hassan flayed the writhing buttocks with the switch, each stroke sounding loud as the crowd watched in stunned silence, seeing the bright red lines left each time it struck. The slave's screams made them shudder as they tried to understand the terrible agony she was enduring.

The potion was certainly working! The pain was unbearable and she did not even have the solace of an arousal to ease her suffering. For the first time under punishment, Juliette prayed fervently for unconsciousness to descend on her and release her from the agony she was suffering. But it did not, and would not, come! She writhed and squirmed so much that, after the tenth stroke, Quinell halted the proceedings while he tightened a strap round her waist and the beam. Now her bottom was held immobile. Completely submerged in a dense fog of excruciating pain, Juliette's head jerked violently from side to side each time the switch wrapped round her taut cheeks. She could no longer scream and only a loud moaning and mewing, lie a beaten dog, could be heard following the sharp report of each stroke. Her body was drenched in sweat that, with her tears, dripped to the ground.

Juliette was unaware of the number of strokes she had received and only realised that the thrashing was over when the switch no longer cut into her bottom. Her limbs were released and she sank to the ground, clutching tightly to the base of the post over which she had been bent. It took two strong men to prise her grip away and pull her to her feet. She was half dragged, half carried back to stand before her Master. As the tears cleared from her eyes, she saw that a long padded bench had been put in front of the dais. The two men lifted her onto the bench and stretched her body along its length. Straps were tightened round her ankles, thighs, waist and back. Her wrists were tied to the front legs of the bench. Juliette looked up in time to see Aylena approach. A flagon and cloth in her hands. She knelt beside the trussed slave.

"Forgive me, child," she whispered.

Looking back over her shoulder, Juliette saw tears in the woman's eyes as she removed the stopper from the flagon. Not knowing what to expect, other than more terrible pain, Juliette looked away and gripped the legs of the bench as tightly as she could with her small hands. She felt a welcome coldness in her buttocks as the woman wiped the damp cloth over her bleeding cheeks. Then she felt the liquid poured slowly over her buttocks. For a moment nothing! Then the most searing pain coursed through her cheeks as the spirit seeped into the cuts made by the switch. Not even the severest beating she could have imagined would have prepared her for the torture inflicted by the spirit. She lost all sense of reason. She screamed terribly, yelling her hatred of her Master and every man living.

It was the first time anyone in the audience, except

Aylena, had ever seen the spirits used. As soon as Lord Charles had left, they drifted out of the yard, the slave's screams ringing in their ears and following them as they dispersed to continue with their work. At the Master's orders Juliette was to be left there for an hour, strapped to the bench, whilst the spirit inflicted the remainder of her punishment. It was sometime before the sounds of her suffering died down, as exhaustion over came her strength to scream.

When Maya and Sarita came to release her an hour later, she was mewing quietly, her body jerking spasmodically as the spirit continued to burn in the cuts. They gently released her bonds and eased her to her feet. The slave's body was covered in a mass of weals where the whip had struck and the girls had difficulty in holding her without touching them. They assisted her back to the kitchen where Aylena awaited, ready to administer to the punished slave's body. They laid her down on the couch where Moona set about putting the cream on the weals left by the whip. Aylena insisted on dealing with the girl's bottom. This was in a terrible mess, covered in a thin film of blood, her sweat and the sprits. They worked in silence, broken only by the low moaning of the girl when they touched the worst and most painful areas. They, even Aylena, were horrified at the barbarity, as they thought, of the second beating. It was something they would not have wished even on their worst enemy.

Slowly, Juliette recovered enough of her senses to take notice of what was going on around her. She looked at her three friends.

"I am truly sorry," she said. "Can you ever forgive me?"

"Of course you are forgiven," they said together, wanting to hug and cuddle her but frightened to even touch her in case they hurt her more.

"Will I be scarred?" Juliette asked, looking at Aylena.

"No, my child," Aylena reassured her. "The punishment was very severe and your body is badly marked. The weals from the whip have not broken the skin and the cream will soon make them disappear. Hassan applied the switch with just enough force to make shallow cuts. Those will heal perfectly without trace."

"I wish I could believe you," Juliette said, a shudder passing over her throbbing body. "It feels as if I have been cut to the bone."

"Just trust me, child," Aylena said.

The intensity of the woman's reply surprised Juliette and, before she realised it, she asked. "How can you be so certain?"

"I was a slave before Lord Charles found me and brought me to his country. I, too, have had the spirits used on me, several times. I am afraid I was not a good slave. The burning will continue for a day but, after that, you will feel just the same as if you had just had an ordinary caning."

The confession answered many questions that had been buzzing around in Juliette's mind for some time. It explained the woman's gentleness, kindness and her concern for any of the slaves who had been beaten.

"Knowing what it is like, I should be asking your forgiveness for putting the spirits on your poor bottom," Aylena continued.

"There is nothing to forgive," Juliette responded. "You were only obeying the Master's orders. It is he that should be begging my forgiveness, not you."

"Hush, child!" Aylena admonished quietly. "Talk like that could earn you another beating."

"He can have me beaten as much as he likes," Juliette said angrily. "I will never be a true slave to him now. The switching and spirits were not in our agreement. He betrayed me!"

"Hush, hush, child," Aylena said a little sternly, alarmed at the venom with which the girl had spoken. "You may have got used to being beaten and can take it well. What worries me though, is just how many can you take before your mind suffers. I have seen girls go mad when their brain could take no more!"

"I can take whatever he wishes," Juliette hissed. "He will break my body before he breaks my determination never to give in to him. I have learned to hate him this morning, more than I ever thought I could hate anybody."

Aylena, deciding against pursuing the topic further, worked on in silence. Once she thought Juliette had sufficiently recovered, she let the girl rise and continue her work. Having washed and made herself presentable, Juliette did, in fact, feel better. She went about naked for the rest of the day and was pleased when the other servants, instead of ignoring her, were very pleasant, wishing her well and hoping she recovered from her ordeal quickly. The one exception was Mehmet who, no longer satisfied at merely looking at the marks on her body, insisted in running his podgy fingers all over the weals.

Whilst outwardly calm, Juliette continued to seethe inwardly. Any affection she might have nurtured for her Master had been driven out of her by the switching. During the course of those few hours in the yard, she had writhed under the whip willingly to earn her friend's forgiveness, but his order for her to be beaten with the switch, followed by the torture of the spirits had ruined his image in her eyes. It had proved to her that the tenderness he sometimes showed to her was merely a sham. He was a fraud and, if she was to accept any man as her master, it would not be one who practised such deceits on his slave.

Contrary to what she had believed at the time, Aylena's prognosis on her condition proved right. The evidence of the whipping soon disappeared due to the magical qualities of the cream. It was some time later that her buttocks healed completely. Looking at her backside in the mirror, she was thankful to see that her cheeks had reverted to their original pale smoothness and no marks of the switching remained.

It was wonderful that her friends had not only forgiven her but, from that terrible morning on, applied themselves conscientiously to their duties. Consequently, although Mehmet did manage to find a few minor faults, which only resulted in mild beatings from Hassan, the girls escaped any major thrashings for some considerable time. Juliette was still ordered to dance for her Master and serve him in bed but she now obeyed, not because it pleased her to do so, but merely to spare her back and bottom from pain.

CHAPTER 8.

It was on one sunny afternoon as Juliette and her two friends were walking in the garden when Mehmet came rushing up to them and, gasping for breath, ordered Juliette to find Moona and for the pair of them to report immediately to the Master's study.

The two slaves knelt before their Master's desk, wondering on the reason for the summons and scared that it would result in a unpleasant interlude in Hassan's yard. Lord Charles was busy with papers on his desk and it was some minutes before he looked up and told them the reason for the summons. The two slaves listened to him in a stunned silence.

They learned that their Master intended to make a trip abroad to visit one of the strangely dressed guests for whom the girls had danced that evening some months ago. He was to take a small entourage with him, which was to include the two slaves. Quinell was also to come, not to ensure they did not attempt an escape, he told them, but to protect them during the journey. They were to depart in two day's time. That they might need protection filled the girls with alarm. Such concern for a slave's safety seemed out of character and they put it down to the fact that Lord Charles was concerned that someone might try and steal them from him.

The household was alive with the preparations for the journey and the slave's were kept busy. Sarita and Maya were very frightened as the learned that both Mehmet and Hassan were to stay behind. The thought of being left in the old lecher's control filled them with alarm. The morning of departure arrived and, after a tearful farewell of their friends, the two slaves who were to go were taken down to the main hall. Their wrists were manacled together and their ankles fettered with manacles with a short chain joining them. Long black cloaks with large hoods, with gauze panels in the front, were put over their dancing costumes. They were then taken outside and put into a cart with the luggage.

They travelled like this for two days until they arrived at the major port for the island. Here they embarked on a large ship with one main mast and rows of cannon on the deck and, lower down, rows of long heavy oars protruded from the sides. There was a lot of activity on deck as the captain prepared to set sail and, just before they were ushered below, Juliette noticed that, inboard, there were many half naked men sitting on benches and chained to the oars. They were, Juliette assumed, criminals who had been sentenced to the galleys for their crimes. The two slaves were locked in a small cabin and the ship soon got under way to the sound of the captain's shouted orders and the oar-master's whip encouraging the rowers to greater efforts.

The two girls were kept locked in the cabin for the whole of the journey, only being allowed up on deck for short periods to exercise and, even then, they were behind large awnings that kept them out of sight of the crew. On the seventh day they felt the motion of the ship slow down and heard the sounds of strange voices and activity, both on and off the ship. They correctly assumed that they had arrived at the destination port. Once more they were confined in the manacles and enshrouded in the cloaks and hoods and led down the gangplank to the dockside, where they were again bundled into a cart with the luggage. Quinell climbed onto the cart and they set off behind the coach in which their Master travelled. Looking through their gauze panels, the girls were amazed. The buildings were very strange in design and the people they saw wore strange clothes. Some, obviously the wealthier ones, were dressed like the three strangers who had visited Lord Charles some months before.

Soon the buildings gave way to a sea of sand from which the sun's rays seemed to give off a burning heat. Juliette felt stifled under the cloak but realised that was preferable to being exposed to the searing heat of the sun on her body. The desert seemed to stretch for ever and it was with some relief that they saw signs of human habitation in the distance. As they approached, they saw a small town surrounded by a high stone wall. They passed through an open gate and along a dusty street with the same strange looking buildings on each side. Some of the buildings were open-fronted and they could see merchants bargaining with customers over their wares. The buildings gave way to open land as the cart began to mount a rise at the top of which was another high wall with heavy wooden gates. At their approach the gates opened and the caravan passed through. The girls gasped in amazement. Instead of dusty sand, they looked out on well tended green lawns with flower beds filled with a blaze of colour from many exotic flowers. The air was filled with a delicious mixture of their scent.

The procession came to a large rambling building and halted. An imposing looking figure came out of the building and ran down the flight of stone steps and took the reins of the coach, bringing it to a halt. As the cart in which they were sitting passed the coach and turned into an arch in the building they heard a shout of welcome. Juliette turned her head just in time to see another man coming out of the building. She recognised him as one of the strange visitors to her Master's residence a few months ago. The one she had served on their last night. The one who had been the most demanding.

The cart went through the archway and proceeded along the side of the building, eventually coming to a halt outside a heavy wooden door. The door opened and a huge black man, naked from the waists up emerged, followed by another. They greeted Quinell and he ordered the girls to alight from the cart. Whilst one of the men began unloading the cart, the other beckoned the girls follow him into the building. They followed him along a long corridor and out through a door into a beautiful garden. They were not given any chance to stand and admire the perfect lawns and colourful flowerbeds. The huge black followed a path across the garden and through yet another door. This led into a large hall on the opposite side of which was a metal studded door either side of which stood two heavily built men with fierce looking light brown faces. They were dressed in some sort of uniform and held wicked looking curved swords across their chests. Their escort knocked on the door. A spy hole opened and they were inspected from within and then the door was opened and the black led them through.

They were in another large hall from which several doors led off. They were ushered through one of these into a luxurious washroom where they saw a large sunken bath, filled with hot water. Their escort ordered them to strip and bathe. The two quickly obeyed and were soon immersed in the bath enjoying the luxury of the hot water and washing the dust and fatigue of the journey from their bodies. Under the eyes of the black, they splashed around for a while until another man entered the room. He was even bigger and blacker than the first. In a voice that brooked no disobedience, he ordered them to emerge from the bath and dry themselves. Standing in front of these men made Juliette feel nervous. They were too large and imposing, this one in particular, whose baggy trousers and embroidered waistcoat was clearly of better quality than the first's, and she felt so small and vulnerable.

"I am Abdul," the new arrival informed them. "I am the Chief Eunuch."

His high-pitched voice seemed utterly out of character with his huge build and Juliette only just managed to conceal a snigger. His demeanour immediately told her that this man was accustomed to being obeyed. Although he had no jurisdiction over them, she thought it prudent not to upset him. He might report them to their Master, who would surely punish them on their return home. Any thoughts along these lines were quickly dispelled as the man continued to address them in his stern voice.

"Lord Charles' orders are that you be kept in the harem during his stay, under my orders. You will obey me, and my assistants, without hesitation or question."

Both girls were taken aback at his announcement. "What do we call you?" Moona asked, bringing a deep frown to his face.

"You are slaves and you will address me, and my assistants, as 'Sir'," he said with a hint of anger in his tone. "You will kneel when any one of us speaks to you. You will not speak unless spoken to. If you wish to speak to us, you will kneel first and then ask permission to do so."

The two girls looked at each other. It dawned on them that their stay there was not going to be the pleasant holiday they had thought. They were not to be treated as guests but as slaves. They had both read stories, and heard tales, of life in a harem and began to shiver with fear.

"Follow me," the man ordered.

"But we are naked!" Juliette said, rather more aggressively than she intended. "Where are our clothes?"

The black turned on them with a look of thunder on his face. "You will get them back when the Master orders and not until." As he spoke he took a thin book from a pocket in his trousers and made a note in it.

Juliette felt the colour drain from her face. Had she just earned herself a punishment? The black turned his back to them and strode out of the room. Trotting to keep up with him, the two followed.

They re-crossed the hall and, as she did so, Juliette quickly gazed around. The style and decorations seemed very familiar. Then she remembered the changes Lord Charles had made to his mansion. So this is where he got his ideas from, she thought. Through the door, they entered yet another delightful garden. The green lawns and brightly coloured flowers set off beautifully the fountains playing in the sunlight. On three sides of the garden were cloisters offering shade from the hot sun behind which were either high buildings or just plain walls. The fourth side had a long cloister on marble pillars, offering a cool shaded area to the garden. In this wall was a door and it was through this that the eunuch led the two slaves.

The sight that met their eyes as they entered a very large, luxuriously decorated, room made them gasp with surprise. One side of the room was open and beyond they could see yet another beautiful garden. Scattered round the room and garden were low divans and huge cushions on which reclined numerous naked girls. They were all young and very beautiful and seemed, by their appearance, to come from many different countries. They were all staring at the two newcomers with inscrutable looks on their faces.

The chief eunuch looked round and called out, "Suki."

An olive skinned beauty rose from one of the divans and, taking short steps, hurried across the room and sank to her knees before the giant.

"These two slaves are called Juliette and Moona. They are the property of your Master's guest and will remain in the harem during his stay. You will be responsible for them."

"Yes, Sir," the girl replied. The newcomers did not fail to notice the submissiveness of her voice. As the eunuch turned and marched back out of the room, the girl rose to her feet and smiled sweetly at the two new arrivals.

"I am Suki," she said, her voice no longer submissive but soft and seductively husky. "I am the senior girl in the harem. I am responsible for seeing that all the others behave properly. Abdul is very strict and we have to be very careful. I try and keep the girls out of trouble," she added, winking her eye at them.

Suki proceeded to show them around the various rooms and gardens that comprised the harem quarters. As they went round, they saw one or two blacks, dressed like the first man they had seen. Suki said these were young trainee eunuchs who watched over the girls to see that they obeyed the rules. Each had the symbol of their authority hanging from the belts at their waists. A long thin cane! Seeing her charges shiver, Suki explained that the canes were merely symbolic. The eunuchs were not allowed to use them. They were carried by the eunuchs to remind the girls of the fate that awaited them if they stepped out of line. They passed from one room to another, all beautifully decorated, as Suki explained the rules of the harem, and were introduced to the girls who, now realising they were not competitors for the Master's favours, greeted them in a friendly manner.

To the two girls, the place looked idyllic. A veritable Garden of Eden! That was until they came to a door which Suki passed quickly without opening it. That, she said, led to the punishment room. A room to be avoided at all costs! This was brought home to them as they passed an alcove where a naked girl lay stretched out on her stomach. Suki whispered that the girl had been punished that morning. Juliette did not see the signs of any beating on the girl's back or buttocks and was about to question her guide when she noticed the girl's feet. The soles of both were raw. As soon as they were out of the poor girl's hearing, Suki explained that the girl had tripped and stepped on a flowerbed, crushing some of the blooms. She had been sentenced to the bastinado. Twenty strokes of a thin cane across the soles of her feet, to teach her to be more careful in the future! It would be a week, at least, before the girl could walk comfortably. The tour of the harem completed, Suki led them back to the main room where the other slaves had settled down again. The apparent lack of activity made Juliette ask when they did any work. Suki laughed at this, explaining that they did not do any work. They were there solely to serve the Master's requirements!

The day passed slowly until, in the evening one of the eunuchs brought their costumes, which had been carefully washed, and ordered them to dress. Then, Juliette and Moona were taken from the harem to the host's banqueting hall and led to where their Master sat on a large cushion with a small table at his side. At his signal, they knelt on the other side of him. As some of the slave girls from the harem, all naked, served the men with food and drink, the two girls watched the entertainment in wonder and fascination. Acrobats and jugglers performed feats of surprising skill and were followed by a magician who had them spellbound with his tricks. After he had departed, there was a small hiatus, during which some men, carrying strange looking instruments, took up their position in a corner of the hall.

There was a clash of cymbals and six young slave girls rushed into the hall and fell to their knees, facing the diners. Juliette recognised them as girls she had been introduced to in the harem during the day. They were all dressed in matching flowing skirts and tiny boleros that hardly covered their breasts. The musicians struck up a weird sounding rhythm and the six girls rose to their feet and danced for their Master and his guest. Moona and Juliette thought they were quite good but these girls outshone anything they had ever dreamed of. Juliette, realising that she and Moona had been brought there for a purpose, watched the girls carefully, trying to remember as much of their movements as she could. After being allowed to watch this display, she was sure her Master would expect a much-improved performance from her when she next danced for him.

After a while, the slaves' dance ended and they sank to their knees in a wide circle around the edge of the hall. Again the musicians struck up and there was movement at the other end of the hall. Suki, dressed only in a number of veils hung from her body and head under which she was clearly naked, came spinning across the hall and fell to her knees before her Master. More movement at the other end of the hall and Abdul, holding a whip with a long lash, strode onto the floor. At a signal from the host, he cracked the whip loudly along the floor. This was the signal for the musicians to play. Slowly and seductively, Suki began to sway to the rhythm. If the other six had seemed perfect, their performance was poor compared with the lithe girl who now danced around the room. After a while, the tempo of the music changed and Suki's movements became more provocative. She really was superb and Juliette, glancing sideways at her Master, was not surprised to see his eyes glued to the girl.

Suddenly Abdul, who had remained as still as a statue so far, raised his arm. The lash sped through the air and, as a loud 'crack' echoed above the music, one of Suki's veils fell to the floor. During the next five minutes, one by one, the girl's veils were whipped from her body, gradually exposing more and more of her luscious charms to her audience. The last veil was swept aside as Suki stood in front of her Master, perfectly still except for the rapid undulating of her stomach. As the last veil floated away and the girl dropped to her knees panting heavily, Juliette was astounded to see that there was not one mark from the whip on her body.

The sight of Abdul lashing the whip at the girl's soft body had re-awakened Juliette's nightmare. Abaddon standing there, lashing at her body as she swung by her arms from a high beam, not to carefully sweep away filmy veils, but to cut into her tender flesh. She shivered at her mind's vision and shook her head to dispel the horror. Would she never rid her mind of that ogre and the threat he had so cruelly made to her so long ago?

Suki's dance was the finale to the entertainment and she and Abdul hurried from the room. One of the eunuchs escorted Juliette and Moona back to the harem and they settled down for the night. Due to the disturbed state of her nerves after the mental vision of Abaddon, Juliette found it hard to sleep. Under the watchful eye of the night eunuch, she wandered round the harem, careful not to disturb the other girls. It was thus that she noticed that Suki and another girl were missing. With no feeling of jealousy, she wondered which of the two was in her Master's bed, pandering to his needs. She also wondered whether she, Moona, or both of them would be ordered by their Master to their host's bed one night.

She and Moona were taken to the dining hall each night where they watched the entertainment, kneeling alongside their Master. During the day, being used to working even though their tasks were not onerous, the two found the enforced idleness hard to bear. They wandered round the rooms and gardens under the watchful eyes of one eunuch or another. Suki, sensing their restlessness and worried that they might get into trouble, started to give them dancing lessons. Fortunately their bodies were supple enough and they only required loosening exercises at the start of each lesson. Whether it was the relief from boredom or genuine interest, neither was sure, but they followed Suki's instructions and advise carefully and soon even they noticed an improvement in their skills. The other slaves, also grateful for the diversion, watched and applauded, encouraging the pupils to greater efforts.

One evening, at the end of the meal, instead of taking Juliette back to the harem quarters, the eunuch explained that her Master had ordered that she serve their host that night. She was led to a washroom where she was made to lie on a bench while an older woman depilated her body and then to bathe. Cosmetics were put on her face and nipples and her body sprayed with a subtle perfume. She was then led to a room in their host's suite. The eunuch handed her over to two others who took her into a room devoid of furniture other than a single divan to one side of the room. Juliette looked at the divan where she expected to serve the man and she also noticed a large rug in the centre of the floor. She was ordered to lay, face up, on the rug. Padded leather cuffs, attached to ropes hanging from pulleys in the ceiling, were secured round her wrists and ankles. She saw the ropes pulled taut until she was lifted about three feet from the floor. The ropes were looped round hooks and the eunuchs left the room, leaving her suspended in mid air, her body stretched rigidly horizontal and her legs spread wide apart, wondering what was about to happen. Whatever it was, she hoped it would happen soon, before her slight weight put too much strain on her limbs.

She heard the door open and let her head drop back so she could see. Everything was upside down but that didn't prevent her seeing the host enter, stark naked, his manhood already rising. She remembered that night, so long ago, when she had worried in case its thickness and length tore her open. Her eyes followed him as he walked round, ending up standing between her spread legs. Fear of his monstrous weapon tearing into her, caused her body to sag in a shallow 'V'. The movement did not go unnoticed by the man who called out loud in his own tongue. Two eunuchs rushed into the room. He spoke to them, again in his own tongue and they hurried from the room, only to return in a matter of seconds. They each carried a candlestick with a lighted candle flickering in the holder, which they placed on the floor immediately under Juliette's buttocks. She felt the heat of the flames and jerked her body up again.

She looked along her suspended body; saw the smile of satisfaction on the man's face. She shuddered as she saw that his penis was now fully erect, standing out thick and hard from his loins.

He edged closer to her and she felt the hard throbbing tip press against her sex lips as he leaned forward and began stroking her breasts. Her body immediately responded, her nipples growing hard and her sex damp with her juices, which began to seep from her. Slowly but surely, the man entered her until she could feel him in the deepest recesses of her body. Her muscles tightened around him in a vice like grip.

Already her arms and legs were aching with the strain on them. Each time that she allowed them to relax, her bottom sagged and the flames licked round her cheeks, forcing her to straighten up quickly, forcing the man's lance even deeper into her. This sent waves of delicious sensations coursing through her body until she became oblivious to all but the craving needs within her. The man continued to use her, not violently but slowly and thoroughly until she was moaning with the desires raging in her, fuelled by his possession and the repeated licking of the flames on her cheeks each time she let her body relax.

Suddenly he withdrew from her. He had not ejaculated and she quivered in terror in case he was not satisfied with her. He called out and the two eunuchs returned. To her relief they lowered her to the floor and removed the ropes from her limbs. The eunuchs ordered her to stand at the foot of the divan. They pulled her ankles apart and tied them to the legs. Obeying their orders, she bent over until her shoulders were pressing onto the surface. She nearly screamed in terror as they each held her pressed down with one hand and she felt their other hands on her cheeks, pulling them even wider apart. The arousal coursing through her body was dampened as she realised to her horror that her anus bud was now on full display to the man standing behind her.

She felt something hot touch her bud. She had to bite her lips hard to stifle the scream of horror, disgust and terror that formed in her throat. Surely he did not intend to use her there! Slowly he forced his entry sending sharp

175

spasms of agony through her passage. She tried to relax her muscles to ease the pain, not to fight against his possession. This was degrading, her brain screamed in her head, but she was serving her Master's host, under his orders and must, on pain of terrible retribution, please him. She had never in her life been used in this way before and her hatred of her Master for submitting her to this disgusting ordeal raged so strongly that she wanted to scream her hatred out loud. Only fear of the whip kept her silent! The man's momentum began to increase until, with a final searing plunge, he ejaculated his satisfaction deep inside her body.

The two eunuchs, who had witnessed her shaming, released her and turned her round and forced her to her knees. She saw the man's rod before her face, a drip of his secretion glistening in the distended slit. Choking back the sickening revulsion that blocked her throat, she opened her mouth and took the organ in. She felt nausea in her stomach when she tasted the flavour of his juices mixed with that of her own body. Knowing she had no choice, she licked him clean. She choked as an unexpected stream of his secretion shot against the back of her throat. She could not prevent a sliver of it from running down her chin before she forced herself to swallow, clearing the remainder from her mouth.

She was turned and laid on her back on the divan and the man dismissed the two eunuchs. He lay down beside her and she felt his hands lightly stroking over her body. Her breasts, stomach and sex tingled at the touch and she, despite her disgust at the way he had just treated her, responded to the caresses. He had already instilled his mastery over her and was now playing with her! Warm sensations surged through her as her body responded willingly to his attentions. She had never been made to feel this way before, not even on the rare occasions when her Master was kind and gentle with her. She wanted time to stand still so this bliss could last forever. Instinctively, against her mind's urging, she reached out for his manhood and began to stroke and tease it, feeling it grow and throb as she revived the life in it. All through the night, with short intervals for rest, he took his pleasure of her and, in return, sent her to the dizziest heights of passion, even permitting her to orgasm on several occasions, to her intense joy.

All too soon for Juliette, Abdul came to return her to the harem quarters. Juliette spent the day resting. In between short periods when she dozed, she relived the glorious experience of the previous night. She had, she hoped, served her Master's host well and her rewards had been ecstatic.

CHAPTER 9.

In all, Juliette and Moona spent four weeks confined in the harem. Had it not been for the lessons Suki regularly gave them, the two girls would have been terribly bored. A life of luxury is all very well but, even that, can become tedious. Due to the ever present watchful eunuchs, and the languid life style of the inmates, very few incidents of note occurred. In fact, only twice during their stay, did the two girls witness the application of harem discipline.

The first occurred one morning when Abdul, accompanied by several eunuchs suddenly descended on the harem and ushered all the girls out into one of the gardens. Here they were made to wait, under the guardianship of one of the eunuchs, while Abdul and the others disappeared inside the harem building. The slave girls all stood round waiting for permission to return to their tranquil existence.

"What is happening?" Juliette whispered to Suki.

"Abdul is carrying out one of his spot checks. He is looking to see if there are any forbidden things that have been smuggled in to us," Suki answered.

After what seemed an age, Abdul reappeared and stood scrutinising the girls carefully, looking for any signs of fear that might betray a guilty conscience. All but one of his minions came out and reported to him that they had not found anything. After a short pause the last appeared a smile of satisfaction on his face. He handed a small jar to Abdul, who scowled as he removed the lid and held it to his nose.

"Suki. Here," he commanded, his face red with anger.

Suki detached herself from the group and knelt at his feet.

"This jar contains honey," he announced, his high-pitched voice echoing round the garden. "This is forbidden. You will bring the offender to me within fifteen minutes." He signalled to his minions and marched away.

Suki, looking stunned and alarmed, rose and faced the slaves. "Whose jar was that?"

There was no reply.

"If the one who had that jar does not come forward and own up we shall all be punished. Abdul will expect me in fifteen minutes and if I do not take the offender with me there will be serious trouble. You all saw his anger. It will surely be the whip for all of us. Now, whose was it? If the culprit does not own up, I will have to ask each one of you if you know the owner."

Slowly, shaking with terror, one of the girls stepped forward. She was a petite Chinese girl, who had only been brought to the harem two weeks earlier.

"Su Lin," Suki gasped. "Where did you get it? Don't you know it is forbidden for us to have sweet things in the harem?"

"Please Suki," the girl said, falling to her knees and clutching at Suki's legs. "Please Suki don't let them punish me. My father gave it to me and I had it with me when I arrived. I didn't know it was forbidden. Please do not let them beat me."

"You will have to come with me to Abdul. I will try my best to make things as easy as possible for you. Just pray the Master is in a good mood."

Su Lin, casting a terrified glance at the other girls, followed Suki. A terrible silence fell over the harem as the girls returned to what they were doing before the search. After a while, Suki returned. Her eyes were red and the thin smock she had been wearing had disappeared. One hand was tentatively rubbing her behind.

"What ever happened?" Juliette asked.

"Abdul gave me twenty strokes of the cane for not checking the girl properly when she arrived. I got off lightly considering."

"What will happen to Su Lin?" Juliette asked, concern at her friend's suffering and the fate of the little Chinese girl etched on her face.

"She will be punished," Suki replied. "It is strictly forbidden for us to have sweet things. They are given to us only as special treats if we have been very good. I have pleaded with the Master and Abdul on her behalf.

179

Fortunately the Master was in a good mood, that's why I got off so lightly. We can only hope she does also."

Whether she was right or not was to be found out soon after the midday meal. One of the eunuchs came and escorted the slaves to the dreaded punishment room and ordered them to kneel, in line, along one wall. The Master, accompanied by Lord Charles, entered and took their seats at one end of the room. Soon a door opened and Abdul, followed by a naked Su Lin held between two eunuchs entered. The shaking girl was led to a tall thick post and ordered to sit with her back to it. A long metal bar was attached to each ankle, spreading her legs wide. Manacles, attached to a long rope suspended from a pulley at the top of the post, were attached to each ankle and the rope pulled tight until the girl hung suspended with her long black hair sweeping the floor. Her arms were pulled round the post and her wrists tied together.

Abdul stepped forward and looked at the kneeling slaves. "The slave, Su Lin," he announced in a loud voice. "Is guilty of possessing a forbidden luxury. The Master has ordered her to be whipped. Twenty-five lashes across her buttocks." He turned and checked the slave's bonds and nodded to one of his minions. The man stepped forward and handed Abdul the whip with which the unfortunate girl was to be punished. Abdul removed his jacket and handed it to the man.

Juliette, who like the others had been commanded to watch the punishment carefully, saw that the whip was unlike any she had seen before. From a thick handle two heavy, plaited thongs hung, about three feet long. Abdul took up his position behind the shuddering and weeping girl and turned to face the kneeling slaves.

"All will count the strokes out loud after each," he said. "This will remind you that disobedience will not be tolerated."

He raised the whip and brought it whistling down across the slave's buttocks. A terrible scream followed the sharp report. The slaves' count of 'one' followed the scream.

"It is the first time she has been punished," Suki

whispered to Juliette, as if to explain the slave's scream on the first stroke.

One by one, to the count of the slaves and a terrible scream from Su Lin, Abdul lashed the thongs across the writhing girl's bottom for the first ten strokes. It dawned on Juliette that, because the two thongs were landing slightly spaced apart, the girl was actually getting the equivalent of two strokes each time the whip descended.

"I hope she passes out," Juliette whispered to Suki, saddened at the pain the young girl was enduring, just for a small jar of honey.

"She will have been made to drink a potion to ensure she does not," Suki answered, to Juliette's horror.

The slaves continued to count as the slave's punishment was meted out. The girl writhed and twisted, trying to avoid the punishing thongs, her body dripping sweat. Her small bottom was terribly bruised by the time she had taken fifteen strokes and, from then on, the thongs rained down on previous weals. As the final ten strokes were applied, the girl had ceased screaming and writhing and only a low moaning and mewing showed that she was conscious. The volume of her moans, and the thud as her body was thrown against the post, sounded in the room as the slaves counted to the end of the slave's ordeal. Juliette was relieved as the thongs lashed the girl's blazing buttocks for the last time. Relief on behalf of the suffering girl, and for herself as she had felt her body's arousal at the flogging reaching towards the limit of her control. She would have been mortified if this had been noticed by Suki!

The slaves were escorted back to the harem while two eunuchs carried the flogged girl to her bed. Two slaves immediately set to work to ease the girl's suffering by applying cold towels to her burning bottom.

"Thank heavens our Master does not own a whip like that," Juliette whispered to Suki as they walked back together. "It must hurt terribly."

"Thankfully the Master was lenient with her. That whip is not as bad as the usual whip that is used," Suki said. "Su Lin got off very lightly, although she, the poor girl, probably does not realise it. If I had not successfully pleaded on her behalf, her back would have felt Abduls' bull whip, or even the dreaded sjambok."

"What on earth is that?" Juliette asked.

"It is a whip made out of rhinoceros hide. The Master got it from a country to the south. One single stroke of it can even cut a man's flesh to the bone."

"That is terrible," Juliette said horrified, just talking about it sent a shiver of terror down her spine. "Surely her offence was not bad enough to be flogged so severely."

"Disobedience is a very serious matter here," Suki said. "Anyone who is guilty can expect no mercy. The Master and Abdul will not tolerate disobedience of any sort. Even I, who am the Master's favourite, am not safe."

"But surely, as favourite, you would not be beaten as badly as the others?" Juliette asked.

"That's what you think," Suki said. "A few months ago, I disobeyed one of the junior eunuchs. I had thirty lashes with a horsewhip, ten of them across by breasts. I don't think I have screamed so much, before or since."

This revelation stunned Juliette so much that she remained silent until she was back in the harem.

The second incident took place a day or so before Juliette and Moona were due to leave for home. All the slaves were ordered to prepare for the monthly punishment parade. There was a bustle of activity in the harem as the girls quickly applied what ever cosmetics were necessary to their faces and put on a pair of gossamer trousers, a bolero jacked and a yashmak. As soon as they were ready they were escorted to a small hall and made to kneel along one wall. In the centre of the hall, a heavy padded stool had been bolted to the floor. Two chairs were arranged on a dais on the opposite side to the slaves. As soon as the slaves were settled, Abdul entered followed by Juliette's master and their host. The latter two settled on the chairs as Abdul stood to one side. Two of his minions had followed them in and stood behind Abdul. One held a long thin rattan cane in his hand and the other a thin switch. At a signal from their host, Abdul stepped forward, consulting a sheet of paper in his hands.

"You have been summoned here to atone for the black marks that you may have earned during the past four weeks," he announced. "The following slaves have earned no marks."

He called out six names. As each girl's name was called, she rose and walked round the stool and knelt in front of her master, facing into the room.

Abdul consulted the list. "The slave Jasmin, six marks."

One of the slaves rose to her feet and went and stood facing the stool. She slipped her trousers down to her ankles, took a step forward and bent over the stool, gripping the legs tight. One of the eunuchs walked forward and lashed his cane across the bared buttocks six stinging times. The girl remained still and silent except for a sharp hiss as she sucked in her breath each time the cane cut across her cheeks. After the last stroke, the weeping girl stood up, replaced her trousers and turned to face her Master.

"Thank you, Master, for my beating. I promise to do better in future," she said and returned to her place in line.

One by one, Abdul called out another ten names. Each time a girl rose and went to the stool and followed the same routine. All of them received between five and twelve strokes.

"The slave, Suki. Fifteen marks," Abdul announced.

Suki rose and walked round the stool and stood facing her Master. She removed each of the items of her costume and then took her place over the stool. Her wrists and ankles were secured to the legs. The other eunuch walked forward. Fifteen times the switch lashed across Suki's taut buttocks, She took four in silence, moaned on the next two and cried our on the rest. Her ordeal over, she returned to her position, leaving her garments in a heap on the floor. As she approached, she managed to give Juliette a weak smile, although tears flowed down her face.

The three remaining girls were called forward, one at a time. One had earned twenty marks, another eighteen and the last sixteen. As the last girl returned to her place in the line of weeping slaves, the host began to rise but was stopped when Lord Charles placed his hand on his arm. They whispered together for a few moments, then their host nodded in agreement.

Lord Charles looked across, over the stool, at the kneeling slaves. "The slave Moona," he said loudly. "Eight marks."

Both Moona and Juliette were astonished that her name had been called. They were aware of the marks system but had never imagined it would apply to them.

"The slave Moona, ten marks," Lord Charles repeated, his voice betraying his anger at the girl's hesitation and adding two marks for the delay.

Moona, not daring to delay further, rose and walked to the stool, dropped her trousers and bent over. The eunuch stepped forward and laid ten searing strokes of the cane across her bottom. Moona managed to retain her grip on the stool, although her buttocks writhed and she yelled on the sixth and subsequent strokes. She eased herself upright, turned a weeping face to her Master and thanked him for the caning and returned to her place.

Juliette was horrified when she had heard Moona summoned forward. There was no doubt in her mind that she would be next and she cringed at the thought. Watching the punishments had fuelled an arousal in her body and she was terrified that, when she was called forward the others would notice.

"The slave Juliette, sixteen marks," Lord Charles announced.

Juliette rose quickly, she didn't want to earn extra, as Moona had just done, for being dilatory. She stood in front of her Master and stripped and bent over the stool. As her ankles were secured, she felt relief that her legs were together and not facing the kneeling girls. She watched the eunuch approach, the switch in his hand, and braced herself. The switch lashed across her taut bottom sixteen times, rhythmically and hard. She managed to stay silent for six, yelled on the next four and screamed on the rest, fighting to restrain the arousal from becoming evident to the watchers. She dutifully thanked her master for the switching and returned to her place in line.

The punishments over, Lord Charles and his host rose and left the room. The slaves, those that were naked first recovering their clothes, were ushered back to the main hall of the harem. The girls paired off, rubbing soothing cream into each other's sore bottoms.

CHAPTER 10.

The morning of their departure arrived and Moona and Juliette bade a fond farewell to the friends they had made in the harem. Abdul came for them and they were again put into the black cloaks and hoods, with their wrists manacled together. Her took them to the door at the rear of the building where Quinell awaited, the cart already filled with the luggage. The cart moved round to the front of the building where Lord Charles was taking his leave of his host. Once they passed out through the gates, the pleasant gardens gave way to the desert. As they travelled along, the girls, now free from the watchful eyes and ears of the eunuchs, huddled together and talked in whispers.

"I am glad we are owned by Lord Charles and not by someone like Suki's Master," Juliette mused.

"Oh, I don't know," Moona said. "Just think. No more work. Just to spend one's time lazing around in those beautiful surroundings until called to serve the Master. It must be heaven."

"I don't think I would like it," Juliette said. "Just think of the terrible punishments they are given. Poor Su Lin will take weeks to recover and the other girl we saw first could not walk at all for a week. Did you get a close look at poor Su Lin's bottom?"

"Yes, I did. It wasn't such a bad whipping, considering," Moona said.

"Maybe not! But the thought of a horsewhip being used on me terrifies me. Heaven knows what that sjambok thing would be like. I think I would just die with fright before the first stroke landed."

Moona shuddered at the idea. "Well, perhaps you are right and we are not so badly off."

They fell silent, each lost in her thoughts. The journey to the ship was uneventful and they eventually arrived at the docks. The girls were immediately locked in their cabin and were relieved to get out of the stifling cloaks. The next morning they heard the sounds of the ship getting underway and the noise from the dockside gradually faded. As before, the girls were only allowed on deck for short periods and spent most of the time locked in the cabin.

During the third day at sea, they heard a terrible commotion on deck. Running footsteps everywhere and the oars master's shouts seemed to have an air of panic about them. This went on for some time, the rowers being exhorted to greater efforts by the overseer's whip. The ship seemed to be shooting over the water. For about a half-hour this went on until there was a violent thud against the side of the ship and it nearly keeled over. The noises on deck increased alarmingly and the sound of sword play filtered down to the girl's cabin. Eventually things quietened down and the two girls heard footsteps echo on the companion way and the door to their cabin opened.

"By Allah!" a deep voice exclaimed. "Look what we have here."

The owner of the voice was a fierce looking individual dressed in colourful strange garments. The thick gold ring in his ear swung dazzlingly in the sunlight that streamed in from the deck above. The two girls clung together in a corner of the cabin. The man was certainly not a member of the crew! An even fiercer man, who pushed him aside and marched into the cabin, joined the stranger. He looked at the girls and then at a piece of paper in his hands.

"Yes!" the man said eventually. "These are the ones. Cover them up and take them to our ship and lock them into a cabin."

"But capt'n," the first man said. "They are part of the ship's cargo and should be shared between the crew like everything else."

"They are the ones we were sent to get," the captain said, turning on the man in anger. "They are to be delivered to Balyan unharmed, or we will not get paid. Any man who lays so much as a finger on them will answer to me. I'll cut his balls off!"

The man obviously took heed of the threat. He made the girls put on the black cloaks and hoods and, wrapping a long chain round their necks, joining them together, he marched them up on deck. Looking through the gauze panel, Juliette saw Lord Charles, and most of the crew, huddled in a corner under guard. Another of the pirates, for that was what they were, was releasing the men from the oars. There were several dead, from both sides, lying around the deck. It must have been a fierce struggle before the pirates overcame the resistance. Moona and Juliette were swung across from one ship to another and taken below and locked in an evil smelling cabin. They had exchanged one prison for another!

As they cowered in the cabin, they heard the noise of cargo being transferred from one ship to another. Eventually the noise subsided and they felt the ship moving. Several days later they heard the sounds of the ship entering harbour then all motion stopped. The usual noises of the cargo being unloaded filtered down to them. They had been left alone since being taken on board, except when a man, under the close supervision of the captain, had come to bring them food and empty their waste bucket. On the one occasion when the man had come alone, they had tried to question him. Either he had been under strict orders not to speak to them, or he just didn't speak their language, so the girls received no answer to the frightening thoughts chasing round in their minds. They had hardly spoken, each being immersed in their own thoughts.

The door to the cabin was unlocked and thrown open and the captain marched in, accompanied by the man who had brought them aboard, and stood glowering at them. They were still dressed in their dancing costumes and his mouth watered at the thought of possessing their delicious bodies. For a moment he was tempted to keep them for himself, but the slaver, who was acting as the middleman, had hinted at the man on whose commission he was working. If he had worked it out right, that man was not one to cross. He was the one and only man the captain feared! Better hand the wenches over rather than get on the wrong side of the fellow. After all, there were plenty more women to fill the seraglio he was collecting for when he got too old for pirating.

"Kneel!" he shouted at the cowering females, his frustration putting an edge to his tongue.

Automatically, the two fell to their knees, lowering their heads to the floor. He smiled at their quick response. Yes, they would surely be a nice pair to own, he thought enviously.

"Permission to speak, Master?" Juliette asked, her inquisitiveness for their future overcoming her fear of the man.

"Speak, then if your must," he answered, his envy growing as he heard the soft submissiveness in the girl's seductive voice

"Please, Master," Juliette continued. "Where are we and what is to be done with us?"

"The where does not concern you," the captain answered gruffly. "As to what is to become of you, that you may know. You are to be taken to a slave dealer. He has a customer who, it seems, is particularly interested in owning you. In short, you are to become slaves."

The two girls shook with fear. The man might have answered Juliette's question, but he had made their agitation worse. Now they faced the riddle of whom this mysterious stranger was, who would dare attack Lord Charles' ship and abduct them from under his nose. Juliette, in particular was terrified. If she was to be passed through the hands of a slave dealer, she was merely changing one master for another, being traded about like an animal again. Just how many masters would own her body before she was released from the bonds of slavery? Just how many would she have to bow down to and serve with her young body? But, she knew in her heart that she would always be a slave. There would never be any release for her. The injustice had begun that day in the House of Correction when she had been flogged and her freedom so unfairly taken from her and she had been condemned to a life as a slave to any man who owned her.

The latent need had been awakened in her body and, as much as she cared to fight against it, she knew that slavery was the only way she could satisfy that need. Even if a

189

miracle should occur and she found herself free, she knew in her heart she would only seek out a man to enslave her again. One that would satisfy the needs in her and force her to submit to him and love him as a complete slave. She had, once, thought Lord Charles might be that man, but he had betrayed her trust that day when he had had her switched so cruelly and the spirits poured over her cut bottom.

"Bind and hood these two and take them to Baylan." The pirate captain's order to the two men who had followed him into the cabin disrupted her thoughts.

Hers and Moona's wrists were bound together and the hooded cloaks put over them. A manacle was put on each of their left ankles and joined to a length of chain. Thus hooded and hobbled, the men led them up on deck and onto the dockside. As they were led through the streets, Juliette looked around at the fierce men whom she passed, wondering if one of these was to be her master. Her apprehension grew steadily, enshrouding her in a sea of terror. Eventually they came to a heavy wooden door, set in a high windowless wall. One of the men knocked, responded to a challenge from within and, as the door opened, ushered them inside.

As the door closed with an ominous clang behind them, the cloaks were removed. The two girls stared at their surroundings in fear and astonishment. Fear, because standing in front of them was a huge black man. He was naked from the waist up, had a curled whip hanging at his waist and his muscular arms and chest rippled as he moved. His face was fearsome, made more so by the scars across both of his cheeks.

"These are the slaves your Master is expecting," one of her escort said. "Our captain expects prompt payment."

"Once it has been checked that these are the two, there will be no delay. Come back in two days time and, by then, the question will have been resolved." The black looked the pair up and down critically, assessing their value on a slave block. They were still wearing the dancing costumes in which they had set out a few days earlier and, due to the travelling, they did not look at their best. "I don't see what the man sees in them," the black finally commented. "We have had far better through our hands."

The men removed the manacles from the girls' ankles and wrists and departed, leaving the girls in charge of the black. The man's last comment had reawakened the panic that had, until then, begun to fade from Juliette's mind. Who was this mysterious stranger, who was going to so much trouble to get them in his power? The black walked slowly round them, muttering to himself in his own language in a tone of disgust. Finally he ordered them to follow him. Under his watchful eye, they removed their costume and lay on benches while an older woman depilated their bodies. Then they were ordered to bath and wash their bodies and hair thoroughly. Once they were dried, he led them down a flight of stone cells to the basement. All round the walls were metal barred cages with small doors. He unlocked the doors to two adjoining cells and ordered them to crawl through the small opening. He closed and locked the doors, leaving the girls alone.

Juliette looked round in disgust. The cages were no more than three feet high and wide and six feet deep. The girls had to remain on their hands and knees in the straw that covered the floor. A deep silence descended as the man closed the door at the top of the stairs. The other cages were empty and the two girls, left on their own, were too terrified to voice the questions that coursed through their minds. Eventually the silence was broken as another black man came down the stairs carrying two bowls, which he pushed through a space at the base of the cell door. It was, apparently, feeding time. The girls crawled to the dishes and a look of disgust passed over their faces as they saw the mess of gruel in the bowls. The gruel that had been dished up for Juliette in the kitchens at Lord Reythal's had been bad enough, but this was infinitely worse.

"Eat!" the man commanded, seeing their reaction. He emphasised his order by rattling the bars of the cages with a cane.

Too frightened by the implied threat to disobey, the two girls ate the mess. They just managed to keep it down. True,

191

they were hungry but the fodder tasted vile. It did, however, stave off the hunger pains that were making their stomachs rumble. When they had licked the dishes clean, they pushed them back through the space and the man collected them and disappeared up the stairs. The girls spent three days in the cells, only being allowed out for half an hour each day to wash and exercise. The cramped conditions made their backs and limbs ache. It was, therefore, a welcome relief when, after washing and exercising on the third day, they had only been back in the cells for two hours when the black who they had seen them the day that they arrived, came and ordered them to follow him. They crawled out of the low doors and, standing up, stretched their aching back and limbs.

"Kneel!" the black ordered angrily. When they had quickly obeyed, he waved his cane in front of their faces. "Slaves should know better," he ranted at them. "You show respect to all men. Remember this when you approach the Master. Now rise and follow me."

Casting frightened glances at each other, the two girls followed the man up the stone stairs into the passage above, through a door into a large room where baths of hot water stood ready. Two older women creamed and depilated their bodies and then, ordering them into the baths, proceeded to scrub them clean. Half an hour later, the two slaves stood, dried and clean but still naked as the black inspected them carefully. All signs of their travels and sojourn in the cells had disappeared and, if it was not for the unknown future ahead, they would have felt overjoyed to be clean and presentable again. When the black seemed satisfied, he again ordered them to follow him.

They soon found themselves in a large luxuriously furnished room where a huge, expensively dressed, fat man reclined on a couch. His fierce eyes watched them closely as they approached. The girls saw this and, remembering the black's warning, sank to their knees in front of the man.

"So, Yousef! These are the two our client has specifically asked for."

"Yes, Master," the black replied, wrinkling his nose in

disgust. "They are not up to the usual standard of your merchandise."

"True!" the fat man replied. "But they are what he is prepared to pay for! My spies tell me they are quite accomplished dancers. I would like to judge this for myself. If the rumour is right, I may increase the price. If he wants them as badly as I believe, he will pay. If not, I can always put them in the sale of second-class merchandise. There they will, at least, cover my expenses in capturing them." He looked down again at the kneeling slaves. "Take them away and prepare them. Then bring them back with the musicians and I will assess their value."

Yousef again ordered the girls to follow him. He took them to a preparation room where two younger girls waited. Soon Juliette and Moona were made up with cosmetics and perfumed and dressed in the same fashion as the dancers who had preceded Suki the evening she had performed the whip dance for her Master. Slave bands also decorated their upper arms and fine gold chains with tiny bells attached put round their ankles. Castanets were placed on their fingers. Juliette was grateful that Suki had taught them how and when to use these when dancing. They were then led back to the room where Baylan, the slave dealer, waited. As they again crossed the room, they did not fail to notice that there were three things that had not been there before. Several musicians had appeared and were seated in one corner. A trestle with a padded top had been placed in another corner and a long whippy cane lay on the floor at the slaver's feet. The sight of these last two additions to the room sent shivers of excitement and dread coursing through both slaves.

Baylan looked down at the slaves, now kneeling submissively before him. "You will dance," he said sternly. "If you do not please me you will be thrashed."

The two slaves quailed with fear. They had seen the dancers at their master's hosts that evening and knew they could no way match their standard. It seemed that a thrashing was inevitable! How good would this ogre expect them to be? They would soon find out, and probably in a painful manner. First Moona, then Juliette, was ordered to dance. Juliette watched as Moona twisted and turned seductively to the music and then her turn came and she tried to outshine her friend. Watching the trained dancers and Suki's lessons helped and both thought their performance better than any they had done before. The two knelt before the slaver, panting and waiting his verdict. It was a long time coming as the man thought carefully over what he had seen. At last he turned to Yousef and gave his verdict.

"Not too bad, Yousef," he said. "They have a lot to learn before I could classify them as trained dancers."

"You wish them trained, Master?" Yousef asked.

"No, Yousef," the man replied, shaking his head. "The cost would be too great. I will present them as partly trained, that should still be a good bargaining point and, hopefully, increase out client's desires enough to squeeze a thousand or so more dinars out of him."

"Please, Master," Moona broke into their conversation. "Please have us trained. We promise to learn fast and it will increase our value."

"Yes, please do, Master," Juliette added her plea. She hoped that improved skills would make their life easier with the man who wanted them so bad, whoever he might be.

"I understand," Baylan said, looking at Yousef, "that these wenches were already slaves before being captured by our pirate friends."

"Yes, Master. But only in their own country," Yousef replied.

"Then they should know better than to speak without permission. They need a reminder, Yousef. Let's see how well they can take a thrashing. Twelve strokes each." He pointed to Moona. "Her first!"

Yousef pulled the trestle into the centre of the room and looked at Moona. "Go and bend over, slave. Facing away from your Master."

Moona rose and walked to the trestle and bent over as ordered.

Yousef looked at Juliette. "Bring me the cane and then

bare the slave's behind."

Juliette picked up the cane. It seemed longer and thinner than the ones she was used to. Not for the first time, she wondered that such an inanimate object could come to life in the hands of a man and cause so much pain in a girl's bottom. She handed the cane to the black and walked over to Moona. Yousef had already clamped her wrists and ankles in place. As she stooped and lifted the girl's skirt up over her back, she noticed that the girl's thighs were twitching and her buttocks clenching and relaxing as they anticipated the kiss of the cane. Juliette felt her own nipples begin to harden and a tingling in her sex as she watched the black raise the cane high over his shoulder. Moona's knuckles turned white as she increased her grip on the trestle legs. The cane whistled through the air and landed with a resounding report across Moona's trembling cheeks. Her body jerked up on her toes as a loud hiss escaped her clenched teeth.

Juliette, to her amazement, watched Moona take four strokes in silence, her knuckles gleaming white as she gripped the legs as tight as she could. The fifth stroke broke her control and a shrill cry followed the report as the slave began to writhe in her bonds. She moaned and cried out as the sixth added its share of pain to her bottom. Juliette counted the strokes silently to herself as Moona's bottom absorbed the full twelve strokes of her beating. To Juliette's surprise, Moona managed to take the full beating without actually screaming. The scene stimulated the craving that, as usual, coursed through her body.

Now it was Juliette's turn! She bent over the stool and gripped the legs as Yousef secured her limbs. She felt tears fall on her as Moona raised her skirt and drew it up over her back. She felt her legs trembling as her bottom waited for the beating to start. Her arousal, stimulated by watching Moona writhe under the cane, began to soar. She heard the cane swish through the air and the loud report of rattan on bare flesh. A line of fire spread across her cheeks as the cane fell away. She tried to remain still and silent as she concentrated on restraining the arousal that the pain and domination was fuelling. Six times the punishing cane burned lines of pain across her throbbing bottom, the strokes curling round so that each stroke left a burning streak the full width of her cheeks. She could not hold back a deep moan of pain and despair as the seventh stroke lashed her buttocks. She was writhing, trying to avoid the cane but Yousef was well experienced in thrashing the bare buttocks of slave girls and her movements did not spoil his aim.

The once pale cheeks now boasted twelve hard raised ridges, standing out clear from her white flesh. Like Moona before her, she had not screamed, only a deep moaning and mewing was heard above the report of the impact of the rod on her bottom. The man released her limbs and, with Moona, ordered her to go and show their behinds to the slaver. The two gingerly walked the few paces, side by side, turned their backs to the slaver and bent over, holding their ankles.

Baylan was no stranger to the sight of young girls being flogged. It was, to him, merely part of his job to train the slaves well so that they presented themselves perfectly on the slave block at auction. It had, by most standards, been a mild beating but both girls had shown remarkable control and taken it well. He had not failed to see how both of their bodies had been sexually aroused, both during their own caning and watching the other. Whilst not an unknown phenomenon, he was not slow to realise that this could increase their appeal and value in certain quarters. Where these two were concerned, he was working under commission, but the terms had been quite flexible and he would use all means in his power to increase his profit on the deal. He regretted that he would not be able to put them to auction. As a pair, correctly displayed, they would fetch a remarkable price. He thrust the temptation aside. His patron, whilst fairly new in the area, had, as the pirate also had known, earned a reputation for taking swift and severe revenge on anyone who crossed him.

"Take them away, Yousef, and clean them up," he ordered with a sigh. "Our client's representative will be here soon to check the merchandise."

Yousef ordered the slaves to follow him. He took them to a washroom, ordered them to clean themselves and then locked them in a cell on the ground floor. The girls, still sobbing quietly, collapsed on benches in the cell.

"What is to happen to us?" Moona asked.

"At least we are not to suffer the degrading process of being put on an auction block and sold like animals," Juliette said, remembering with shame that that had once been her fate. "He has a client who has paid him to capture us."

"I wonder who that could be?" Moona asked. "I hope he will not be cruel to us."

"I don't know who he could be," Juliette replied. "Obviously someone who has seen us sometime in the past. Probably one of the visitors to Lord Charles' mansion who took a fancy to us."

"But why us in particular?" Moona queried. "As we have both seen, there are lots of very beautiful trained slaves around."

"I don't know," Juliette answered. "Either way, we will still be slaves subject to the whims of the man who owns us. We will spend the rest of our lives as slaves in this foreign land with no chance of escape."

"I suppose so," Moona sighed. "It is all so unfair."

"More so for me," Juliette replied. "At least you had done something wrong to end up like this. I was not guilty of any crime but no one would listen to me."

"Oh, come on!" Moona replied tartly, feeling that she was being got at. "You enjoy being a slave, don't deny it. You even enjoy being flogged. I've seen you, don't forget!"

"Maybe," Juliette agreed quietly. "But I prefer to chose the man to be my master." She refrained from reminding Moona that she also responded to pain, and domination, the same way she did.

"Don't be silly," Moona scoffed. "Then you would not be a true slave."

At this observation, which Juliette had to admit to herself was true, the girls fell silent, each immersed in her own thoughts.

It was some hours later that Yousef came and took them from the cell and led them into a round room, around the edges of which, many tall wooden posts had been erected. This, they assumed was the pre-auction display room. The girls were made to stand with their backs to a post and their arms were drawn over their heads and their wrists secured to rings in the post. A few minutes later, Baylan waddled in, followed by a figure in an all-concealing cloak. The figure approached the girls and inspected them closely. Yousef had warned the girls of this and told them that, whatever the man did to them, they must remain silent. Juliette shivered as the man inspected her. He forced her mouth open and looked hard at her teeth. Then his hands slid down over her body, feeling the firmness of her breasts and bouncing them in the palms of his hands, his fingers teasing her nipples until they became erect. Down over her slim waist to her stomach and then her mound, the hands stroked. She felt her thighs forced apart and fingers inserted into her slit from which her juices were seeping. Then she was turned to face the post and the process continued. The stranger's hands glided over her soft back, pulling her hair aside, then down passed her waist to her buttocks. They seemed to linger there as fingers traced the cane weals before pulling her cheeks apart and feeling her anus.

Then it was Moona's turn for inspection and the man went through the same routine. Juliette heard several stifled gasps come from her friend as the man's fingers entered her sex and anus. Finally the man stepped back and turned to Baylan, who had stood nervously during the inspection.

"They are the correct ones," the stranger confirmed. "I said I wanted them unharmed, though. I see the signs of a recent thrashing on their backsides."

"They were disrespectful and needed teaching a lesson," the fat man wailed. "They only had a dozen strokes each."

"They will be collected in the morning. See that they are prepared and ready," the stranger said. "In the meantime, see that they are not touched again. Another will teach them any lessons they need."

"It shall be as you say, my Lord," Baylan said, wringing his hands. "Shall we retire and complete the financial business, now that you are satisfied?"

The two men departed and Yousef released the slaves and returned them to the ground floor cell. The two girls were left alone for the rest of the day and night; the only person they saw was the black who brought them their bowl of gruel and water to drink. The girls chatted for a while, trying to identify whom the stranger might be. The slaver seemed in awe, if not actually frightened, of the man and they wondered if he was to be their new master. The cloak had hidden his features and muffled his voice, so they were unable to even guess if he was someone they had already met. The next morning, Yousef came for them. They were taken to a wash room where the same women depilated them and then scrubbed their bodies and hair clean. They were dried and their hair brushed until it shone in waves down their backs. Cosmetics were applied to their faces, nipples and sex lips and they were given the costumes, which had been cleaned, and jewellery in which they had been attired on arrival and told to put them on.

They were then taken to a room where the stranger of the day before, still muffled in the cloak, awaited them. After a brief inspection, their hands were manacled together and more manacles, separated by a short chain, put on their ankles. A long black cloak and hood was put over them and, finally, a metal collar attached to a chain was put round their necks. Led by the chains, the stranger took them out of the building and bundled them into a covered cart, locking the chain between their ankles to a bar running along the centre of the floor. The stranger mounted the cart and, accompanied by several heavily armed horsemen, the cart set off on the journey taking the two girls to their destiny.

The journey took several days. It was hot and stuffy in the cart and the girls were only allowed out at night when the party halted to make camp. Even then, they were still dressed in the cloaks and hoods. At these times, they saw nothing of the stranger, only one of the horsemen who had been delegated to watch over them. They were fed and watered twice a day, once in the morning before setting off and once at night when they camped. As they were allowed out of the cart to exercise at night, they noticed that the camp was well guarded. The men made no attempt to conceal their features and they all looked terribly fierce and strong.

CHAPTER 11.

After they had been travelling for several hours on the fifth morning, the girls sensed an air of excitement and expectation among the escort. Shortly after there was shouted challenge and one of the escort responded. Juliette had discovered a small gap in the covering at the front of the cart and immediately put her eye to the opening. She saw a high wall, which seemed to stretch away in the distance on both sides of two heavy wooden doors, which were swinging open. The cart and escort passed through and Juliette gasped in surprise. Inside the walls, the empty desert had given way to what appeared to be a large village. Sandstone buildings lined the streets and people sauntered by. She saw no signs of shops and all the men were dressed alike in what appeared a form of livery, the same as their mounted escort.

The escort left them once the gates had been closed and the cart proceeded along a wide street towards a large imposing building to the far end. Again, this was surrounded by a high wall, in which a large gate opened at their approach. Armed guards stood either side inside the gate, which was closed behind them with a menacing finality. They had arrived at their destination. Looking out of the small gap, Juliette saw bright green lawns stretching to either side with flowerbeds full of exotic, colourful, plants. Ahead, the long drive approached a large range of buildings and it was to the largest of these that the cart was driven. Juliette was surprised to see that there was not one window anywhere in the walls. The cart was driven past the front of the building and round to the rear until it came to a halt outside a door. The door opened and a tall, well built, man emerged. Juliette, expecting him to be another giant black, was not disappointed. He was dressed in long baggy trousers held up at the waist by a wide leather belt from which hung a curved sword and dagger.

The man released the manacles from their ankles and ordered them to dismount from the cart and follow him.

They were led through the door and along a short passage and ushered into a small room. The cloaks and hoods were removed and their escort departed, locking the door behind him. Juliette looked round. There were two couches against the walls, several cushions on the floor and two buckets in a corner. One contained fresh water, and the other was empty. The two girls looked at each other, unspoken questions in their eyes. Since leaving Baylan's establishment, they had been forbidden to speak to each other or anyone else. This imposed silence had put a strain on them but they dared not risk breaking it even to whisper together at night. From the little they had seen of their new Master, and listening to the pirate captain and Baylan, they had gathered that he was not one to stand for disobedience. Even when a young black brought food to them, it was done in silence.

The couches were reasonably comfortable and the food very good compared with what they were used to. Apart from the shaming necessity of using the bucket, they passed as reasonably a comfortable night as their individual fears would allow. The next morning, after they had been fed, the door opened and a tall, well built man entered. He was dressed in the same livery as the others but, in his case, it was much finer and more luxurious. His skin was a light brown, more olive than brown, and he had sharp dark brown eyes set in a stern weather beaten face. The sword and dagger at his waist were heavily embossed with jewels as were the scabbards into which they were sheathed. Two half naked black men had entered the cell behind him and the girls did not fail to see the long thin canes hanging from the belts at their waists. Instinctively, the girls fell to their knees before him.

"I am Haroun," the man said in a deep commanding voice. "I am your new Master's major-domo. You will always address me, and my assistants, as 'Sir'. You will not speak unless spoken to or before kneeling and asking permission. You will be respectful and obedient at all times." The sheer authority in the man's voice informed them that he was not one to be trifled with. "Failure to observe these, and the other rules, will earn you a severe whipping."

The savagery with which these last words were spoken left them in no doubt about where they stood. Juliette felt very small and vulnerable in his presence and a thrill of excitement surged through her, and she felt a tingling in her loins. If her new Master was of the same mould as this man, life could be interesting here. Would he be the man who would finally master her and teach her to be a true slave? The omens were promising and the thought sent a shiver of excited anticipation down her spine.

With a command to follow him the man turned and marched out of the cell. The girls rose and, with a guard at their sides, obeyed. They were taken to a washroom where two young naked girls waited. Their bodies were depilated and they were ordered in to a bath of hot water. The young girls followed them in and began to wash their bodies and hair. Juliette surrendered willingly to these attentions, lying back in the water and enjoying the luxury. She did not fail, however, to see dark red stripes across the buttocks of one of the girls where she had been recently thrashed. This reminder of her own position did not detract from the pleasure of the bath and the girl's ministrations. All too soon, one of the guards ordered them out. They were rubbed dry and their hair brushed until it shone. Then they were made to keep still as the usual cosmetics and perfumes were applied to their faces and bodies. They were then given long flowing, brightly coloured, skirts, tiny embroidered boleros and face veils to put on. They were handed golden snake shaped bands to put on their upper arms and fine chains, from which hung tiny bells, for their ankles.

Haroun reappeared at this moment and carefully inspected them. The girls looked at their reflections in long mirrors, wondering what all these preparations were for and what would happen next. A strange sense of doom clouded over them, Juliette in particular, as some instinct warned her that something was going on which she could not fathom out. Haroun completed his inspection and stood back, clearly satisfied. He dismissed the two girls who scurried away.

"You are now to be taken to your new Master," he announced. "You are to dance for his entertainment. Do not displease him. You will remain silent at all times, unless spoken to. Now, follow me."

Juliette and Moona, escorted by the two guards, obeyed the man as he led them through the building. Juliette was amazed at the décor. It was similar to that of Suki's Master's but much more elaborate and ornate. Clearly their new Master was a man of great wealth and substance! They entered a large long room that was empty of furniture except for a beautifully decorated throne on a dais at one end. On this throne sat their Master. He was dressed in a long flowing, expensively embroidered, robe with sandals on his feet. His face was obscured by a gold mask, from which two steely eyes watched the girls' approach. As Juliette followed the major-domo along the room, she noticed several musicians seated to one side. But it was the seated man's eyes that held her gaze. She caught her breath and shivered as the eyes shone menacingly from behind the mask. They seemed to look right through her, into her very soul, as if they could read her like a book and from which no secrets could be kept. This was a man to be wary of, she decided as, with Moona at her side, she sank to her knees before him, lowering her forehead to the floor.

"Excellent, Haroun," the figure said in a voice distorted by the mask. "Proceed."

"The slave Moona will stand," Haroun ordered and, when she had obeyed, continued. "You will dance first for your Master. Musicians, play!"

Juliette, her head still to the floor, heard the music start. The strange chords sent her thoughts travelling back in time, back to her stay in Moona's house, when the two had performed for Lord Charles and at Suki's master's palace. That all seemed a lifetime away now! She heard Moona's bare feet on the floor and the swirl of her skirt as she moved to the rhythm. In her cramped position, from which she dare not move, the dance seemed to go on forever. At last, with a clash of cymbals, Moona sank to the floor at her side, panting heavily.

"The slave, Juliette, will now dance," Haroun ordered. "Musicians, play!"

Juliette rose quickly to her feet, shaking off the cramp in her limbs and stood, left leg slightly bent and her arms raised above her head, hands back to back. The musicians began to play and she moved into her dance. Fearing to displease the man watching her intently, she danced as if her life depended on it. She used all the wiles she had ever learned, even remembering Suki's hints and advice. It seemed terribly important to her to please the man whose eyes never left her sinuous body, and not only to escape the lash. As she moved around the floor, she stole quick glances at those dark piercing eyes, hoping to detect some sign of satisfaction. That there was none, only made her strive all the harder, doing her utmost to seduce him with the body she knew men found desirable. The music came to an end and she sank, panting to the floor beside Moona.

Although no orders were given, the girls heard the sound of movements behind them as the musicians departed. Then other sounds like furniture being moved, heavy objects being placed on the floor, came to their ears. But there had been no furniture in the room! Apprehension flowed over both of them at these sounds. What was going on behind them? Then, for a few moments there was absolute silence in the room.

"Stand, slaves!" The order came from behind them. Neither slave could believe their ears as they recognised the voice. But it couldn't be, they must be mistaken!

"Strip." Again the same voice gave the order, confusing them even more. Both quickly removed the flimsy costumes and stood naked. Juliette glanced quickly at the figure of their Master and shuddered as he gave a low chuckle and she saw the blatant lust shining from his dark eyes as they roved over her naked body.

"Juliette, turn and come here," the voice behind her commanded.

She turned and nearly fainted on the spot. Her ears had not deceived her! Standing there beside a padded bench was the boy, Jason. But he was a boy no longer. His tall frame had filled out and he was very much a young man, now. She saw the bundle of straps he held in his hand and the leather phallus, just like the one she remembered from the past. She walked slowly to him. In no time, he had attached the straps to her body and she was lying, face up, on the bench. She felt a shiver of excitement at what she knew must follow. Once again, she and Moona were to perform the obscene act, but this time before her new Master. How did he know about it? Where had Jason come from?

"Moona. Prepare!" Jason commanded.

Moona turned and halted in mid-stride, a look of total disbelief in her eyes.

"Now!" Jason barked the order at her, breaking the spell that had gripped her.

Moona, apparently in a daze, walked to the bench and stood astride Juliette's prone body, so that the phallus brushed her sex lips. Keeping her legs straight, she bent over and reached forward and gripped the bench above Juliette's head. Looking up, Juliette saw the lovely breasts of her friend as they swung above her. The nipples were hard and prominent in their brown aureoles, just as she had seen them many times before. It was as if her memory was playing tricks with her and she expected to wake up and find she had been dreaming. She saw Jason come into her field of vision as he positioned himself at Moona's side.

"You know the rules, slave. Keep touching the leather, until you are told to impale your body on it," Jason reminded the trembling slave.

Juliette saw Moona turn her head and shudder as she saw the cane he held in his hand. She turned her head away and closed her eyes tight.

Swish. Crack.

Moona's body rocked under the force of the impact. A gasp escaped her clenched jaws as her eyes shot open in utter astonishment. The cane had hurt more than she had anticipated. He had laid it on with the force of a man's arm, far harder than he had ever done before. A fiery streak, running the full width of both buttocks testified that he was no longer a boy. Five more times the cane lashed the girls buttocks, throwing her forward, making her brush back and forth on the phallus, groans of mounting desire sounding from her throat. Six separate lines of fire raged in her cheeks, which were rising into hard ridges where the cane had struck. So far, the girl had not cried out, although the tears flowed from her eyes. Again, Jason lashed another six scorching strokes across the taut throbbing buttocks, each now forcing a shrill cry of agony and despair from her throat as her sex rode back and forth on the phallus.

The tears were falling onto Juliette and she could see the girl's nipples, fully erect, swaying above her. Moona had jerked violently on each of the last six but, somehow, she had kept hold of the bench struggling to maintain her position as the cane had lashed her. Juliette felt her own body responding to the scene being enacted above her. So far, Moona had survived a dozen searing strokes.

"Six more strokes, then you will impale yourself," Jason ordered.

Juliette looked up in compassion at the girl above her. Eighteen strokes she must survive before impaling her body on the phallus! Moona's body was soaking with sweat and Juliette could already feel the girl's juices running down the phallus and onto her body. How her friend survived the next six strokes she would never know. Exhibiting a degree of control Juliette would never have credited her for, Moona survived all six without moving her legs or hands. Her body writhed and bucked on the phallus each time the rattan struck and loud screams of pain and exquisite arousal roared from her open mouth. Eighteen lines of intense fire soared from her buttocks into her body fuelling her arousal. Juliette knew that the girl must be praying for the next stroke, the signal that she could release her control.

"Another six strokes and then you have permission to come. Do so before and you will be whipped. And no cheating," Jason commanded.

Juliette stared in disbelief as she saw Jason grip the cane in both hands and, lifting it high, brought it down with a resounding report across the girl's buttocks. Moona screamed in agony as she bent her legs and descended with a heavy thump onto Juliette, who, looking along her body, saw the phallus disappear into Moona's sex. From then on, Moona rode the phallus frantically, thudding down onto Juliette and driving the air from her lungs. Moona's screams echoed round and round the room as Jason continued to lash the slave's rising buttocks. If Juliette's body was highly aroused, it was nothing compared to the girl being flogged. She was still holding tight to the bench as she fucked the phallus, screaming her pain and ecstasy to the ceiling. As her light body hammered onto Juliette beneath her, Juliette felt the air forced from her lungs. The girl's sweat and tears made their bodies slide about and her juices, flowing down the leather mingled with those oozing from Juliette's open sex.

Juliette, gasping under the onslaught of Moona's thudding body on her own, only just managed to count the next six strokes. How Moona managed it she would never know. The girl rode the phallus frantically, scared of being accused of cheating until the sixth stroke burnt her swollen buttocks. Then she released her grip on the bench and wrapped her arms round Juliette and planted her mouth on that of the girl under her. It only took another five searing strokes before Moona's body arched backwards like a strung bow, and she screamed her surrender to the ceiling as the young body shuddered on one orgasm after another, until it collapsed onto Juliette, her sweat, tears and juices soaking them both.

Haroun, who had been watching from the side in utter mystification, signalled his minions to lift the unconscious girl off and release Juliette. Moona slowly came to and, with Juliette's assistance, staggered to the front of the dais and the pair sank to their knees. Moona let out a soft cry as her heels pressed into her swollen cheeks.

"Interesting! Most interesting!" the voice behind the mask mused. "Now the other way round!"

In no time at all, Juliette found herself standing astride her still sobbing friend, bent over gripping the bench as the wet phallus brushed her open sex.

208

"You will impale yourself after the twentieth stroke," Jason commanded.

Juliette's mind immediately bridled at the injustice! She must take more strokes than Moona! Not only take the strokes, but stay in position, her legs straight, her sex on the top of the phallus and her small hands gripping the bench. To fail on any one of these would surely earn her a terrible whipping. What the fate would be if she failed to control her arousal, did not bear thinking about. It was not fair! Her body was already aroused to a pitch nearing the limit of her control by Moona's thrashing. How could she possibly hold it back as her own buttocks were so savagely flogged? She sought her memory and mentally visualised the terrible whip she had seen used on little Su Lin. That and the heavy single lash whip she had seen hanging on Hassan's wall. At all costs, she must keep the vision of those to the front of her mind. Only the thought of the soft flesh of her back being laid open by one of those would give her the strength to survive the ordeal ahead.

She felt the cane touch her buttocks, then it was taken away. She braced herself and summoned up her control. All went well until the eighth stroke seared across her bottom and her first shrill cry followed the report. As Moona had done before her, she was taken by surprise at the strength now in Jason's arm. Even so soon into her thrashing, she craved to lower her body onto the leather, much as she hated this substitute for a man. But, at all costs she mustn't! Not until permission was given and that would be withheld until her young bottom had endured the full twenty strokes. Twenty strokes during which she must hold position!

She was never sure, afterwards, if it was the mental picture of the whips she kept to the fore of her mind, the fact that she was more used to being thrashed or that she was learning to control her body better, that helped her survive. But she managed to keep the orgasm at bay for the full twenty strokes. She had screamed and yelled, writhed and bucked, all the time dripping sweat, tears and her juices onto Moona lying beneath her. Then the blessed relief after the twentieth stroke had burned a searing path across her cheeks, she descended on the phallus and rode it for all she was worth. The cane still lashed her buttocks but she hardly felt it as she drove her body on, forcing the orgasm into a shattering climax.

When she eventually emerged from the cotton wool cloud of sensual delight into which she had fallen, she found that she, and Moona, were lying side by side in front of the dais. Looking up, she saw the mask looking down on her. The eyes were laughing and the man was chortling in his throat. For some inexplicable reason, she did not hate him as she should have done. She nudged Moona and, together, the beaten and exhausted girls struggled to their knees before their Master.

"That really was most entertaining and interesting. I would not have believed it had I not seen it with my own eyes. Take them away, Haroun and have them cleaned up then put them back in the cell. Then send in the other girl."

Haroun signalled to his assistants and they drew the two slaves to their feet and marched them from the room. Back in the room where they had been prepared, they were cleaned up and then taken back to their cell. The two girls talked quietly together, trying to resolve the many questions that flooded through their minds. Who was the masked figure who they now knew was their new master? Why was his face hidden? Was his face so disfigured that he could not bear any one to see it? Then how had Jason got there? Was it he who had informed their new master of the 'games' she and Moona had played when Juliette had stayed with her those weeks? The master had clearly been very interested since he had watched every moment assiduously. The boy had changed into a man in the relatively short time since they had last seen him, and could wield a cane with a man's strength, as the state of their bottoms could testify.

The questions just went on and on and, now matter how hard they tried, they could find no satisfactory answer. They eventually gave up, completely baffled.

The slaves were confined to the cell for three days after their 'demonstration' before their master.

One of the black men, who they discovered were eunuchs, came to them three times a day with food and water. Each morning, before they were fed, they had to empty their bucket and scrub the cell floor. They were then taken into a small yard and made to exercise for half an hour. An older woman came to the cell four times a day to massage them and rub some sort of ointment into their buttocks. That provided yet another mystery. Considering how hard they had been caned, the marks disappeared even quicker than with Aylena's special cream! The girls refrained from asking these people any questions for fear of earning themselves another beating. They had not had any rules explained to them and, consequently, had to be guided by their common sense.

It was on the afternoon of the third day in the cell that some, at least, of the questions buzzing in Juliette's mind were answered. Haroun came and unlocked the door and ordered her out. She followed him as he led her through the building. She was frightened and felt terribly alone, now that she was separated from Moona. Eventually, she found that she was back in the room where she and Moona had been prepared ready to be presented to the master. Again she was depilated and bathed. Her hair was brushed and her face and body painted and perfumed as before, but this time she wore no jewellery. Haroun watched these preparations carefully and, when he was satisfied, he put the final touches to her appearance. Soft leather cuffs were fitted snugly round her wrists and ankles. She noticed that each had a metal ring attached to it. Haroun handed her a glass containing a colourless liquid and made her drink it all down. Did this mean that she was to be flogged or raped? Her body began to tingle with expectation and she felt her nipples begin to fill and tentative stirrings made themselves felt in her tunnel. What ever was to happen was not going to be delayed or interfered with by her wearing any costume. She was naked and ready!

Having finished her preparation, Haroun ordered her to follow him again. With an escort of a black eunuch on either side of her, she followed the major-domo from the preparation room. Glancing sideways, she watched the blacks with terrible fascination as their muscles rippled over their arms and shoulders. They seemed so strong, making her feel so small and vulnerably weak as they towered over her. At last, just as she was beginning to feel her legs giving way under her with fear, they halted by a door. Haroun opened it and the blacks ushered her through. She stumbled as she looked around. One question had been answered. She was clearly to be flogged, not raped!

Scattered around the courtyard were various pieces of apparatus, stools, benches, beams and others, all designed with the express purpose of completely restraining a victim in numerous positions while pain was inflicted on their body. It was not one of these, however, to which Haroun led her. Two thick upright posts, some eight feet apart, stood in the centre of the yard, with a heavy beam joining the tops. She was halted in the centre of these. The eunuchs proceeded to take hold of her wrists and clip the rings in the leather cuffs to chains hanging wide apart from the beam. Slowly the eunuchs pulled on the chains until she was lifted from the ground, suspended by her slim arms. Chains from the base of the posts were attached to the rings on her ankles and her legs were pulled wide apart. She now hung there, between the posts, her body a white 'X' against the sandy colour of the walls.

Haroun and the eunuchs departed, leaving her alone in the courtyard. She hung there, alone, suspended, terrified at what might be in store for her. Wild thoughts, each more dreadful than the last, flashed through her mind, stirring the arousal that fear and exquisite anticipation had already ignited in her body and which had begun to manifest itself as she had entered the courtyard. She remembered what Aylena had once said to her. The waiting was, sometimes, worse than the beating. Eventually the door, which she was facing, opened and her Master entered. His identity was still hidden behind the mask, but it was the heavy whip, its long lash curled, which he carried in his hand that sent terrible spasms of terror and panic flooding through her.

Juliette watched in dreadful fascination and anticipation,

as he walked slowly and menacingly towards her. The richness of his robe, and the jewelled scimitar and dagger hanging from the ornate belt at his waist, seemed to be emphasised by the bland colour of the wall behind him. He halted a few feet in front of her and scrutinised her hanging body. She saw the lust and cruelty in the eyes behind the mask and her heart seemed to stop. As she had sensed before when she had danced for him, this was a man who would not only master her completely, but make her into his true slave. He would brook no nonsense from her! This time it would be total submission! He laid the whip on the floor at his feet and slowly, so deliberately, raised his hands to the mask on his face.

Juliette's mouth opened in a silent scream of abject terror.

The man had no facial deformity. Nothing to require it to be hidden behind the mask. It was the last face she had expected, or ever wanted, to see!

Abaddon!

She felt her mouth go dry. She was unable to swallow. She felt terror as she had never felt it before. It was he that now owned her. It was he who had poked and prodded her body so intimately at the house of the slaver, Baylan. And it had been he before whom she had danced so seductively just a few days earlier. What terrible quirk of fate had returned her to his clutches?

"I have waited many moons, just for this moment. For this pleasure," he said.

There was none of the old Abaddon about him now. None of the obsequious, crawling, fawning distasteful creature who had served the Lord Reythal. Here was a man who bowed to no one.

"No! No!" Juliette screamed at him, her voice sounding high and strained in the silent courtyard. She wished she would die but, she assumed, the potion she had drunk would see that wish didn't come true. She was condemned to remain alive and conscious, no matter what he did to her!

"Oh, Yes! Yes!" Abaddon mimicked her terror. "You surely were not so stupid to think that you had escaped from me for ever. I still have a debt to collect from you. Anyway, it also pleases me to own such a beauty as you."

"What debt?" Juliette asked as her fear mounted higher.

"Perhaps the words 'Do your worst, you sadistic bastard.' will refresh your memory," Abaddon said with a sneer.

"But I was punished for that," Juliette protested. She shivered as she remembered the flogging with the birch he had given her.

"That was only for calling me a monster. Now you are to be punished for the greater insult." Abaddon leered at her helpless body. "Unless you wish to beg me for mercy," he added.

"Never!" Juliette spat at him

"Also you have spoken without permission, and you have failed, on several occasions to address me properly. I am your Master and you will address me as such," Abaddon said, his voice quiet and loaded with menace.

Juliette shuddered at the sheer authority in is voice. He was so self-assured. He was his own master and would be the master of any who came under his influence. Now he was the one totally in control and answerable to no one. How this had come about, was beyond her understanding. The suspended slave looked into his eyes, defiantly. He returned her gaze until she lowered her eyes, unable to bear the menace in those dark sockets. In that instant, she knew he would make her his, his true slave and with this recognition her body reacted accordingly. A sense of complete submissiveness flowed over her. She knew he would master her to a degree she had not ever imagined possible. She felt her nipples ache with the hardness of their swelling and dampness seep from her sex.

It came as a shock when she realised it was not just the sight of the heavy whip on the ground that caused this reaction in her. The very aura of authority that exuded from him, the realisation that he would demand, and accept, nothing less than total and utter submission from her turned her to jelly. As much as she still hated this man, she knew that in him, just as Moona had once prophesied, she would find a perfect master. Maybe not a love master, but one that would fulfil the desire deep inside her and make her a perfect slave. She looked down at the whip. The whip that she had always dreaded and had prayed that she would never feel its bite. It came as a shock to her as she realised that her tender young body longed to feel its lash. To be made, once and for all, to acknowledge her unconditional surrender and submission!

"Your slave is sorry for having offended you so greatly, Master." She heard her own voice speaking as if from a distance. "I am yours to do with as you may wish. I willingly submit to whatever punishment my Master may decide I deserve."

Abaddon looked at her intently, his face expressionless, masking the thoughts that were coursing through his mind. She had spoken so quietly, in a tone of complete submission that had startled him more than it had done her. He looked hard at her. Her words had sounded sincere! Was she trying to make him go easy on her? Was it only fear of the lash, or was she submitting to him and not the lash? For a moment a satisfied smile tinged his cruel mouth. She, who had hated him so much, submitting to him! Surely this was too good to be true. It was what he desired, yet he could not believe it! He shrugged these thoughts from his mind. Whatever her motive, she must be punished for her insult.

"So be it, slave," he said.

He moved close to her. He reached up and drew her hair forward over her upthrust breasts, feeling her body shiver as her back was bared, ready for the lash. To Juliette's surprise, he took her head in his hands and kissed her fiercely on the mouth. She smelt the sweet odour of his breath and tasted his saliva on her mouth. The aching in her breasts and the tingling sensations in her tunnel increased alarmingly, overshadowing the pain in her arms caused by the strain of supporting her slim body.

Juliette felt the sun on her back as her hair was drawn forward, preparing her back to receive the kiss of the whip. She felt the savagery of his kiss on her mouth, making her catch her breath as he instilled the first stage of his ownership over her. She watched, hypnotised, as he stepped back and, stooping to the ground, picked up the whip and shook loose the long lash. The moment had come! The moment that she knew would come sometime and which she both dreaded and longed for. She shut her eyes tight and clamped her jaw tight shut, and waited. She heard him walk behind her.

"Twenty lashes." Abaddon's voice behind her informed the slave of the extent of the whipping she was to receive.

"Yes, Master. Please whip me for my offence and make me your slave," Juliette heard her voice reply, through her clenched teeth.

She heard the sound of the lash cutting through the air and then the dreaded report. She screamed in terror. There was no pain! Had her body gone numb with fear? Then she realised that he had merely struck one of the upright posts as he tested the weight of the whip. She let her head drop until her chin rested on her chest and tightened her grip on the chains that suspended her. She was to be given twenty lashes of that terrible whip. The thought made her shudder with dread. It was to be the worst flogging she had ever received, even worse than those that occasionally intensified her nightmares. She prayed that she would be able to survive it. She hung there, waiting, wondering why he did not get on with it. Now that the moment had come, she wanted the whipping to start and take her on that terrible journey to complete submission. Perversely, something inside her made her resolve to take the flogging as bravely as she could.

Once again, she heard the dreaded sound of the long thong slithering back over the sand. She heard it whistle through the air.

Crack.

The report of the leather striking her bare flesh echoed round the courtyard as a searing line of sheer agony blazed across her back and shoulders, making the pain in her arms seem to disappear. She bit her lip to stifle the scream that welled up in her throat.

Crack.

Another line of exquisite fire joined the first. She felt her body swing against her bonds as pain, far worse than she had ever thought could exist flared through her back. She tasted blood in her mouth where her teeth had bitten through her lip.

Crack.

A deep groan issued from her throat as her body writhed under the blow, reawakening the pain in her stretched arms. She felt the sweat break out all over her body. Her nipples ached in her raised breasts and she felt the juices flowing from her open sex lips. Only three lashes from the whip had caused a more intensive reaction than a dozen with the cane usually did.

Crack.

Crack.

Twice more the cruel thong snaked across her back and shoulders sending another two lines of burning flames through her slim body. Somehow she had managed, so far, to hold back the screams that rose in her throat so that they only emerged as deep groans. Now, she knew she had reached the limit of her control. She had promised herself to take the whipping bravely. To try and make a good impression on the man who was instilling the true meaning of slavery into her! As she heard the lash slide along the sand for the next stroke, she turned her head to the side and sank her teeth deep into the aching flesh of her arm, as her tears flowed freely from her eyes.

Crack.

The lash had curled lower down across her back and the tip snaked round and cut into the under belly of her breast. Her mouth opened in a grimace of agony and a shrill scream of pain and surrender followed the report round the courtyard. She felt the sweat running over her skin, her breasts felt so swollen she feared they would burst and her nipples ached more than they had ever done before. Her juices were flowing freely down her thighs as the arousal soared through her body.

Six livid lines of fire burned across her white back. Six signatures of the lash! For the first time in her life she knew

217

what true slavery meant. The whip, wielded by a man she hated, was teaching her the real meaning of complete and utter submission.

Unusually for him, Abaddon had been wielding the whip dispassionately. Slowly savouring the taking of his revenge for the terrible insult she had heaped on him and his parentage. He had waited so long and the waiting had, somehow, tempered his usual sadistic pleasure in inflicting pain on a young girl's helpless body. The things she had said before he started whipping her buzzed round in his mind. The bravery with which she had taken the lashes so far had impressed, rather than angered, him. He paused and looked at the suspended girl, saw the lines of pain etched on her white skin, the tears and sweat dripping from her and the evidence of the way her arousal was raging through her young body.

Until now, the only slave girls that he had encountered had been reluctant to fully accept their fate. This had fuelled his sadistic tendency until it had almost become second nature to him. The male element in his nature had recognised that this girl was different. She might hate him but the whipping, even the six lashes she had so far received, had awakened the true slave girl in her that he had sensed lay, latent, deep inside her. He looked hard at her back and was pleased to note that the lash had not cut into her skin. Only light abrasions showed so far! Having awakened the real slave girl in her he realised that she was now his and he would enjoy many more opportunities to use and beat her young body. But he would not wish her to come to him naked, her body marred by scars left behind by the whip. That would spoil his pleasure! But the girl must be punished for the serious offence she had committed!

Crack.

Juliette screamed as the onslaught on her back continued. She was writhing and twisting against the chains, trying to avoid the biting of the lash, but she had been secured too well. Time after time, as the whipping continued, she screamed her submission. The potion she had drunk, whilst keeping her conscious, had restricted the stimulation the whipping was arousing in her. She felt it teetering on the edge of an orgasm that would never come. Consequently, the delights that flowed through her were prolonged and thus more delightful. Strangely, unlike the other times when she had been beaten, she did not have to fight back the orgasm and the continued presence of heightened arousal, was divine.

Taking care to moderate the force of the strokes so as to cause infinite pain without lacerating the slave's sweet flesh, Abaddon continued with the flogging until there were only five more strokes to administer. He paused to wipe the sweat from his own brow and looked at the suspended girl, writhing in the chains. She had ceased to scream now, only a loud moaning and mewing and the violent jerk each time the lash struck, signifying that she was still conscious. Her back was covered with a mass of raised weals, each a line of pain surging through her body. Instinctively his gaze dropped to her buttocks. They shone white and inviting, compared with her girl's bruised back. A wicked smile curled the corners of his mouth as he resolved to remedy his omission. The next stroke whistled through the air and wrapped the lash round the relaxed and unprepared cheeks of her bottom, the leather indenting her soft flesh. Her body jerked violently and the moaning stopped as a shrill scream of pain and shock followed the report. A thin red weal instantly formed across the full width of her cheeks as her buttocks spasmodically clenched and relaxed against the unexpected pain. He smiled and lashed the next stroke in the same place. His aim must have been a little out of true. The tip of the lash curled round her hips and found the sensitive open sex lips and the swollen clitoris.

Juliette, taken by surprise by the first stroke across her buttocks, was prepared for the second. But she was not prepared for the effect of the tip curling round and flicking her bud. If the lash across her back had made her into a true slave, the effect of this stroke was completely astonishing to both her and the man who was whipping her. As her shrill scream died away, she turned her head and her tear filled eyes sought his.

"I love you, Master," she yelled out as the pain broke down the last vestiges of her resistance to her true self.

Abaddon, again stunned by her reaction, unthinkingly, laid the next stroke in exactly the same place. The arousal raging inside the girl's body fought against the effect of the potion, which was prohibiting the orgasm that was striving to reach fulfilment. As a consequence, the delectable sensations raging in her were soaring to heights of absolute bliss.

"I love you, Master. I am your slave. I love you," Juliette screamed her final submission and acknowledgement of him as her complete master. Her love master!

Abaddon, her cries ringing like music in his ears, laid on the last three strokes of her punishment, one across her back and two across her buttocks.

Juliette was not aware that she had now reached the end of her punishment. The exquisite pain in her back, and now her bottom and sex had swamped over her, even driving the agony in her slim arms from her mind. Someone, somewhere, her mind recalled had told her that a girl would never know herself as a true slave until a man laid the whip on her and taught her. Abaddon had now done this and proved just how right that person had been. She had screamed her submission, and her new found love, to the man who, until now she had hated with all her being.

Abaddon dropped the whip to the floor and looked at the suspended body of his slave as he wiped the sweat from his brow. It was only then that he realised that, whilst his sadistic instincts had been pushed aside, the desire that flogging a girl usually induced in his loins had not been quelled. His penis, hard and erect struggled against his garments to be released. So great was the need raging in him that he couldn't wait to get this girl back to his harem. He had to have her there and then! He torn off his robe and breeches and hurried in front of her. Fortunately, he had, unwittingly, suspended her at the right height. His hands reached round and clasped her throbbing buttocks as he thrust his lance deep into her tunnel. He took her, savagely and thoroughly, until, with a shout of triumph he felt her muscles squeeze his manhood as he ejaculated his satisfaction deep inside her.

Juliette had felt his hands grip her cheeks, sending fresh waves of pain shooting through them as his penis penetrated deep inside her. His possession of her added explosive fuel to her arousal and sent it soaring beyond the control of the potion she had drunk. Stars flashed before her eyes as her body surrendered to one shattering orgasm after another, arching rigid in the chains as her muscles milked his penis to the last drop. She emerged from the delicious cloud of satisfaction to find herself lying in a crumpled heap on the ground. She heard a voice, as if coming from a distance, calling her. She raised her head and, through her tears, saw Abaddon standing a few feet away from her. He was naked and his manhood was still protruding from his loins. Slowly, mewing with the pain that had again made itself felt throughout her body, she crawled to him and struggled to a kneeling position, knees wide spread. Dutifully, as a slave should, she leaned forward and took his penis into her mouth and tenderly licked it clean. Then she leaned back and looked up into his dark penetrating eyes.

"Master," Juliette said, submissively as she stared into his dark sockets. "You have made me your slave. I am yours to do with as you wish. I will serve and love you perfectly in all ways, in all things and at all times. If I should fail to give perfect satisfaction, I humbly beg that you will not hesitate to have your slave thoroughly beaten."

Abaddon looked down on the kneeling slave. His natural desires having been satisfied, scepticism raised its ugly head. Suddenly it all seemed too simple. Knowing the girl as he thought he did, it seemed unbelievable that a few lashes of a whip could have triggered such a dramatic change in her. As much as he wanted to believe it, cynicism won the day.

"As to being my slave," he said sternly. "You have no choice. Your body is mine since I now own you. You will serve me perfectly, whether you want to or not. As for beatings, I assure you, you will get more than you desire, whether you deserve them or not." He pushed her aside with his foot and she fell sideways on the sand. "Go now and have the old woman see to your weals. Then tell her to have Haroun take you and Moona to the harem."

Feeling absolutely devastated and dejected, Juliette struggled to her feet. With tears of misery cascading down her face, she returned to the preparation room and surrendered herself to the ministrations of the old woman. Once her bruises had been attended to, she lay face down on a bench, while the old woman sought out the major-domo. Some while later, the door opened and Haroun, followed by Moona, entered. Moona let out a cry of horror as she saw the state of her friend's back and bottom. She gently helped Juliette to her feet and, supporting her as best as she could, followed Haroun through the building.

They eventually halted outside a door guarded by a fierce looking man with an unsheathed scimitar held across his massive chest. Haroun knocked on the door and, in response to his answer to a challenge from within, the door opened and the two girls were ushered through. The two slaves stood looking round in amazement. They were in a very large room, the ceiling supported on thick marble pillars. The room was beautifully decorated and airy, one side opening out onto a large garden where cooling fountains played amid green lawns and colourful flowerbeds. Scattered about the room were numerous couches and cushions on which perhaps a dozen very beautiful naked girls reclined. The two new arrivals gasped in horror at the sight of a naked girl tied to one of the pillars by her wrists high above her head. The girl's back and buttocks bore a mass of terrible weals, obviously made by the savage application of a whip.

Four days passed during which Juliette and Moona got to know the other girls. They learned that the girl at the pillar, who had been released shortly after their arrival, had been disciplined for disobeying one of the eunuchs who were ever present in the harem. The old woman came four or five times a day and tended to Juliette's weals until, after the fourth day the marks had disappeared although she was still stiff and sore. Neither Juliette nor Moona were sent for by Abaddon during this time, although the eunuchs collected other girls each evening and took them to serve their Master. In the morning these girls returned exhausted and those who had not been found completely satisfactory, were taken away to be disciplined. All the girls were kept naked and, at any one time, there was at least one bottom bearing the marks of a recent punishment.

Juliette had told Moona of everything that had happened to her in the courtyard, leaving nothing out. Even confessing how she had yelled out her complete submission. To her surprise, Moona fully understood her sister slave's actions. She realised that, although Juliette had detested and feared the man for so long, he had fulfilled her prophesy and turned the girl into his devoted love slave. It was surprising, she said, how a whip in the right hands could bring happiness to a girl in the wake of terrible pain as it awakened the latent slave, which was present in all women.

This had certainly happened to Juliette, but had not brought about the happiness it should have done. Her master did not believe her and she was in a state of misery. Why would he not believe that it was not fear of the whip that had awakened her inner slave and made her submit to him? Moona, fully understanding her friend's dilemma, tried to help Juliette to think of a way to convince Abaddon of her sincerity. Although Moona was a little jealous now of Juliette, since she craved a true master for herself, she promised she would do all she could to solve the problem.

It was the afternoon and Juliette and Moona were lounging in the garden, when Juliette broached an idea that had been slowly germinating in her mind. The two discussed this for a while and, when neither could find any fault with it, decided to put it to the test. Juliette begged an audience with Haroun and, when this was granted, she begged for some writing materials. The Major-domo was reluctant at first, since these items were forbidden in the harem. When Juliette had convinced him that she only wished to write a letter to her Master, he relented, on condition he was present when she wrote it. She selected the wording very carefully so to intrigue Abaddon and placed it in the envelope and sealed it and begged Haroun to deliver it to the Master as soon as possible.

Juliette waited impatiently until the next day before Haroun brought a reply. To her utter joy, Abaddon had agreed to the request in the letter and said she may see him in the main hall the following afternoon. Juliette, with Moona in attendance this time, begged another audience with Haroun. The major-domo was angry at first when they asked him to keep the matter secret from the Master. However, once they had convinced him that the Master would be pleased, they unfolded their plan to him, without divulging Juliette's true reasons The major-domo chuckled inwardly as the plan was explained. He was well aware of Juliette's declaration to the Master and the cynicism with which it had been received. He saw the real reasons behind her plan immediately, but kept the knowledge to himself. Knowing the Master, he was sure that even if the girl's scheme did not succeed, the Master would not be angry. On the contrary, he would see it as a big joke! The two slaves explained what they would need and Haroun promised to make the necessary arrangements.

Once again Juliette had to wait patiently for the rest of that day and night. She was putting all her faith in the success of the idea and the thought of failure, and its consequences, she would not even consider. At last the time arrived. Mid-morning the next day, Haroun, with two eunuchs in tow, entered the harem and called the two slaves to him. They ran and fell to their knees in front of him.

"Come," he commanded. He was going to enjoy this. He had not, he hoped correctly, said anything to Abaddon about what was to happen.

He led the slaves from the harem to the room where Juliette would be prepared. The old woman, with two younger female slaves was waiting and set to work on the girl as soon as she arrived. Juliette lay on a bench while her body was depilated, then into a hot bath, where she was scrubbed from head to toe. Then she lay on a bench while the young slaves massaged fragrant oils into her skin. This treatment was both luxurious and invigorating and when it was completed, she felt on top of the world. Moona smiled to see her friend so happy for the first time since she had first met her. The oils had made her skin shine, matching the lustre in her hair that had been well brushed. Cosmetics and a subtle perfume were applied to her face and body, and snake bracelets put on her upper arms and tiny chains with tiny bells attached, locked round her ankles.

Juliette surveyed her reflection critically in a full-length mirror. She smiled happily at what she saw. She thought she had never looked so lovely and seductive and prayed that Abaddon would find her both irresistible and convincing. Moona's praise in her ear confirmed her opinion and Haroun's approving glances endorsed the matter. Moona then supervised the attire that they had decided upon. She walked slowly round Juliette making minor adjustments here and there until she was satisfied. Juliette looked at Haroun and asked him if the other arrangements she had asked for had been attended to. The major-domo laughingly replied and assured her that they had. Now all that they had to do was wait until Haroun's assistant eunuch came to tell them that the Master was ready.

Abaddon entered the hall and took his place on the throne at one end. He had been completely mystified, yet very intrigued, by the letter the slave had had the audacity to send to him. He had nearly ordered her to be flogged again, but curiosity overcame the urge. Having nothing better to do, and thinking it might be entertaining to lead her on he had agreed to her request. He had no idea what she wanted to say to him, she had only asked to see him. He wondered if she was going to show him, somehow, that the episode in the courtyard had only been a passing moment. If so, he thought, the little bitch would smart terribly for it. He would have her flayed, and enjoy watching it done. He saw the door at the far end of the hall open and several musicians enter and sit along one side wall. His curiosity was further aroused when one of the eunuchs entered and placed two coiled whips on the floor in front of him, the ends of their handles touching. His natural impatience at being kept waiting began to rise. Then the door opened again and Haroun entered, leading a figure completely enveloped in a long cloak and hood. The pair halted in the centre of the hall facing him. He leaned forward in his seat, intrigued by this development. Whatever was going on, Haroun was in on it!

"Master," Haroun's strong voice broke the silence. "A slave begs your indulgence and requests your permission to dance for your pleasure."

Abaddon looked hard at his major-domo. The slave had merely requested to be allowed to speak to him. He had not expected all this paraphernalia. If this was all some practical joke, the man would pay for it as well as the slave!

"Permission granted," he said at last, thinking to get it over with and he could find some soft slave girl to soothe away the anger that was mounting inside him.

"The slave, Juliette, thanks her Master and, for his pleasure, will perform the dance of the submissive slave." So saying, Haroun whipped the cloak and hood away from the figure at his side. He retreated to the side of the hall, nodding to the musicians.

Immediately the musicians lifted their instruments and began to play. The music filled the room as Juliette, looking straight into the hooded eyes of her master, walked slowly forward. Across the upraised palms of her hands lay the heavy whip with which Abaddon had flogged her, its lash neatly coiled. She halted in front of her Master and, crouching down, laid the whip on the floor, between the two already there. Still crouching, she edged her way back to the centre of the hall.

She stood erect, almost defiantly, placing her hands, back to back, above her head. Gradually, her body began to sway to the rhythm. Abaddon, for all his feigned disinterest in the proceedings, leaned forward as her movement revealed that her young, slim, white body was concealed by a number of translucent veils. He felt his interest kindled.

Juliette, looking over her yashmak saw his interest

226

aroused. She began to move her body seductively around the hall, the veils floating around her and occasionally revealing parts of her body as she moved. Although she had never performed this dance before, it was not so difficult. Suki had explained it in detail, including various hints to make the performance more seductive and erotic. It was based on the dance of the 'Seven Veils' and Juliette had quickly picked it up, at least in theory. The dance passed gradually through three stages in a slave's existence.

The first stage was the new frightened slave, introduced for the first time to the dominance of a Master. Juliette moved gracefully, keeping pace with the slow soft rhythm. Her eyes peered over the yashmak, frightened, while her body, although moving seductively, spoke clearly of the fear that was gradually consuming the slave as her mind realised the helplessness of her future.

The tempo of the music increased as the dance moved into the second stage. Now she was no longer a new slave and her Master was enforcing his ownership, conquering her reluctance to submit to his will. The drummer, at intervals, made the sound of a whiplash rise above the music, making the slave's body jerk violently as if struck. The terror clearly showed in the slave's movements and in her eyes. As she reached the end of this stage, Juliette, for the first time since the music had taken control of her body, dared to glance quickly at her Master. To her joy, the anger that she had seen lurking in his eyes when she had entered the hall had been replaced by intense interest and there was a smile on his mouth. Not the cruel smirk she had expected!

Again the tempo changed. Still moving smoothly and seductively, the dancer's portrayal changed to that of a slave tempting her Master with the promised delights of her body. Deftly, one by one, she released the veils, letting them float away, gradually revealing more and more of her seductive charms. Finally only one veil remained. This was secured by a small ring on the top of her head and floated in a wide circle about her body to the floor. The material was so fine that every detail of her luscious form was clearly visible. Juliette waited until the steps took her immediately in front of her Master and then stopped dead, facing him. As her belly undulated rapidly she raised her hands under the veil and slowly lifted it off her head. The music stopped, save for the drummer who gave a roll on his instrument, increasing the speed and volume. Juliette timed it perfectly. As the drummer reached a crescendo, she allowed the final veil to float away from her body. In the silence that followed, for a few moments she stood perfectly still, naked, with her arms raised above her head, her lovely breasts rising and falling as she sucked air into her lungs. Then she gracefully sank to her knees and lowered her panting body prone to the floor with her arms stretched out sideways. Her mouth was on the coiled lash of the whip and she kissed it lovingly.

Abaddon, fully aroused by the sheer eroticism, and symbolism, of the dance looked lustfully and triumphantly at the naked slave spread submissively at his feet. It had gradually dawned on him, during her performance, that her submission and declaration of love the other day had been genuine. He had conquered her at last! Not by the whip, although this had probably been the catalyst that had finally awakened the true slave within her. She had, herself, recognised in him her true master at last. This was far better than he had ever dreamed possible. Now he would be able to enjoy the many ways he had planned to take his pleasure of her, knowing that she would surrender willingly and strive to make his pleasure even more enjoyable. He was just about to order her to his room, when her soft seductive voice rose to his ears.

"Master," Juliette said sweetly and submissively. "I submit myself to you as your true slave, not from fear of the whip, but because your slave truly recognises you as her true Master. She loves you and desires to serve and please you for the rest of her days." Abaddon sat stunned by her words. "Master." Juliette continued, before he could speak. "Your slave humbly begs you to accept her submission and love."

"Your submission and love are accepted," Abaddon replied, looking down on her lovely nakedness.

Slowly, Juliette eased herself up until she knelt, knees wide spread, her buttocks on her heels and her eyes demurely lowered. She reached forward and picked up the whip and, with it lying across her upturned hands, raised it towards her master.

"Your slave thanks her Master for the honour." Juliette's voice trembled slightly as her eyes looked at the whip. "I beg to ask one favour."

Juliette shuddered as, through her eyelashes, she saw a scowl appear on his face. "Speak." His tone was suddenly harsh.

"Master," Juliette said softly, as she approached the final act she had planned for her performance. "Your slave humbly requests that you will signify your acceptance of her submission in the appropriate manner. By marking your slave's back with the symbol of your authority. Then, once a year on the anniversary of this day, my Master will order me to the courtyard and there lash his slave with this whip, exactly as he did seven days ago."

"That is a request I will be happy to grant," Abaddon said, a cruel smile of anticipation on his face. The scowl left his face as he looked down on his kneeling slave. The slave had actually begged for the whip. This was better than ever! Then he looked into her sweet face. Did he see a faint glimmer of success there? That would not do! He put a stern expression on his face.

"I have accepted your submission and love and granted your request," his voice thundered in the hall. "I am your Master, now and until I tire of you and dispose of you. Never, never, make the mistake of dreaming otherwise." He turned his head and ordered Haroun to clear the hall.

As the door closed behind the last one to leave, he reached out and took the whip from the trembling hands of his slave. He stood up and quickly removed his own clothing. He stepped down from the dais and walked behind his slave. She heard the lash snake along the floor, then it curled across her back. She gritted her teeth and forced herself to remain stationery and the lash laced across her shoulders twice more. Three lines of fire burned where it had struck. Abaddon threw the whip to one side and, grabbing his slave by her shoulders, turned her round and forced her to the floor.

Juliette blinked the tears from her eyes and looked up. She saw his rampant manhood and quickly spread her legs wide. He descended on her and proceeded to savagely take his pleasure of her, just as she wanted him to do. She struggled to control the arousal that had gradually been building up inside her from the moment she had entered the hall. As he used her fiercely and thoroughly, the sheer irony of the situation dawned on her. The man she had hated and dreaded for so long had, in the end, turned out to be the true Master she had sought! With that thought in mind the arousal soared out of control. As he shed his satisfaction deep into her, her body surrendered to the ecstasy of a multiple shattering orgasm, she realised that she had come without permission and that she would soon pay for this lapse with a beating.

Surely there was no justice in this world for a slave. But then — who needs justice!

The End

TITLES IN PRINT
SILVER MOON
ISBN 1-897809-50-6 Naked Truth, *Nicole Dere*
ISBN 1-897809-54-9 The Confessions of Amy Mansfield, *R. Hurst*
ISBN 1-897809-59-X Slaves for the Sheik *Allan Aldiss*
ISBN 1-897809-62-X Slavegirl from Suburbia *Mark Slade*
ISBN 1-897809-64-6 Submission of a Clan Girl *Mark Stewart*
ISBN 1-897809-65-4 Taming the Brat *Sean O'Kane*
ISBN 1-897809-66-2 Slave for Sale *J.T. Pearce*
ISBN 1-897809-69-7 Caged! *Dr. Gerald Rochelle*
ISBN 1-897809-71-9 Rachel in servitude *J.L. Jones*
ISBN 1-897809-72-2 Beaucastel *Caroline Swift*
ISBN 1-897809-73-5 Slaveworld *Steven Douglas*
ISBN 1-897809-76-X Sisters in Slavery *Charles Graham*
ISBN 1-897809-78-6 Eve in Eden *Stephen Rawlings*
ISBN 1-897809-80-8 Inside the Fortress *John Sternes*
ISBN 1-897809-84-0 No Justice for Juliette *Mark Stewart*
ISBN 1-903687-00-4 The Brotherhood *Falconer Bridges*
ISBN 1-903687-01-2 Both Master and Slave *Martin Sharpe*
ISBN 1-903687-03-9 Slaves of the Girlspell *William Avon*
ISBN 1-903687-04-7 Royal Slave; Slaveworld Story *Stephen Douglas*
ISBN 1-903687-05-5 Castle of Torment *Caroline Swift*
ISBN 1-903687-08-X The Art of Submission *Tessa Valmur*
ISBN 1-903687-09-8 Theatre of Slaves *Mark Stewart*
ISBN 1-903687-10-1 Painful Prize *Stephen Rawlings*
ISBN 1-903687-12-8 The Story of Emma *Sean O'Kane*
ISBN 1-903687-14-4 Savage Journey *John Argus*
ISBN 1-903687-15-2 Slave School *Stephen Douglas*
ISBN 1-903687-16-0 Slaves of the Circle T *Charles Graham*
ISBN 1-903687-17-9 Amber in Chains *Francine Whittaker*
ISBN 1-903687-18-7 Linda's Trials *Nicole Dere*
ISBN 1-903687-19-5 Hannah's Trials *Stephen Rawlings*
ISBN 1-903687-20-9 The Pit of Pain *Falconer Bridges*
ISBN 1-903687-21-7 The Sufferers *Caroline Swift*
ISBN 1-903687-22-5 Bought and Sold *Tessa Valmur*
ISBN 1-903687-23-3 Slaveworld Embassy *Stephen Douglas*
ISBN 1-903687-24-1 Trained in the Harem *Mark Stewart*
ISBN 1-903687-25-X Dark Surrender *Kim Knight*
ISBN 1-903687-26-8 Into the Arena *Sean O'Kane*
ISBN 1-903687-27-6 The Slave Path *Francine Whittaker*
ISBN 1-903687-30-6 The Initiate *Miranda Lake*
ISBN 1-903687-31-4 Darker Dreams *Tessa Valmur*
ISBN 1-903687-33-0 Pain and Passion *Mark Stewart*
ISBN 1-903687-35-7 The Gladiator *Sean O'Kane*
ISBN 1-903687-36-5 Divine Cruelty *Lee Ash*

TITLES IN PRINT

SILVER MOON CLASSICS
ISBN 1-897809-23-9 Slave to the System, *Rosetta Stone*
ISBN 1-903687-32-8 The Contract *Sarah Fisher*
ISBN 1-897809-37-9 Bush Slave, *Lia Anderssen*
ISBN 1-897809-39-5 Training Jenny, *Rosetta Stone*
ISBN 1-897809-43-3 Selling Stephanie, *Rosetta Stone*
ISBN 1-903687-36-9 Olivia, *Charles Graham*
ISBN 1-903687-42-5 Naked Plunder, *J T Pearce*
ISBN 1-903687-55-7 Gentleman's Club, *John Argus*

SILVER MINK
ISBN 1-897809-22-0 The Captive *Amber Jameson*
ISBN 1-897809-24-7 Dear Master *Terry Smith*
ISBN 1-897809-26-3 Sisters in Servitude *Nicole Dere*
ISBN 1-897809-49-2 The Penitent *Charles Arnold*
ISBN 1-897809-58-1 Private Tuition *Jay Merson*
ISBN 1-897809-61-1 Little One *Rachel Hurst*
ISBN 1-897809-63-8 Naked Truth II *Nicole Dere*
ISBN 1-897809-67-0 Tales from the Lodge *Bridges/O'Kane*
ISBN 1-897809-68-9 Your Obedient Servant Charlotte *Anna Grant*
ISBN 1-897809-70-0 Bush Slave II *Lia Anderssen*
ISBN 1-897809-74-3 Further Private Tuition *Jay Merson*
ISBN 1-897809-75-1 The Connoisseur *Francine Whittaker*
ISBN 1-897809-77-8 Slave to her Desires *Samantha Austen*
ISBN 1-897809-79-4 The Girlspell *William Avon*
ISBN 1-897809-81-6 The Stonehurst Letters *J.L. Jones*
ISBN 1-903687-07-1 Punishment Bound *Francine Whittaker*
ISBN 1-903687-11-X Naked Deliverance *Lia Anderssen*
ISBN 1-903687-13-6 Lani's Initiation *Danielle Richards*

STILETTO SM
ISBN 1-897809-88-3 Stern Manor *Denise la Croix*
ISBN 1-897809-93-X Military Discipline *Anna Grant*
ISBN 1-897809-94-8 Mistress Blackheart *Francine Whittaker*
ISBN 1-897809-97-2 Slaves of the Sisterhood *Anna Grant*
ISBN 1-897809-98-0 The Rich Bitch *Becky Ball*
ISBN 1-897809-99-9 Maria's Fulfilment *Jay Merson*
ISBN 1-903687-02-0 The Daughters of de Sade *Falconer Bridges*

SPECIAL DOUBLE ISSUES
ISBN 1-897809-06-9 Biker's Girl + Caravan of Slaves
ISBN 1-897809-12-3 Biker's Girl on the Run + A Toy for Jay